"This is your first Surprise filtered through his voice.

Abby nodded.

And her first time ever in Texas.

And her first time ever being face to horse with a real cowboy.

And her first time experiencing such an overwhelmingly instant awareness of a man. That was merely a by-product of the full sun beating down on her, burning her nose and scrambling her common sense.

Besides, she'd left her broken heart back in California. Another relationship was the last thing she'd come to Texas for.

Dear Reader,

As a child, our family moved quite often. I was always envious of my cousins who got to remain in the same town in the Upper Peninsula of Michigan their entire childhoods. When I was around eight years old, I asked my mom where my home was. My mom told me simply, *Home is where your family is.*

As it turns out, that was all I needed. Those are the same words I gave to my daughters when we moved for the first time. Family is at the core of my books. Family is blood relatives, rich history and connections to past generations that help us build a foundation for the future. Family is also those people we choose—the ones who start out as strangers and turn into lifelong friends. That for me is the definition of a true family. And when I need to find home, I always look to them.

In *The Texas SEAL's Surprise*, Abby James and Wes Tanner find themselves redefining family and what home really means. Welcome to Three Springs, Texas, where the tumbleweeds are large, roots run deep and family is the heart of everything.

I love to connect with readers. Check out my website, carilynnwebb.com, or chat with me on Facebook (carilynnwebb) or Twitter (@carilynnwebb).

Happy reading!

Cari

HEARTWARMING

The Texas SEAL's Surprise

—

Cari Lynn Webb

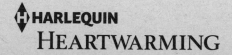

H HARLEQUIN
HEARTWARMING

If you purchased this book without a cover you should be aware that this book is stolen property. It was reported as "unsold and destroyed" to the publisher, and neither the author nor the publisher has received any payment for this "stripped book."

ISBN-13: 978-1-335-42640-6

The Texas SEAL's Surprise

Copyright © 2021 by Cari Lynn Webb

Recycling programs for this product may not exist in your area.

All rights reserved. No part of this book may be used or reproduced in any manner whatsoever without written permission except in the case of brief quotations embodied in critical articles and reviews.

This is a work of fiction. Names, characters, places and incidents are either the product of the author's imagination or are used fictitiously. Any resemblance to actual persons, living or dead, businesses, companies, events or locales is entirely coincidental.

This edition published by arrangement with Harlequin Books S.A.

For questions and comments about the quality of this book, please contact us at CustomerService@Harlequin.com.

Harlequin Enterprises ULC
22 Adelaide St. West, 40th Floor
Toronto, Ontario M5H 4E3, Canada
www.Harlequin.com

Printed in U.S.A.

Cari Lynn Webb lives in South Carolina with her husband, daughters and assorted four-legged family members. She's been blessed to see the power of true love in her grandparents' seventy-year marriage and her parents' marriage of over fifty years. She knows love isn't always sweet and perfect—it can be challenging, complicated and risky. But she believes happily-ever-afters are worth fighting for. She loves to connect with readers.

Books by Cari Lynn Webb

Harlequin Heartwarming

City by the Bay Stories

The Charm Offensive
The Doctor's Recovery
Ava's Prize
Single Dad to the Rescue
In Love by Christmas
Her Surprise Engagement
Three Makes a Family

Return of the Blackwell Brothers

The Rancher's Rescue

The Blackwell Sisters

Montana Wedding

Visit the Author Profile page
at Harlequin.com for more titles.

To my dad... I'm so blessed to have a dad like you. You live your faith, love your family and never hesitate to help others. You inspire me every day to be a better person—to be like you. I love you!

Special thanks to my writing tribe for answering every text and email with patience and humor. To my family for rallying when I'm on deadline, whether it's going to the grocery store, working through one of my plot problems or reminding me to laugh. I couldn't do this without your continuous encouragement and endless support. I love you!

CHAPTER ONE

ABBY JAMES SHOVED her car into Park and waited for the dust cloud surrounding her to settle.

Her jamming on the brakes of her compact two-door convertible had caused a mini tornado on the dirt road outside Three Springs, Texas. And all because of a flat tire.

But it was the cowboy sitting on a massive chestnut-colored horse in the middle of the road only a puddle jump away that captured Abby's full attention.

He shifted in the saddle and pointed at her front wheel. "If you'd been driving the right way down this one-way road, you might have missed that pothole back there."

If Abby had been going the right way, she'd already be in Three Springs, inside her cousin's apartment with her face pressed against the air-conditioning vent. The AC in her car had given out several hundred miles ago, forcing her to lower her convertible top. And man, it was hot. "I wouldn't have swerved into the pothole if you and your mammoth Clydesdale hadn't been barreling down the road right at me."

"Dan is a Belgian draft horse." The cowboy rubbed the horse's thick neck as if Abby had insulted him. "And Dan barely canters on his fastest day."

Whatever the pair had been doing they'd made quite the image. Powerful horse and real-life cowboy set against the backdrop of a brilliant clear-blue sky and wide-open plains. It was the perfect setting for a classic Western movie. Captivated, Abby had locked her gaze on the pair and not on where she had been going. She was lucky she hadn't driven off the road altogether. She blew a stray piece of hair out of her eye. "You really named your horse Dan?"

"He's an old soul." The cowboy's fingers tangled in Dan's light blond mane. "He's understanding, patient and loyal. That's a Dan in my book."

In Abby's book the horse was a giant and deserved a grander name than Dan. His sheer height and muscles daunting. But his demeanor was rather calm, from his dark eyes to his stillness. Yet when Abby glanced at Dan's owner, calm wasn't her first reaction. Something about the cowboy made her pulse kick up and her nerves fire. Most likely lingering adrenaline from her collision with the pothole. "If you could point me in the direction of a real road to Three Springs, I'll let you and Dan get on with your day."

The cowboy nudged his hat up his forehead and frowned. "A real road isn't going to help you."

Neither, it seemed, was her cowboy. Wasn't there a cowboy rule book? *Always help damsels in distress.*

"You barely have any tire left on your wheel," he continued. "Dirt or pavement, you aren't going to make it far."

His voice was dry and gravelly like the dust she kept inhaling. Only, unlike the dust, she breathed in the deep timbre. Wanted him to keep talking. Abby unbuckled her seat belt and leaned over her car door to peer at her flat tire and disrupt her sudden fixation with her cowboy. "I just need it to go a few more miles." She'd already driven over thirteen hundred miles from Santa Cruz in just two days. She was so close to starting her future. "I don't have a spare."

Or another plan. This was it.

"You drove from California without a spare." He tipped his chin toward her front license plate. Disappointment shone in his eyes.

Abby pushed aside the worry that this was a bad sign. She raised both hands to shade her eyes. Not even her fancy brand-name sunglasses were powerful enough to block the unrelenting sun or the cowboy's intense stare. "I've owned this car for years. Never had a flat before, despite all the potholes I hit in the city."

"This is your first flat tire ever." Surprise filtered through his voice.

Abby nodded.

And her first time ever in Texas.

And her first time ever being face-to-horse with a real cowboy.

And her first time experiencing such overwhelmingly instant awareness of a man. That was merely a by-product of the full sun beating down on her, burning her nose and scrambling her common sense. Besides, she'd left her broken heart in California. Another relationship was the last thing she'd come to Texas for.

"Well, for your first flat, you went all out. You bent the rim of your wheel too."

Abby leaned against the headrest. That worry pulsed faster. Hightailing it out of California had been rash. But had it been a mistake too? "Now what?"

"You need a tow truck." He guided Dan closer to her car. "I'll give you a ride to town."

On his horse. Not happening. Panic tripped through her. The pair might look like they belonged in an award-winning Western film. But not Abby. She belonged in the audience.

True, she was moving to Texas to build a new life. And she'd planned to embrace the country lifestyle, but she'd meant by buying cowboy boots and a hat, not riding a horse only hours into her first day in the state.

"Dan is one of the most reliable ways to travel around here." The cowboy scratched his cheek and watched her as if confused by her resistance.

Abby tugged her car keys from the ignition. "Thanks, but I'll walk. It'll be good to stretch my legs."

"Three Springs is almost five miles away." He lifted his gaze to the sky, then glanced at Abby.

"My GPS says…" Abby grabbed her phone from the console and squinted at the screen. Even the bright sunshine failed to hide the blank map screen. "It says nothing. There's no connection."

"Happens out here a lot." He nodded as if he approved of the relentless heat and lack of cell reception.

Who enjoyed that? If she wanted to disconnect, she chose a full day at the spa. Still, she couldn't remember the last time she'd indulged in more than a quick soak in her bathtub. Abby picked up her purse from the passenger seat and locked her car doors.

Her cowboy chuckled.

"I've lived in cities my entire life. We always lock our doors." Never trust strangers. And always remain alert. She swung her oversize fringe bag onto her shoulder cross-body-style, then brushed past the cowboy and his horse.

He cleared his throat. The low rumble warmed Abby from the inside out.

She stopped and glanced up at him. "Three Springs is the other way, isn't it?"

He nodded and slid off his horse, landing directly inside her personal space. Granting her an up-close and personal view. He was much taller than she expected. His jawline more chiseled. And his direct gaze was especially piercing.

That awareness spiked again.

It was dehydration. She'd finished the last of her water at the state line between New Mexico and Texas. The same place her air-conditioning had quit. She'd opened her convertible top and driven on, determined to let nothing derail her. That included handsome cowboys. "What are you doing?"

He looped the reins around his hand and motioned her on with the other. "Escorting you to town."

"That's not necessary." Even more unnecessary was her small sigh at his consideration.

"Maybe not." He shrugged. "But my mom taught me better, and she'd be disappointed if I left you here alone. I'm Wes Tanner, by the way."

Abby introduced herself and concentrated on the road. Not on the fact that being so close to Wes made her feel safe. Except there was nothing but cactus, and flat, flat land all around her. Surely, she could handle herself against a tumbleweed attack. "Do you rescue people out here often?"

"No," Wes replied. Dan shook his head and whinnied as if laughing at her. Wes added, "This road is hardly accessible from the main highway."

Abby winced. She'd had to make a hairpin turn and jump the curb to get where her GPS was telling her to be, namely this dirt road. Perhaps that should have been a clear warning to her to turn around. But a fresh start waited in Three Springs, and rock bottom required fresh starts. She just had to get there.

Wes's voice disrupted the silence. "What's in Three Springs that you can't find in California?"

Happiness. Family. "My cousin, Tess Palmer, recently moved there."

"Tess reopened Silver Penny General Store a few months back," Wes said.

"Our grandparents owned it." Abby smiled, hearing her grandfather's laughter. Grandpa Harlan had described the general store and the array of customers that had filled their days in his favorite small town. But he'd left out key details like the blistering heat and surprise cowboy encounters. Sweat dripped down her spine, sealing her shirt to her skin. Dust and dirt wedged between her bare toes thanks to her open sandals. "Tess came to collect family heirlooms and decided to stay."

"Now you've decided to join her."

"Something like that." Tess had offered Abby a safe place to land. Abby could've dealt with the sudden loss of her job as a matchmaker. But throw in a cheating boyfriend and unexpected pregnancy, and Abby's world had simply tilted too far to rebalance it alone. And she was tired of being alone. Her hand brushed against Wes's arm. She edged away. She had to get out of the heat before she lost her way and did the unthinkable. Like holding Wes's hand. "Are we almost there?"

"We've barely begun." He pointed over his shoulder at her convertible.

Her car was so close. As in lunging-distance close. Abby stopped, touched the back of her damp neck and slanted her gaze toward the horse. "I'm not going to make it by walking. It's too hot."

Wes tipped the rim of his hat back and lifted his gaze to the sky as if only then noticing the sweltering heat. "What do you want to do?"

"I'm working that out." She frowned.

"He's very gentle." Affection slipped into Wes's voice. "You don't need to be scared of Dan."

Abby wasn't scared. She was pregnant. Eight weeks pregnant. She didn't know if pregnant women were even allowed to ride horses. She knew nothing about being pregnant. Nothing about living in the country. And even less about her cousin, Tess.

The last time the cousins had been together in person they'd both been in grade school. They'd gotten along quite well, but it'd been a Christmas spent at their grandparents' house. The entire visit had been magical. And something Abby had been searching for, yet failed to find again, over the years.

But she knew she wanted to reestablish that bond with her cousin. Find those roots she'd been missing her whole life. She touched her stomach and steadied herself. Her baby needed family too.

She gazed at Wes. He was a stranger, she

reminded herself, even if he had manners and listened to his mom's advice. Still, he wasn't there for her to spill her worries to. She chose another revelation instead. "I've never been on a horse before."

"Never?"

She chewed on her bottom lip. "Not a pony. Or even a mule."

A smile cracked into the corner of his mouth. "I can't imagine there'd be a lot of opportunities to ride mules in California."

"Not where I lived."

He grabbed her hand and squeezed her fingers. "How about we take it slow?"

There was nothing slow about her pulse. Or her racing heart. And he was only holding her hand. She tugged her fingers free, curled them around the strap of her oversize purse and tried to collect herself.

She eyed the saddle, rather than her cowboy. "I need a ladder. I cannot get up there."

Wes linked his fingers together and opened his palms. "You're going to step here, and I'll lift you up."

"What do I grab onto?" *Because I want to grab onto you.* Making this one of the worst ideas ever. Abby clenched her fingers around the purse strap. Sweat trailed along the back of her neck. How could she be flushed and shivery at the same time?

"Reach for the saddle horn, and swing your leg over the saddle." Wes lowered his joined hands.

Easy. Or so he made it sound. Three tries later, Abby wiped her palm across her forehead and blew out a hot breath. Dan waited patiently beside her.

Wes simply relinked his hands and smiled at her. "I promise I won't let you fall."

She wanted that promise in writing. Notarized and legally binding. Because Abby had vowed never to be swept off her feet again. She fully intended to keep her new cowboy boots firmly planted in the dirt and her heart permanently locked away. She hadn't listened to over nineteen hours of podcasts on how to succeed in life and forgo love as a single, strong woman for nothing.

She shook out her arms and wiggled her shoulders, then focused on her cowboy. "Ready?"

He never looked away. Simply nodded, composed and confident.

Abby grabbed the saddle horn and swung her leg. Wes assisted, one nudge around her waist, and she settled herself on Dan's muscular back. Seconds later, Wes found his place behind her, wrapped his arms around her and gripped the reins. Abby gripped the saddle horn, but lost hold of her racing heart. She reconsidered starring in that Western film, admitting rather reluctantly there was something very appealing about her current predicament.

"What's the next stop after Three Springs?" Wes's clear, smooth voice skipped along her spine.

Her shoulders relaxed. "Why do you think there's a next stop?"

"Three Springs is never the destination." Wes chuckled. "It's the place you stop along the way to your real destination."

"Not for my cousin." *Not for me.*

"You aren't your cousin."

She stiffened and straightened. Grateful for the criticism in his voice and the reminder that he wasn't hers to lean on. His arms were not the ones she wanted around her. And this wasn't the fresh start she'd come to Three Springs for. "What does that mean?"

"Tess arrived in town quieter than a whisper on Christmas Eve." He adjusted the reins. "It was days before anyone knew Tess was even living in the apartment at the general store."

"Once you knew she was in town, what happened?" Abby tried to turn around to look at Wes. But with the stiff saddle and the slow side-to-side sway of the horse, every shift put her further inside his embrace.

"Don't worry." His tone was amused, as if he recognized her battle not to get too close. "The entire town has been looking after your cousin as much as she'll let us."

Abby nodded. Tess had always been reserved as a child, preferring the background to watch and observe. Tess had also been the caretaker, always looking after her younger sister and Abby when she visited. Six months ago, Tess had become a widow, and her quiet reserve had morphed into private and isolated. Now it was Abby's turn to take care of her cousin. "I'm here now. I'll look out for her."

Dan turned onto a road. His hooves clip-clopped on the asphalt. Buildings, some historic, others modern, sprouted in front of them. The smallest of road signs indicated Three Springs and the population of four thousand six hundred and thirty-two. That was the only welcome sign, as if proving Wes's claim that the town was truly never a destination.

"When your cousin no longer needs someone to look out for her, what then?"

Wes's deep voice pulled Abby away from her inspection of the town. "Why are you so certain I came to Three Springs intent on leaving as soon as possible?"

"Because you don't belong here." He reined Dan in outside the Silver Penny General Store. Then he guided Abby off Dan's back and onto the wooden sidewalk before she could finish sputtering.

She wanted to adjust her shorts. Shake the steadiness back into her legs and rub the knots from her backside. But she refused to wobble in front of Wes. Refused to let him know his horse and his words had unsettled her. She set her hand on a wooden post and glared at the infuriating cowboy. "You know nothing about me or where I belong."

He shifted in the saddle and leaned toward her. Only half of his smile reached his cheek. "You have a collection of flowery sandals, matching necklaces and fancy sundresses packed in your car, don't you?"

She curled her toes into her sunflower sandals and pressed her lips together. Cute sandals made her happy. Bold colors, feminine dresses and chunky jewelry did too. Nothing wrong with that.

He nodded as if her silence confirmed his guess. "You've never been on a horse until today. Most likely never caught a blue catfish or driven a tractor."

She crossed her arms over her chest, covering her bulky turquoise bead necklace. "That matters why?"

Wes eyed her. "Because that's all Three Springs is."

"There's more to this town than fishing and tractors." And there was more to her too. More than cute, impractical sandals and pretty sundresses. More than the fluff, head-in-the-clouds daydreamer she'd been accused of being.

"That's another thing." He shook his head, and his full grin fell loose. "You're too optimistic. Too hopeful."

"And that's a problem now too?" She frowned at him. He was sounding more and more like everything she'd left behind in California.

"We're more levelheaded and practical around here."

More like stubborn and overly critical. She added her cowboy to her list of people she intended to prove wrong.

He glanced over her shoulder and tipped his hat. "Hey, Tess."

Abby swung around, away from the aggravating cowboy and into her cousin's welcome embrace. "Tess. It's so good to finally be here."

Tess hugged her, then leaned away to look Abby over. "Where's your car?" she asked with concern.

"Flat tire. Wes brought me into town." Abby

kept her arm around her cousin's too-thin waist and peered at Wes. "Thanks for that. Who do I call about a tow?"

"I'll take care of it," Wes said.

"That's not necessary." Abby stepped closer to Dan and held Wes's gaze. Her voice edged into her own version of inflexible and determined. "I wouldn't want to impose on you any further. I'm sure you have fish bait to locate, tractors that need driving and cattle to rope."

Tess coughed discreetly behind her.

Wes's jaw slid back and forth as if he was grinding away his smile. "It's no problem. Trey Ramsey owns the auto shop, and he's part of my roping team."

Abby narrowed her eyes at him. He tipped his hat and walked Dan down the street.

Tess touched Abby's arm. "Wes is…"

"I'm not talking about that particular cowboy anymore." Abby clapped her hands together like a schoolteacher capturing her student's attention with one firm word. "I'm here. With you. And that's all that matters now."

CHAPTER TWO

WITH DAN'S SADDLE STORED in the stable and the horse brushed down, Wes decided his Tuesday was finally returning to its normal routine. Tuesday mornings always included a sunrise ride with Dan. Followed by cleaning the stables, working with the horse rescues in the paddock and checking off ranch repairs on the to-do list.

Tuesday mornings had never included cherry-red convertibles, flat tires or an out-of-towner with sun-soaked blond hair and a smile that had charmed Wes from his head to his boots. Wes chuckled. "Nothing but trouble there, Dan."

The giant horse nudged Wes's shoulder.

"Right. It's time to get on with our day." He led the horse out of the stable and grinned at the older cowboy stepping off the wraparound porch of the single-story ranch house.

Boone Bradley walked across the driveway and opened the gate to the main pasture. His gait was the same ambling one he'd had when he'd first shaken Wes's hand two years ago, before inviting the younger man inside for dinner.

Wes wondered if Boone had ever regretted that invitation. After all, it was Boone's grandson, Jake Bradley, who should've been returning home that day from their latest SEAL mission. Not Wes, who had sobering news and nowhere else to go.

Wes guided Dan into the pasture and released the gentle horse to check on the other rescues.

"Got a call from C&H Horse Haven." Boone rested his arms on the top rail of the wooden fence. "We're getting new arrivals tomorrow afternoon."

"You can't keep telling them yes, or we're going to need to find more land." Wes latched the pasture gate. He knew the incoming horses' condition without asking: malnourished, neglected and desperate for help. The C&H specialized in removing horses from the most dire situations and finding them new homes. Boone and Wes had already taken three horses from the rescue group, including Dan. And despite the seven horses grazing right now in the main pasture, Wes wasn't operating a horse rescue.

"It's a mare and her new foal." The earnest waver in Boone's voice was at odds with his chiseled frown. The old cowboy had a heart he preferred to keep hidden under layers of grit and determination. "They're family. Can't separate them. Can't leave them where they are. Can't abandon them either."

Family wasn't a topic Wes had any interest in discussing. He braced his foot on the bottom post of the fence. Too bad the unrest inside him wasn't as easily steadied. But it was nothing he hadn't been handling, and furthermore it was nothing he cared to share. "The horses will have to quarantine in the birthing stall."

"We have time before Cinder will need it." Boone pointed to the dappled gray quarter horse in the pasture.

Cinder had been saved from an auction house and her pregnancy discovered after she'd been placed into quarantine. Boone had argued they had an unused birthing stall and room to spare at the time, unlike the C&H, whose stables were often full. Boone had claimed they had an obligation to help since he and Wes were experienced ranchers, who understood and liked horses. Wes had struggled to disagree. And Cinder had arrived the following morning.

He pushed away from the fence and declined to argue now. His own family might be broken, but he'd never split up another one. "I'm going to add more fresh straw and a larger bucket for fresh water to the birthing stall. Make sure it's stocked and ready."

"I'll lend a hand." Boone walked beside Wes

to the stable. "Speaking of lending a hand, heard you and Dan brought a woman into town today."

Wes wasn't surprised Boone already knew about Abby's arrival. Life in Three Springs was slow, except for the gossip. That flowed faster than rainfall in a monsoon. Still, he frowned.

"It's not every day Wes Tanner escorts a pretty lady around town on his horse." Boone's grin softened across his weathered face, raising his thick salt-and-pepper eyebrows. "Even the folks living outside the county lines are talking about you this morning."

Wes's frown deepened. He disliked the excess chatter, and he liked it even less when it was about him. "I couldn't leave her out there."

"It was the right thing." Boone headed for the bales of fresh straw stacked in neat rows against the back wall of the large stable. "Same as taking in all the horses."

Abby and the rescue horses were entirely different. Wes had given Abby a ride into town. He hadn't invited her into his home. And as far as he could tell, Abby didn't require looking after, especially from him. If his guess was right, she would be moving on from Three Springs before the next full moon. Abby, with her striking steely blue-gray eyes and her enchanting manner, belonged in a fast-paced, bustling locale. She was as temporary in town as Wes considered himself to be. Three Springs was only a stop along the journey before they both transitioned to their futures.

"How'd she get her fancy car out on Old Copper Mill Road anyhow?" Boone cut the binding around a hale bay with the pocketknife he kept strapped to his belt. "That road hasn't been open to traffic since the seventies. Can't barely access it from the highway these days, let alone see it."

Wes had no idea why Abby had continued on the back road. Or why she believed Three Springs would be enough for her. Sure, her cousin lived here, but for how long? As far as he knew, the Silver Penny General Store wasn't ready for customers, and that was assuming it would be able to turn even a small profit once it was open. And there wasn't much of a market for impractical sandals and positivity quotes in town. The locals here needed reliable work boots and favored straight talk.

Wes secured another water bucket inside the birthing stall and considered the flooring. He wanted the mare and her foal to feel comfortable and safe. As for Abby, he wanted her out of his thoughts. One more Abby-related task, and he'd do just that. "I'm meeting Trey out on Old Copper Mill Road to have Abby's car towed, then heading to the bar."

His usual Tuesday-evening routine included

managing the Feisty Owl Bar and Grill. The bar that Boone had opened decades ago.

"Sam and I are paying a visit to the general store later this afternoon." Boone's tone was bland as if he was reciting the weather forecast for the week: hot and hotter.

"Is there something particular you need?" Wes eyed the old cowboy. "I wasn't aware Tess had officially opened for business."

"Tess is only accepting special orders." Boone swept the stray pieces of straw into a pile and leaned on the broom handle. "Last week, she found an original nineteenth-century cast-iron dinner bell for Cassie Weaver's mom. The bell was quite remarkable. The last time I saw a dinner bell like that I was running across the yard to my grandmother's dinner table."

"Are you in the market for a cast-iron dinner bell now too?" Wes latched the door on the stall. He'd add clean straw and more mats to the floor tomorrow before the pair arrived.

"Might be." Boone rocked back on his well-worn boot heels and eyed Wes. "Also, might be that Sam and I want to welcome our newcomer to town."

"When exactly did you and Sam become the Three Springs welcoming committee?" A twinge of unease tapped along the back of Wes's neck. Sam Sloan and Boone had been best friends since grade school. The duo were harmless and meant well but meddled all the same. Even more disturbing, the pair considered themselves the town's matchmakers.

"Nothing wrong with being neighborly." Boone ran his palms over his plaid shirt as if smoothing out the wrinkles. "The Silver Penny General Store and the Feisty Owl are a horseshoe throw away from each other."

"I feel like I've been neighborly enough for one day." If he kept helping Abby, she'd feel as if she needed to return the favor. And that would only upset Wes's peace of mind.

"Sam and I grew up with Harlan Palmer. He was the girls' grandfather." Boone hooked his thumbs in his belt loops. "Harlan isn't here to watch over them. Sam and I want to check in."

"As long as that's all you're planning on doing," Wes said. "Checking in."

"We're two old-time cowboys. How much trouble can we cause?" Boone headed for the stable doors.

Wes tilted his head and watched Boone's departure. A hasty one at that. It was the fastest he'd seen Boone walk in a while. And if Wes wasn't mistaken, a different sort of energy surrounded the old man. Wes's unease grew.

Last fall, Sam and Boone had come across a runaway bride. They'd given her a ride to the Owl and discovered the bride's cold-footed groom already seated at the bar. Two hours of heartfelt talk and two servings of Boone's special potato-and-bacon soup later, they'd ushered the reunited couple back to the old church to exchange their vows. Sam and Boone had then declared themselves the town's relationship experts, offering advice and introductions to both locals and guests at the Owl. Their machinations had quieted down over the past few months so Wes had assumed they'd retired from playing Cupid for Three Springs.

Now he wasn't so certain.

Now he'd have to watch the wily cowboy duo more carefully.

And warn Abby to duck if she wanted to miss Cupid's arrows.

Sam and Boone might not have the best aim, but they were nothing if not relentless once they settled on a goal.

Wes fastened the stable doors and checked one last time on Dan and the rescues in the pasture. Then he climbed into his truck and headed out to Old Copper Mill Road.

Trey Ramsey, owner of Ramsey & Son's Repair Shop, had already arrived. He climbed out from under Abby's car, wiped his palms on his jeans and shook Wes's hand.

"Thanks for coming out, Trey." Wes shifted to look at Abby's ruined tire.

"Always happy to get out of the shop." Trey tapped his fist against Wes's shoulder. "Cute ride by the way. Never took you as the candy-apple-red sports car type."

"Belongs to Abby James." Wes saw Abby behind the wheel. Heard the upbeat eighties song she'd been playing. Recalled her sunburned cheeks and wind-loosened blond braids. He wanted to forget her honey-glazed voice. Her perceptive gaze and wit. "She's Tess Palmer's cousin and just got to town today."

"That makes more sense." Trey knelt beside the flat tire and touched the bent rim. "This might be an expensive repair. Of course, I'll give her the friends and family discount on account of you and her being…"

Trey's eyebrow lifted. His voice faded into the hot wind. Yet the speculation hovered.

Was Wes the only one in the whole county who hit Mute on the town's chatterbox? Abby had only just arrived in town. How could she possibly be Wes's anything? Wes crossed his arms over his chest. "You'll have to take up the cost with Abby."

"Where is she?" Trey adjusted his baseball hat. *Not with me. As it should be.* "She's staying with her cousin."

"That works." Trey pulled his truck keys from his pocket. "I need to drop by and see if Tess can find a vintage glass casserole dish to match my wife's set that her great-grandmother gave her."

Not his friend too. When had Silver Penny General Store become the go-to place for everyone's special requests?

"I'll let Abby know I have her car at the shop." Trey opened his truck door and glanced at Wes. "I'm looking forward to meeting her as well."

Wes considered his friend, then rubbed his forehead. Heat was messing with him something fierce today. Or perhaps it was Boone's sneaky ways. Trey was only doing his job. And Wes hardly cared what Trey wanted to order from the general store. The man had his own personal business same as Wes.

Yet when it came to Abby… Wes rolled his shoulders and stretched his neck. When it came to Abby, something felt funny inside him. And that he didn't care for.

Trey maneuvered the tow truck around to the front of Abby's car. Five minutes later the convertible was loaded onto the flatbed and secured.

Trey took off his work gloves and slapped them against his thigh. "You hear the latest talk about the land developers sniffing around town?"

That was talk Wes had heard and listened to.

He nodded and checked the clouds. Rain hung on the horizon, and he expected a storm to roll in before evening. "You might want to put Abby's top back up when you get to your shop."

"Will do." Trey glanced at the sky, then back at Wes. "Think this time will be any different than the last?"

"That company never stayed longer than a day." Wes ground a stone into the dirt with his boot. "I suppose it depends on what the land developers want to do here."

"Three Springs works fine as it is," Trey said. "Can't think of anything that needs to be done."

Wes agreed and looked at Abby's car. Too fancy for Three Springs. Too impractical. "But that's not progress."

"Progress." Trey grimaced at Wes as if he was watching something troublesome, like a rattler, and was annoyed at its presence. "I didn't think you'd climb on the change wagon too."

"I'm not." After all, Wes didn't intend to make Three Springs his permanent home. Still, he managed the Feisty Owl for Boone and took care of operations on the ranch. He had to look out for the town if only to ensure Boone's legacy and the Owl prospered, even after Wes had moved on.

"Guess we have to wait and see if the chatter becomes real talk." Trey opened his truck door and swung into the seat. "In the meantime, I'm going to keep on keeping on. My land and business aren't for sale. I know from experience, if you sell your family legacy, you're left with nothing."

Wes eyed his friend. "They say everyone has a number. A price. If those land developers offered that, would you sell?"

"You can't put a price on hard work and family loyalty. If I sell out, what have I taught my kids?" Trey slammed the truck door and leaned out the open window. "If I do my job right, my boys will know hard work builds a bank account. Besides, some things matter more than a quick sale and a fat wallet."

"You're a good father, Trey." The kind Wes would've wanted as a kid. The kind Wes would've wanted to be if that had been his path.

"Thanks." Trey rapped his knuckles against the truck door and grinned. "You should consider it one day."

"I'm good." More than that, Wes wasn't interested in a relationship now or in the future, and what might come with it. He pushed his cowboy hat lower on his head. "Taking in another pair of horses from C&H tomorrow. A mare and her foal."

"What's your plan for them?" Trey asked.

"You interested in adopting? Kids can learn

a lot from caring for horses." Wes certainly had growing up.

"I'm definitely not saying no." Trey laughed.

Wes worked the disbelief from his face. Ever since Wes had met Trey at the Owl, the man had been adamant about no livestock ever living on his land. That he'd consider it now was more than a little surprising.

Trey started his truck and yelled over the deep rumble of the engine, "See you tonight for the Owl's pulled pork nachos. Tuesday's special is the family's favorite."

Wes watched the vehicle kick up a dust cloud and walked over to his own. A single flower sprouted from a tall and lanky cactus feet away from where he'd parked. The dark pink color was at odds with the monotone, earthy colors surrounding it. The bloom was late. The rest of the cactus's flowers had already given way to fruit. The bloom shouldn't be there.

Yet there it was: brilliant, eye-catching and startling. Like an omen.

Wes climbed into his truck, started it and headed into town.

Change was coming. He was as certain of that as he was of the approaching storm.

He didn't like it. Not one bit.

CHAPTER THREE

ABBY FOLLOWED TESS. They took the outside staircase to the apartment on the second floor above the Silver Penny General Store. The store had been in the Palmer family for more generations than Abby could count. The same location. The same building. The stairs creaked under Abby's feet as if underscoring the building's age and its resilience.

Tess opened a plain front door and stepped inside. "Welcome home. Oh, the air conditioner seems to have a mind of its own."

A dozen brown tiles and a round welcome mat created the boundaries of the small entryway. Abby stepped farther into the apartment and the stifling heat. Apparently, the air conditioner didn't mind if it worked or not.

Tess pointed at the half dozen portable fans situated around the quaint apartment. The colorful fans were perched on top of unpacked boxes, the refrigerator and even the TV. "I can get more fans."

"Or we could fix the air-conditioning." Abby

reached to pull her hair into a bun only to realize she'd already braided it. She twisted the ends of her braids together and clipped them on top of her head. More sweat beaded on the back of her neck and forehead.

Tess maneuvered around a stack of unopened boxes and shoved the window all the way open. "The AC unit needs to be completely replaced."

Abby set her purse on the two-seater sofa. Stacks of cardboard moving boxes crowded every corner of the apartment. The boxes overwhelmed the family room and the kitchen, blocking the natural light from the pair of windows and covering the only work space on the kitchen island. Each one had been labeled with a thick black marker. *Photographs. Office. Christmas. Kitchen. Wedding.*

Abby's heart ached.

Every box was a memory for Tess. A connection to the husband and life she had lost only six months earlier. Abby wanted to help Tess unpack and organize the apartment, but she feared pushing her cousin. She wanted to rebuild their bond, not cause Tess more pain. Tess was a widow and deserved to grieve on her terms. Abby decided to start slow. "Who do we call to replace the air conditioner?"

"Here's the thing." Tess shifted a box, aligning it into a straight line with the ones underneath it. Her gaze remained fixed on the tower as if the stack was part of her design aesthetic. "I don't have the money."

"I do," Abby said. Well, not really. Abby had a modest savings account. Had been offered no severance from her most recent job termination. But she had a credit card for emergencies. She touched her forehead. Her entire scalp had started to sweat. No, air-conditioning definitely qualified as an emergency.

"I can't let you pay for a new air conditioner." Tess moved to another tower, putting the boxes back into perfect alignment as if the apartment only needed to be straightened up to make things right. "It's really expensive. I invited you to stay with me. Not fix my problems too."

Problems. Was Tess implying there were more problems than a broken AC? Abby straightened, suddenly alert. "Is everything okay, Tess?"

"It will be." Tess tucked her dark hair behind her ear, offered Abby a smile, then turned away.

But her cousin's smile wavered. Her voice was hesitant, not confident. There was worry in Tess's wide green eyes. Abby scooted around several boxes and followed her cousin into the kitchen.

Tess opened the refrigerator. "Once the general store shows a profit, improvements can be made."

"How far from a profit are you?" Abby accepted a bottled lemonade from her cousin.

Tess had moved to Three Springs from Chicago one month after her husband's unexpected death. She claimed she and Eric had been discussing leaving the city for Three Springs. Tess had been certain Eric would want her to reopen the family general store just as Tess and Abby's grandfather had always advocated.

Abby had assumed the store was ready for her to help guide it to the next level. Tess had never implied anything else.

Abby twisted the cap off the lemonade bottle and took a deep sip. The cold drink barely cooled her down. The tart taste only sharpened her growing concern. Had she been wrong to come here? To stake her future on a historic store in a sleepy, don't-blink-or-you'll-miss-it Texas town?

"I'm a lot far from a profit. But it's fine. It's all going to be fine." Tess set her lemonade bottle on the counter with a thump, as if punctuating her conviction. "Besides it's not about me. How are you? The baby? Everyone feeling okay?" Tess flung her arms open. "It's really good to see you, Abs. It's been way too long."

"It's good to be here." Abby stepped into her cousin's embrace. She wasn't certain who was propping up whom. Tess was too thin, her hug more fragile than a crush of affection. Abby held on, and the shadow of loneliness that had been trailing her for weeks retreated. She wanted to give her cousin the same sense of hope.

And in that moment, she knew that the cousins needed each other. Everything would work out. She would make sure of it—for herself and Tess. "Thanks for the invite."

"If the AC hasn't changed your mind, you may start to rethink things once you see your room." Tess wrinkled her nose and walked down a narrow hallway. "The entire apartment seems to have been an afterthought. The store space downstairs is nothing like this. It's open and spacious. High ceilings and good ventilation."

"I can't wait to see it." And share her vision for the growth of the store. Abby exhaled, long and slow, pulling her eagerness back. Even her breath couldn't stir the heavy, hot air surrounding her or the feeling that her cousin might not be as prepared for Abby's ideas as she'd thought.

Tess stepped into the room across from a compact bathroom. "I looked everywhere, but I can't seem to find the closet door that belongs in here."

"It doesn't matter." Abby stood in the doorway of a tiny room. The cushion on the futon bed brushed against a small wooden folding table under the narrow window with another one of Tess's neon-colored desktop fans. The doorless closet looked as if it could hold nothing taller or wider than an ironing board.

Tess had added a cheery comforter and half a dozen plump pillows to brighten the space. Abby pressed her palm against a purple sequined pillow and grinned. "This looks like a really comfortable place to sleep. It's going to be perfect."

"You always were the most positive one among us." Tess squeezed Abby's arm, then switched on the fan. "I still remember that first Christmas we met at Grandma and Grandpa's house. Remember that blizzard that locked us indoors without power for three days?"

"It was my first time seeing snow." Her first time spending a holiday with her extended family. And one of her favorite Christmases to date. Abby hugged the pillow.

"And we couldn't even open the front door to go outside and play. We couldn't even bake cookies for Santa without the power." Tess shook her head. "You never complained. Not once, unlike Paige and me."

Abby had been in second grade, Tess in third and Tess's younger sister Paige in first. Abby had spent her early childhood overseas, traveling with her archaeologist mother and

English-teacher father. They'd returned to the US to spend that Christmas in northern Wisconsin with Abby's grandparents and her aunt and uncle. Abby hadn't wanted to leave to return to her mother's archaeological site in Bolivia. She'd begged her parents to let her move in permanently with her grandparents. But her parents had wanted Abby to explore the world with them. Except Abby had sometimes wanted to explore her own backyard instead, just like her cousins did at their home.

Over the years, pictures and Christmas cards would arrive of her two cousins and grandparents opening presents together in front of the Christmas tree, and Abby had only ever wished to be there with them. Her parents never understood why she didn't share their passion for adventure and travel.

Even now, her parents were in Peru, exploring the history of an ancient civilization. And all Abby wanted to discover was her own family history right here in Three Springs, Texas. "That was the best Christmas ever."

Tess laughed. "You convinced Paige and me that Santa would still be able to come. That he'd find the house even buried under all the snow."

"And he did." Abby set the pillow on the bed. "Santa brought us matching fleece pajamas." Abby had also received a tie-dyed plush unicorn she'd taken on every move around the globe and to college when she'd returned to the States.

"That's right." Tess straightened the comforter and smiled at Abby. "One of my favorite memories was the three of us sleeping together in front of the fireplace in the family room, telling stories and giggling too late into the night."

"Grandpa would come to warn us to quiet down, then curl up on the couch and tell us a story about growing up in Three Springs." Abby had listened to and memorized her grandfather's stories that week and retold the stories to her stuffed unicorn on the nights she couldn't sleep.

"Then Grandpa would fall asleep and Grandma would have to come and get him," Tess said. "Telling us he'd be too stiff to move the next morning if he slept on the couch all night."

"I would've slept on the couch here," Abby confessed. Anything not to be alone. Anything to be with her family.

"We'll save the couch for Paige." Tess slipped around Abby and stepped into the hallway.

"Is she coming for a visit?" Abby had seen Tess and Paige at Eric's funeral, but the visit had been too brief.

"I haven't spoken to Paige in a while. Only texts." Concern could be heard in Tess's voice before she cleared her throat. "But every message I send, I tell her to come down here to see us."

Abby had only shared text messages with Paige too over the past few months. Her cousin's replies were always brief and assured Abby that she was okay and simply overworked. Like Tess, Abby still worried about Paige. "Maybe the hospital where she works will find another vet as good as Paige, and she'll get time off soon."

Tess nodded. "That's exactly what I'm hoping for."

Abby skirted a stack of boxes marked *Kitchen* and picked up her lemonade. The bottle had already warmed from the few minutes sitting on the counter. "What can I do to help in here? Line cabinets? Unpack essentials?"

"This place is on hold." Tess waved her hand, and her gaze skipped over the boxes. "The store has been my priority."

Her cousin wasn't ready to confront her memories. Abby respected that. She would be there when Tess felt differently. Meantime, there was the store and the future she planned to stake here. She motioned toward the front door. "Then, lead the way. I'm ready to get to work."

"Are you sure?" Tess's gaze dipped to Abby's stomach.

"I'm pregnant, not injured." Abby laughed. "And I came here to help you. I can't do that lying around on the couch."

Besides, Abby had ideas for a new store website and expansion. Things that would get the Silver Penny noticed beyond the town limits. Things that would build profits and ensure the general store's success. Abby was determined this time she would be a success too.

"Still, if you need a nap or to put your feet up, you have to do that." Tess's voice dipped into determined. "I can handle things alone."

Tess had been handling things alone for too long. The same as Abby. That changed now. "But you aren't alone anymore. I'm here. And I'm not napping either."

She refused to be a burden to her cousin. Tess's shoulders were already too weighed down, and Abby wasn't certain how much more her cousin could handle.

Tess picked up her keys and lemonade from the counter. She tapped her bottle against Abby's. "Have I mentioned I'm really glad you're here?"

"I am too." Abby grinned and together they went outside, down the creaky staircase to the front of the building. A wooden sidewalk connected the row of stores lining one side of the main street. The same wooden sidewalk was used across the street, joining another dozen eclectic-looking buildings.

Tess jingled the keys. "Downtown Three Springs consists of Fortune Street, which is our street. Then the square, two blocks down. City Hall, the historic church and the original Stagecoach Inn make up the three main points around the square. Five Star Grocery Depot, the gas station and Ramsey's auto repair, where I'm sure your car is going, are on the opposite side of town."

"I can acquaint myself with Three Springs later." Abby turned and pressed her hand against the wrought iron double doors with original etched glass and scrolled handles. She could hear her Grandpa Harlan's laughing voice greet the customers. *Welcome to the Silver Penny, where we have what you need and the gossip is free.* "I can't believe I'm finally here."

Tess pushed the doors open and stood aside to allow Abby in. "Welcome to our grandparents' pride and joy. The place they treasured for decades."

The treasure was hard to find beneath the layers of grime. The store may once have been a sparkling gem, but now it was a neglected afterthought. A remnant of a time long past.

Only the checkout counter and front windows had been cleaned and polished. A collection of more than a dozen shelves stood empty and waiting. Note cards taped to the shelves marked their intended use, except most of the words on the cards had been crossed out and written over with different items several times. Two large archways were roped off, keeping the areas dark, uninviting and unexplored.

Abby turned in a slow circle, trying to recall her grandparents' descriptions to superimpose those memories on her current view. She'd designed her vision for the store on her grandparents' narrative of a thriving business. Not on this ramshackle version.

This place would require a complete overhaul to become functional. Profitable was more fantasy than reality. She pictured her ex-boyfriend shaking his camera-ready head and reminding her, *Wishful thinking isn't a viable career, Abby. You can't even support yourself. How do you expect to take care of a child?* She curled her fingers into her palms. Her ex had doubted. Even her cowboy today doubted her.

She'd faced the truth, left her cheating ex and her failures back in California. Listened to all those self-help podcasts on living an extraordinary life, scaling up her strengths and finding success on the drive here. Now, it was time to usher in the new version of Abby James. The one who could achieve anything, including taking care of herself and her baby on her own.

No matter that her cousin couldn't pay her. That the store was barely functional. She would find a way that wasn't built on daydreams and stargazing.

A book box near the window caught her attention. The four shelves had been filled with hardcovers and paperbacks. The glass doors gleamed. A neat sign perched on top of the large case read *Book Exchange. Please take one and leave one.*

"I might not be working in a library now." Tess touched the book box. "But I'm still a librarian."

"It's a lovely addition to the store." Abby moved to face the bare shelves again.

"The rest of it is a work in progress as you can tell." Tess brushed her hands together.

Nothing to do now but start at the beginning and build from there. "Where should we begin?"

"I've been trying to plot out what I want to sell and where I want to put it in the store." Tess removed a sticky note from an empty shelf and crumpled it up. "Like the sections in a library."

Except a library often had books to put on those shelves and fill those sections. Abby walked behind the long checkout counter and peered inside the storeroom. Only more antiques and dust-covered boxes. "Where is your inventory?"

"It's been more on an order-as-needed basis."

Tess wiped her hand over the top of a stool and sat down.

Translation: her cousin had no inventory. "How is that working out?"

"Customer orders are increasing." Tess's smile wavered.

Abby searched for her positive. *Drawing a rainbow over your account balance doesn't change it from zero, Abby.* No, but it had dulled her despair. Besides, there was nothing wrong with optimism, despite what her ex and even Wes claimed. "What did Grandma and Grandpa sell?"

"A bit of everything, judging from the old ledgers I found." Excitement showed on Tess's face. She opened a cabinet and lifted a leather-bound book out. Her grip on the ledger was reverent. Her voice was soft and smooth. "These ledgers date all the way back to when the store opened in 1799. In the nineteenth century, they sold basinets and ran an apothecary. In the twentieth century, the store expanded to every type of dry good from silk to suspenders to hats and coffins. Penny candy, groceries and farming equipment were always staple items."

Abby glanced at the ledger. "You mentioned there's a grocery store nearby."

"And a feed and tack store next to Ramsey's

auto shop." Tess set her palm on the tattered ledger. "I don't want to compete."

Abby wandered down an aisle and read the note cards. "What have customers been ordering?"

"Everything from vintage cast-iron dinner bells to antique caster sets to hard-to-find fabric." Tess set her elbow on the counter and rested her chin against her palm.

"Things they can't find in the other stores in town, then."

"And things other stores don't have the time to source or locate," Tess explained. "Especially when it's not something sold in bulk, like caster sets or vintage lanterns."

Abby wiped off the top of a barrel at the end of an aisle. "This looks ready for some of that penny candy."

"Is that what you think this should become? A candy store?" Tess wrinkled her nose as if not convinced that should be the store's direction.

"I think vintage candy is one item you could stock," Abby offered. "Wait. Do you still make your own candy? I always said you could sell your candy creations."

Abby had been in college when Tess had mailed Abby her first birthday candy tin. It had been filled with the most delicious homemade fudge and caramels. Every birthday since,

Tess would send Abby another candy tin filled with a new variety she'd created. Last year had been the first year in over a decade that Abby hadn't received Tess's offering for her November birthday.

"That was just a silly hobby." Tess shook her head, knocking her hair loose from behind her ear but not the lost look from her cloudy gaze. "Something I used to do for fun, but not anymore."

Abby pressed her lips together rather than press her cousin. Tess's candy had been some of the best she'd ever tasted. And Tess's love for candy-making had been evident. Abby wondered why she'd given it up. Tess and her husband had had a whirlwind romance—meeting, getting engaged and eloping in under six months. In that time, Tess had quit her job as a librarian and had given up her candy-making hobby and who knew what else. Abby had assumed Tess and Eric had shared a once-in-a-lifetime love story. After all, that's what her cousin had deserved. Abby began to wonder if there was more to the relationship than what Tess had described as a fairy-tale romance.

Abby refocused on the store, leaving her cousin and her secrets alone. "The place once sold basinets. What about making a section for infants and babies? You could offer home goods for every stage from infant to adult."

Selfishly, Abby wanted that section for her own personal shopping. She had a baby on the way and no idea where to start.

"That's it. It'll be a home goods store." Tess jumped from the stool, then frowned. "But is that too specific? It's supposed to be a general store like it used to be."

"Before we decide what it is," Abby began, "maybe we need to clean the entire space and see what we have."

"But I didn't hire you to clean the store," Tess said. "You're supposed to run the cash register. Help customers and sit on the stool when you need to rest."

"And I will do that." One day sooner than later, she hoped. "But we have to clean first."

Tess dropped back onto the stool, folded her arms on the counter and lowered her head. "There's something you need to know."

Abby walked to the other side of the counter and faced her cousin.

"And if you want to leave, I'll understand." Her voice was muffled.

"Are you selling the store?" Abby wouldn't blame her. The entire space was a bit overwhelming, and overhauling it into a successful business was more than daunting. If Abby were in Tess's shoes, she'd consider selling the place. Though that would leave them both with no place to go. And prove Wes right—Abby didn't belong here.

"No." Tess straightened and blinked. "No way. I'm not selling."

Abby relaxed. She could still prove her cowboy and everyone else wrong.

"I invited you down here because I was lonely." Tess reached across the counter and grabbed Abby's hand. "I took advantage of your situation, and it was selfish and wrong. I wanted you here for me."

"You didn't take advantage of my situation," Abby said. "I called you, remember?"

Abby had sat in her car after watching her boyfriend kiss another woman at the house Abby and her ex had shared for two years. The positive pregnancy results, printed on a paper from the doctor's office, had been on the passenger seat beside her. All her excitement and hopes for their life together had evaporated like a fog.

She'd been lost and alone and scared.

Tess had been her first phone call.

"But I lied to you." Tess squeezed Abby's fingers. An urgency rushed into her words. "Abby, I cannot pay you to work here. I can't pay myself. It's not what I promised you."

Abby covered their joined hands with her other hand. "Tess, you offered me a place to stay. A place to start over and rebuild my life."

"What about the money?" Tess asked.

"We'll figure everything out." There really was no other choice.

Tess eyed her. "You aren't mad?"

Abby shook her head.

Tess exhaled. "Does that mean you're also not leaving?"

"Definitely not leaving," Abby said. "We're family. And I can't think of anyone I'd rather be with right now."

Tess rose and wiped her fingers through a layer of dust on the wall. "We really need to deep clean, don't we?"

"We do." Abby laughed.

"I'll run to Five Star Grocery and get supplies." Tess picked up her keys.

"Where can I find a cup of decaf coffee?" Abby asked. "I haven't had a decent cup since I left Los Angeles County."

"The Feisty Owl," Tess said.

"Isn't that a bar?" She'd seen the barnlike building across the street from the general store.

"Yup," Tess said. "And they serve the best cup of coffee in town."

Abby exited onto the wooden sidewalk and

waited for Tess to lock the doors. "I shouldn't be too long. And then we can begin."

Abby checked the street for oncoming traffic. There wasn't any kind of traffic on the quiet main street, not a car or pedestrian or horse. Her grandfather had never described Three Springs as a sleepy little town. He'd only ever talked about the kind and generous friends and constant flow of customers that had filled the store. Of course, it'd been decades since the store had closed. Towns changed.

Abby crossed the street. Her cousin might not know where to begin, but Abby knew exactly what she needed to do. She had to find another job. Quickly. One that came with a stable paycheck and the ability to help her cousin restore the general store.

Surely, she was qualified for something in Three Springs. Never mind her résumé was more of a series of starts and many more stops in various industries. She'd always begun a new job with high hopes and ended being told she wasn't a good fit for the position.

She opened the heavy door to the Feisty Owl and paused. She'd expected it to be dark and dank with beer-stained, sticky floors and smoke-filled rooms. Instead, an open, airy space greeted her. One side of the room had sit-down dining and the other a massive bar and mechanical bull. One wall in the bar area was made entirely of glass, granting a view to the outdoor patio with a massive fireplace. A small stage and large dance floor in the far corner and dozens of high-top tables completed the bar scene.

Abby headed there.

An older gentleman tipped his worn brown cowboy hat at her from the far corner of the bar. "What brings you to the Owl? An early start on the evening's happy hour, or something to recover from last night? We have cures for all."

"A coffee craving," Abby said. "My cousin told me I could find the best cup of coffee in town here."

"Who's your cousin?" His thick eyebrows pulled together as he studied her.

"Tess Palmer," Abby answered.

"She's a good egg." A quick smile stretched across his weathered face. He rose and made his way around the bar, then reached out his hand. "Boone Bradley. Don't call me Mr. I only answer to Boone these days. And you are?"

"Abby James." Abby shook Boone's hand: his grip was warm. There was something sturdy yet comforting about the older gentleman that reminded Abby of her grandfather. She liked Boone instantly. "Nice to meet you, Boone."

He gestured to the empty bar stool beside

him. "You're the owner of that convertible at Trey's shop."

"That's me." Abby sat. "I didn't know the car had been towed already."

"We don't like to keep friends waiting. I was coming over to the general store this afternoon to meet you. Now you saved me the trip." Boone patted her arm, then hollered toward the swinging door marked *Kitchen*. "We got a customer out here."

The barn-style door swung open, offering a glimpse into a modern kitchen with stainless-steel furnishings. Another cowboy-hat-wearing man stepped through the doorway. This one more than familiar. And unexpected. Abby's mouth dropped open. "Wes?"

Wes blinked and pushed his hat up on his forehead. "Hey, Abby. What can I get you?"

Directions to the one place in town where she wouldn't accidently run into Wes. Was there such a place?

Abby straightened and kept a hint of indifference in her voice. As for the spike to her heartbeat, she ignored that. "From cowboy to bartender. Any other talents you want to share with me?"

"I'm not sure if it's a talent," Boone offered. "But Wes here is…"

"Getting Abby's order from her," Wes finished for him.

"Decaf coffee." And anything that might neutralize her reaction to seeing Wes again.

CHAPTER FOUR

WES SLOWED HIS truck in Boone's wide driveway and parked beside a white four-door sedan.
Boone hadn't mentioned anyone visiting him
this afternoon.

He'd driven Boone home last night after
they'd ensured everything had been tidied thor-
oughly and the money was secure in the safe.
Boone had created a checklist of six items for
the bar's closing procedure years ago and still
insisted on making the final inspection every
night. Boone believed the tone for the following day was determined by how the previous
night ended.

And good days came to those who'd properly
prepared the evening prior.

So far, Wes's day had been good. And pro-
ceeding as he'd planned.

A sunrise ride on Dan along Old Copper
Mill Road. The uneventful delivery of the rescue mare, an American paint horse, and her
foal. A breakfast meeting with his head chef to
plan the weekend menu and order supplies, fol-

lowed by two uninterrupted hours in his office for paperwork and payroll. He'd had no surprise run-ins with a broken-down convertible or one eye-catching and all too intriguing blonde.

Not on his morning ride or at the bar. Wes had brewed a fresh pot of decaf coffee, just in case. He wondered if Abby would linger at the Owl like she had yesterday.

It wasn't exactly that Abby had lingered. She'd left rather quickly after Wes had given her a large to-go cup of decaf. It was more that everything about her had lingered with Wes. From her bright smile to her soft laugh. To that spark within her gaze—the one that hinted at a woman with layers and depth. He had to press pause on his thoughts. In short, he had to stop thinking about Abby.

He had everything he needed for a full life. And one collision with a woman wasn't going to make him reconsider. He'd avoided relationships during his active-duty days in the Navy. And now, he simply preferred his life just as it was. He was single, self-sufficient and satisfied.

Wes checked the Texas license plates on the sedan in Boone's driveway and noted the dirt-coated white paint and mud-splattered tires. In contrast, the interior was clean, spotless and dull like the plain, basic amenities found in a rental car or even a business car.

Boone emerged from the stables and joined Wes in the driveway.

Wes pointed to the sedan. "Whose car is this?"

"The appraiser's." Boone frowned toward the ranch house. "Seems there's been an offer to buy the property."

"I didn't know this place was for sale." Wes crossed his arms over his chest.

Boone had been renting the ranch house and land ever since old man J.R. Dawson had passed away and his heirs had decided they wanted to keep the land in the family. J.R. had run his family's leather- and shoe-repair shop next door to the Feisty Owl for years. J.R. had eventually closed his business, citing the changing times, and retired to spend his days on his ranch.

"Everything is for sale for the right price." Boone's tone was grim.

Even family loyalty could be bought. Wes understood that all too well. His only brother had proven that money had mattered more than blood ties. Wes knocked his anger at his brother aside and turned toward the stables. "Still, someone from the Dawson family should've informed you."

"They did. Today in fact." Boone handed an envelope to Wes. "Out of respect for my relationship with their grandfather, they're giving me first right of refusal."

Wes didn't take the envelope. "And?"

"And I have a decision to make." Boone folded the envelope and tucked it into the front pocket of his plaid shirt.

Wes wiped the back of his hand across his mouth and stopped walking to stare at Boone. "For how much?"

"That's to be determined." Boone hitched his thumb toward the house. "By him."

Wes watched a reedy man come around the corner of the single-story ranch house. He held a clipboard and fumbled with an oversize tape measure. He wore wrinkle-free dress pants and a pale blue polo shirt. No sturdy work boots. No cowboy hat. And no reason to make Wes believe the man knew the first thing about a rancher's life.

An attachment to the land wouldn't factor in the appraised value. Neither would a long-standing friendship with the former owner. Or Boone's deep, unrelenting respect for all living things. None of it would matter once the appraiser dropped his figures onto his spreadsheet and pressed a button to calculate the current property value. "What happens if you can't afford to buy it?"

"Then, the horses and I need to find a new home." Boone's voice was matter-of-fact.

Anger on Boone's behalf surfaced. But emotions always crowded out reason and sound solutions. And they needed both right now. "What can I do?"

Boone leveled his gaze on Wes, steady and serious. The poker face that had won the old cowboy more hands at the card table than anyone else in the county was firmly in place. "Buy me out of the Feisty Owl and become full owner of the bar finally."

Wes ground the toe of his boot into the dirt. Boone had been encouraging Wes to buy the bar for the past two years. But the Feisty Owl Bar and Grill was never supposed to be Wes's inheritance or his legacy. That honor belonged to Boone's grandson, Jake. Wes and Jake's SEAL team had succeeded on their final mission—the target had been neutralized and detained. But their target had also collected three casualties, including Jake. "I can't do that."

"You've turned the place around. Made it profitable." Boone eyed him with the same intensity he used to dissuade patrons from starting a barroom brawl. "Your heart is as much inside that place as mine is."

Wes had come up with improvements to the historic bar and made what he considered sound business decisions.

That wasn't heart.

Wes had taken over as bar manager one day

after he'd informed Boone of his grandson's death overseas. Ten days after Wes had returned to US soil as a decorated veteran and learned his own brother, Dylan, had sold the Tanner family ranch in Colorado and disappeared with the profits from the sale and Wes's entire inheritance.

At the time, Wes had recognized the lost look in Boone's dark gaze. It was the same despair and anguish he saw in his own reflection. Confused and adrift, Wes had accepted Boone's offer to stay in the apartment behind the Feisty Owl and work at the bar until Wes decided on a direction for his future.

He'd been searching for his deceitful brother, following leads, knocking into dead ends and restarting his hunt over and over. Once Wes had his inheritance in his hands, then he'd have a direction. Only then could he rebuild his family's home and legacy on Colorado soil again.

But those painful details were Wes's personal business.

It was exactly like he'd told Abby. Three Springs was only ever a temporary port. Not his permanent future.

Wes pushed his hat up his forehead and tipped his head toward the ranch house. "Looks like the appraiser might be finished. Want me to talk to him?"

"Leave him be." Boone scowled, then turned away from Wes. "Rescued horses and an old man with roots deeper than his family tree aren't in his job description."

"Where are you going?" Wes asked.

"Into town." Boone lifted his cowboy hat off his head and ran his fingers through his hair as if fixing himself before walking into the historic church. "Gonna consult my financial adviser."

"Sam Sloan is not a financial expert," Wes said. The two men were best friends, comrades and coconspirators. But neither one had a degree in finance or a deep retirement fund.

"When you've lived through year-long droughts and tornadoes and been chased by an irate bull on more than one occasion and survived, you become something of an expert on life." Boone stopped and set his hands on his hips. "That's Sam and me."

"I'll come with you," Wes offered. "We can look over your personal financials at the bar. Talk through the options."

"You'll stay here and make sure that new mare and her foal are settling in," Boone ordered. "And you'll come to the bar for your shift as usual. Unless you're ready to discuss the only option that makes the most sense."

Buying the bar outright. Stepping in like an impostor into his best friend's legacy and hometown. Trespassing on his best friend's life. What if Wes failed? What if he couldn't measure up to Jake or to Boone's expectations?

Wes took his hat off and tapped it against his leg. "Tell Sam not to order today's special. The chicken tortilla soup will be too spicy for his stomach to handle."

Boone's smile was weak. "Never thought I'd ever meet a man more stubborn than Sam."

Wes knew one. His name was Boone Bradley. He left him and walked toward the stables.

He'd check on the horses quickly, then run another online search for his brother before he went to the bar. He had to find his inheritance. It was possible he'd have the money to purchase the land for Boone and still have funds leftover to begin his life by buying back his family's land in Colorado.

That was his place, and he knew it.

Rebuilding what his family once had and honoring their memory. Fixing past wrongs. Wrongs that might not have happened if only he'd been there for his family. If only he'd been there working the ranch beside his brother.

But none of it would happen if he failed to find Dylan and the lost inheritance.

CHAPTER FIVE

ABBY SPREAD THE classified section of the Wednesday edition of the *Three Springs Standard* across the checkout counter in the general store. She uncapped her marker and scanned the employment offerings. They included a handful of jobs ranging from ranch hand to cutting-horse trainer to distillery-grain operator.

The listings for resale furniture and roommates outnumbered the available jobs four to one.

"That can't be all." Abby opened the paper wider and smoothed her hand over the black-and-white comics covering the adjoining page. Surely, there were other businesses hiring in Three Springs. More than the ranches and the local whiskey distillery. She had experience in several different fields. Her résumé read like a sampler box of multiple tea varieties. She'd dabbled in everything from retail to media to the corporate world. But that hardly left her uniquely qualified as a heavy-equipment operator or a herd manager.

"What's wrong?" Tess worked to straighten one of the shelving units. An entire section slanted sideways. Inventory would simply slide to the floor if they used it.

Abby folded the paper, picked up the to-go coffee cup from the Feisty Owl and swallowed her worry. She wouldn't dull Tess's good mood. She'd find a job, even if as a last resort she had to convince Wes to hire her. He could use a capable hostess, not that Boone wasn't already the perfect greeter. "I'm already out of decaf coffee."

"There's more across the street." Tess laughed.

"We have a lot to do." Abby tugged on her cleaning gloves. She admitted she found her cowboy attractive and would manage that unwise realization better if she wasn't forced to see him for work every single day. "I'll start over here."

Tess and Abby scrubbed and polished every surface and leveled every shelf. Testing each one for sturdiness and strength. They shared a high five once they finished.

The brass shopkeeper's bell above the main doors chimed.

Abby and Tess turned together to see who was there. A tall, thin gentleman with a herringbone fedora angled on his head held the door open for a petite woman. The woman's wide-brimmed straw hat and crimson lipstick gave her a decidedly retro vibe.

"Frieda. Gordon. Welcome." Tess peeled off her work gloves and brushed her hands on her jeans, then introduced Frieda Hall and Gordon Rivers to Abby. Tess added, "Frieda, your waffle iron hasn't arrived yet. I expect it will be another day or so."

"That's wonderful, dear." Frieda untied the red silk bow under her chin, removed her hat and set it on the counter. "I'll be making fried chicken and waffles this weekend. I'm bringing my award-winning dish to the gardening club on Saturday. You and your cousin should consider joining us."

"We'd love to, but we're quite swamped getting the store ready to open." Tess's voice balanced perfectly between gracious and apologetic.

Abby offered Frieda a soft smile, grateful for her cousin's quick reply.

"Next time, then." Frieda brushed her fingers over her side-swept silver-white bangs and pointed a polished fingernail at Abby and Tess. "Be sure to mark your calendars. We meet the second Saturday of every month, rain or shine. There hasn't been a Roots and Shoots meeting canceled in the last ten years."

That was certainly a dedicated group. Abby's

thumb was more brown than green. And she doubted the garden-club members would appreciate her fondness for artificial-succulent gardens.

"Is there something I can do for you?" Tess asked.

"Boone sent us over. Straightaway." Frieda's smile widened. Her round, dark brown gaze landed and stuck like syrup on Abby.

"We've come to speak to Ms. James." Gordon wiped a handkerchief across his forehead and motioned between himself and Frieda. "Frieda and I sit on the town council."

Abby pulled off her cleaning gloves and dropped them on the counter. What could the town council want with her? She'd been in Three Springs only two days. "Me."

Tess dropped her tools into the toolbox near her feet and whispered, "Abs, you didn't damage any public property when you wrecked your car, did you?"

"Only if a pothole counts as public property." Abby squeezed Tess's arm.

Gordon lifted his fedora and patted at his bald head. "We have bigger problems to focus on at the moment than our county's potholes."

"Corine Bauer is on bed rest." Frieda's hands flew to her face as if she'd just spoken ill of one of her long-lost ancestors. "As of this morning. Full bed rest until the dear soul delivers."

Gordon dabbed his forehead again.

Abby wanted to offer the gentleman water or a fan or a chair. Except the only refrigerator with cold drinks, working fans and comfortable seats were upstairs in the apartment. The store needed a commercial refrigerator. Stools at the counter. And a stronger air conditioner.

"Corine Bauer is the town manager," Tess explained to Abby. "She's pregnant with twins and due in November."

"Corine Bauer keeps the town together." Frieda clutched Gordon's arm and tapped her ivory leather Mary Jane heel.

"That's an understatement," Gordon muttered.

"Now Corine needs an assistant," Frieda said.

"I can do that," Abby blurted.

Gordon paused middab and eyed Abby. "But can you put together a town event by Labor Day weekend?"

Labor Day. That was less than four weeks away. Sure, she'd planned matchmaking events in less time. Of course, she also had been relieved of her matchmaking position. The HR director had cited a company reorganization as the reason. But Abby had read between the lines. She'd been a bad fit for the role. That wasn't relevant now. Only the current job offer was. "What kind of event do you want?"

"The kind that will draw tourists and locals alike." Frieda splayed her hands in the air in front of her. Her words lifted as if she was the soloist in the church choir. "The kind of event that will grow each year and establish Three Springs as a place to visit annually."

"You want all that in less than a month." Doubt and surprise vied in Abby's voice.

"We have to have it." Gordon folded his handkerchief and returned to mopping his forehead. "Or the land developer will walk away and choose another town to invest in."

"Can't allow that." Resolve stiffened Frieda's shoulders. Determination clear in her words. "Three Springs needs opportunity. Growth."

"And the businesses need business." Gordon arched an eyebrow at Tess. He shifted his perceptive gaze to Abby as if he knew full well Tess could not pay the electric bill let alone herself and Abby.

"You want an event that will show the land developer that Three Springs is worth the investment." Sounded simple and impossible at the same time.

Still, excitement uncurled inside her. This was her chance. Forget the general store. She could put Three Springs on people's radar. Turn a sleepy town into a destination hot spot, not just another dot on the map. Then she would have finally made her mark too. No one would be asking her to leave or consider her a failure then.

"That's exactly what we want," Frieda said, beaming.

"Can you do it?" Gordon's sharp gaze settled firmly on Abby.

Abby stopped fidgeting. She had to look confident to be confident. A lesson she'd learned from her temporary stint as a dog groomer. That and proper grooming equipment mattered. She had no equipment to prove she could do this particular job. Except her belief in herself. If she intended to level up like her podcasts advocated, she had to take risks. Step outside her comfort zone. She pushed her shoulders back.

"If you succeed, you'll be hired full-time as Corine's assistant." Frieda held out her hands as if she read the title from a lit marquee sign on the side of a building.

Abby glanced at Tess. Worry shifted through her cousin's gaze. The same worry that wound through Abby. Could she plan and execute the kind of event the town council expected? In time? She couldn't afford not to try.

"Will you excuse us one minute?" Tess tugged Abby into the dark storeroom.

"Vacation and benefits are included," Frieda

said in a singsong as if she'd just explained that she'd added fresh-picked strawberries to her homemade lemonade at the garden-club gathering.

Tess clutched Abby's shoulders and looked her in the eye. "Abs, can you do this?"

"There's medical benefits, Tess." Abby brushed her hand over her stomach.

"It's a big job." Tess never blinked. "Have you ever planned an event on such a large scale before?"

"I planned events for the matchmaking company," Abby said, hedging.

"And…" Tess pressed.

"And I matched five couples that are still together." Never mind that she'd never reached the quota of matches required by her boss during her seven-month tenure. Or that every event she'd put on had gone over budget. "I'm more qualified for this than the ranch-hand positions listed in the newspaper."

"I have insurance money from Eric's policy." Tess chewed on her bottom lip. "It's enough for us to live on for a little while. You don't have to rush into anything."

Abby shook her head. She refused to be a drain on her cousin's finances. It was time she stood on her own. Proved something to herself and everyone around her. "You don't think I can do this, do you?"

Doubt tightened across Tess's face.

Not her cousin too. She forced herself to sound upbeat. She believed in herself—she'd make that be enough for now. "I see no other options, Tess. Besides, what's the worst that can happen?"

"Where do you want me to begin?" Tess blanched. "There's the risk with opening this store and flopping. Where will we go then? There's your baby coming soon. Babies need homes and things. Now the town council has pinned their hopes for the growth of Three Springs on you and your event. You could disappoint an entire town. It's so much."

Put like that, it was heavy and overwhelming. Abby's earlier excitement fizzled into a simmer.

"I'm worried." Tess lowered her arms and grabbed Abby's hands. "For you."

Abby replayed those podcasts she'd listened to, searching for the right words to convince them both this wasn't a mistake. "I heard recently that worrying snowballs and eventually tramples your happiness."

"That's not helping me feel any better." Tess looked defeated.

"Well, we can stand here, keep on worrying, and accomplish nothing." Abby linked her arm to her cousin's and headed for the doorway. "Or we can put our energy into doing something positive and be happy while we do it."

Joy did not infuse Tess's tone. "You're accepting the job, aren't you?"

"I know what I'm doing." She had to prove she could do one thing right. That she could not only imagine but also execute her ideas effectively. Then that would surely start a chain reaction of wins for Abby like the podcasts had preached. Her life would become a series of victories, rather than starts and stops. She would finally add value to the world. Finally be seen.

She stopped behind the checkout counter and smiled. "Frieda and Gordon, I accept the job."

"Wonderful!" Frieda clapped. "Simply wonderful."

Gordon exhaled and nodded slowly. He tucked his handkerchief into the back pocket of his khaki pants as if he'd suddenly overcome his heatstroke.

Tess remained quiet and still behind the counter.

"Tell us what you need, and we'll do our best to help." Frieda settled her straw hat on her head, tied the fabric under her chin to secure it. The entire time, she swayed as if she was humming a tune only she could hear.

Gordon's teeth flashed behind his suddenly

cheerful grin. He held his arm out for Frieda and escorted her to the front doors.

Abby called out, stopping the pair. "I need a large meeting space."

"For how many?" Gordon twisted around. "The largest conference room in the town hall fits about forty-five comfortably."

"Much larger than that." Abby touched the dampness on the back of her neck. Her nerves twisted.

Frieda blinked. "Do you intend to have a meeting with the whole town?"

"That's exactly what I intend." There was nothing like jumping in with both feet as if she knew the landing would be fine. She knew nothing. That was why she wanted to meet with the whole town.

"But—" Gordon started.

Frieda cut him off. "But you'll have to give folk more than a day's notice for this meeting. Saturdays are best."

"Right." Abby reached for the pencil on the counter and one of Tess's note cards from the stack. "People are off on the weekend."

"No one takes time off from their ranch." Gordon's voice turned defensive. "Ranching is a way of life. We live it every single day."

"I don't need long," Abby rushed on. "Only

the lunch hour. Even ranch owners eat lunch, right?"

"There's only one place big enough to hold the locals and feed everyone." Frieda's smile broadened.

Gordon nodded again, slow and precise. He knew the exact place too.

A bad feeling—the kind she got when she'd been called for the unscheduled meeting with the HR director and subsequently lost her job— overtook her.

"The Feisty Owl is the place you'll want." Frieda shrugged as if everything was settled.

Gordon tipped his hat, wished both Tess and Abby a good day, then slipped outside with Frieda.

Of course it was the Feisty Owl. Abby was going to hold a town-hall-style meeting in a bar. Why not? Nothing about her job interview or her hiring had been conventional. The older duo had never even inquired about Abby's qualifications. Never asked for more references than Boone's recommendation and Abby's family ties to Tess. Worse, Abby had never asked about the pay, the job description or the budget for the event.

But she had the promise of a full-time job. She had hope again. And one stubborn cowboy wasn't going to sidetrack her.

"Where are you going?" Tess asked.

Abby pushed the twin doors open. "To secure my meeting venue."

And to prove to that same stubborn cowboy that her new life was definitely in Three Springs.

CHAPTER SIX

"WHATEVER IT IS, it's a no." Wes wiped a thick microfiber towel over a bottle of whiskey and never looked at Abby.

Abby pulled up short on the other side of the aged bar top, set her hands on her hips and stared at Wes. Stubborn man simply went on polishing. Abby batted away her irritation. "How do you know I'm not here for more coffee?"

"Because you're not." Wes returned the whiskey bottle to the glass shelf behind him and picked up a deep blue vodka bottle. "Frieda and Gordon were in here earlier."

"You can't just say no without hearing me out," Abby said.

"I can." Wes lifted his gaze to hers and tipped the top of the vodka bottle toward her. "And I just did."

"What is wrong with you?" Frustration spilled into her words.

"That's just it." Wes grinned. But it wasn't the teeth-revealing, amused kind of smile. It was the dual-sided kind, one part courteous, two parts elusive and all too intriguing. The man had secrets Abby wanted to unravel if she had the time. But a new job and a new baby required all her focus. Her interest in Wes was a brief glitch and nothing she intended to act on.

"Nothing is wrong with me." Wes returned the bottle to the shelf. His polite but implacable grin never wavered. "And that's exactly how I like things."

"You make it sound like I'm here to mess things up for you." When in fact he was the one messing things up for her. That was obvious. Less clear was how she was going to make him understand that.

"You, Abby James, complicate things." Wes set a to-go cup on the bar and reached for the decaf coffeepot. One perfect, long pour filled the cup. Steam drifted from the hot brew. Something else drifted through his copper-tinted gaze. "You definitely complicate things."

"I don't need anything from you. I just need…" Abby accepted the to-go cup and took a sip. It was seriously unfortunate that it was one of the best cups of coffee she'd ever tasted. She would set up shop inside the bar for a continuous supply of decaf if not for this one provoking man. "It's simple really. I just need your bar."

"You want the bar?" His eyebrows rose as if he hadn't expected that.

"And the restaurant," Abby added.

He stilled. His gaze never left her face. He had such singular focus. She might've been flattered. If he wasn't objecting and making it more difficult for her to secure a job that would start her chain reaction of personal triumphs. The very victories that would finally set her on that path to success.

"For an hour. At the most." Abby rambled on, taking his silence as an invitation to keep pleading her case. She clutched the coffee cup and located her nerve.

He'd been telling her how it was going to be. How she didn't belong in Three Springs. How she was temporary. Now, it was her turn to tell him a few truths. "I need to use the bar and grill at noon this Saturday. I'd also like you to provide appetizers too."

His gaze narrowed. "For how many, exactly?"

Abby winced, the smallest break in her bravado. "What's the current population of Three Springs?"

He inhaled, flattened his palms on the bar top and leaned toward her. "This sounds like it's getting *complicated*."

"There's nothing complicated about it." Abby set her cup on the bar and curved her fingers around his hands. "I need to have a meeting with the people of Three Springs. It needs to be here."

"On Saturday." His gaze drifted to their joined hands, held for several beats, before returning to her face. "As in two days from now."

Abby reached for her own singular focus. But his fingers flexed beneath hers. And the warmth of his skin distracted her. She wanted to rearrange her grip, press her palm against his and test how well their hands fit together. She blinked, searched his gaze. Surely, that wasn't heat she saw there too. She had to let go. Step back. She never moved. And couldn't quite slow her racing pulse. "You have the only place large enough to host everyone."

"But you don't need me to do anything."

Need him. Now her fingers tensed around his as if she needed to steady herself. He was a distraction she certainly did not need. "You'd have to arrange the food unless you want me to work with your chef directly."

She tried to recall the matchmaking events she'd hosted. "You have to also coordinate your staff. Open the bar. Set up the microphone. A wireless one works best. But that's all. I promise."

He eased free of her grip, leaned against the back counter and crossed his arms over his chest. "You should always make sure you understand the promise you're making before you make it."

That wasn't an answer. It was more like a prophecy. Abby opened and closed her mouth. She didn't have time to take a deep dive into the particulars of a promise issued. A simple *Yes, the place is yours* or *No* would have sufficed.

The door behind the bar swung open. Boone stepped through and spread his arms wide. "Is that Eagle Springs' new event planner?"

"Boone." Abby rushed toward the older cowboy and wrapped him a tight hug. "How can I thank you?"

Boone patted Abby's shoulder. "I believe you just did, darling."

Abby eased away and quickly adjusted Boone's cowboy hat. Her enthusiasm had knocked it askew. Chagrined, she apologized. "Sorry. I'm a hugger."

"Never apologize for embracing life." Boone linked their arms and guided her around the bar toward his usual stool. "Or hugging with all your heart. That's the proper way to right a person's entire day."

Abby relaxed and found her first real smile of the afternoon. Clint, her ex and an up-and-coming newscaster, had avoided public displays of affection, usually citing his reputation. *Some-*

one is always watching and always recording, Abby. I have an image to maintain. Ironic Clint had forgotten his own decree when he'd shared an intimate embrace with another woman on their porch for all the neighbors and Abby to witness.

Boone waited for Abby to slide onto a stool before settling onto his own. "What brings you into the Owl today?"

"Wes and I are discussing the town meeting I'm going to have here on Saturday." Abby aimed her triumphant grin at Wes.

"Town meeting, you say." Boone set a bowl of roasted peanuts between them and scooped out a handful. "Can't recall the last time we had one of those."

"Then, it's past due to have one." Abby snapped a peanut shell open. "It'll be the perfect way for me to start to plan the Labor Day weekend event."

Boone popped several peanuts into his mouth and chewed. "What do you have in mind?"

"I already have a list of potential ideas." Abby shook several peanuts in her palm. "Can you believe that? But I want to discuss them with everyone."

"What if the town decides we don't want an event?" Wes stretched out the word *event* as if it was stuck in his throat and placed an empty bowl next to Abby for her peanut shells.

Now Boone looked chagrined, staring at Wes.

Abby lost her smile again. No thanks to her cowboy. "Are you telling me the town is content coming here for their entertainment fix night after night? Week after week. Month after month."

"Haven't heard any complaints." Wes shrugged.

"Doesn't mean they aren't complaining." Abby crushed another shell in her fist.

Abby herself had a growing list of complaints against Wes. He was stubborn. Cynical. Arrogant. Worse, he disrupted her balance. Made her heart race. And he continued to intrigue her.

One thing gave her peace of mind. Romance wasn't anywhere on her radar.

Besides, if she'd been looking for love, Wes certainly wasn't the one she'd fall for. Falling in love was supposed to be full of rainbows and butterflies, not potholes and frustration.

Boone's quick burst of laughter erupted around them. "Never thought I'd see the day when Wes was rendered speechless."

Wes yanked a polishing cloth off a hook and scrubbed a spot on the bar. "We're a small town, Abby. If you want more, you have to keep on driving east until you reach Amarillo. They have events every night. Every weekend. Every month."

"It's one weekend, Wes," Abby countered.

"I'm not altering the fabric of Three Springs. I'm planning an occasion as I was tasked to do by the town council, and obviously, I want the town's input."

"Then, you should have the meeting here." Boone slapped his palm on the bar top like a judge with a gavel, declaring the trial over.

"Really?" Abby glanced between Boone and Wes.

"He owns the place." Wes dumped the cracked shells into the trash behind the counter and returned the empty bowl to the bar.

"For now." Boone's words seemed to land like a lit firecracker between the two men.

Abby took in the silent standoff.

She wanted to smooth things over between them, except she didn't know exactly what needed to be smoothed over. If Wes had been implacable before, he was downright rigid and completely closed off now.

She really wanted to take Wes's hand. Offer another promise he wouldn't accept. But, man, she wanted to reach for him. Reach him. For beyond his stiff jaw and unyielding posture, his gaze reflected something lonely.

But Wes had already called Abby a complication. She hardly wanted to become an interference too. Whatever it was between the two men, they'd have to solve it on their own. She had the first of her own personal victories to achieve and a job to secure. "Okay. Looks like I have a presentation to go and prepare. See you Saturday."

"I'll be here." Boone patted Abby's arm. "I'm looking forward to hearing what you have in mind for improving this town."

Wes rolled his shoulders and picked up the coffeepot. He refilled Abby's cup and pushed a lid on top. "I'll talk to my chef about appetizers."

"Nothing extravagant." Abby accepted the cup and slipped off the stool. "Keep the menu simple."

"What about you?" Wes tilted his head and eyed her. "Are you going to keep this Labor Day event simple?"

Abby shook her head and chuckled. "There's nothing fun about simple."

Wes rubbed his chin. He looked mildly uncomfortable, as if he'd swallowed a peanut shell.

What was fun was getting under Wes's skin. "Oh, and Wes, not every complication is a bad thing."

"What is it, then?" One corner of his mouth twitched, his expression blank.

"A complication can be a challenge." She smiled, reveling in her determination. "And my Grandpa Harlan told me to never back down from a challenge."

CHAPTER SEVEN

"Maybe everyone is running late." Abby's smile wavered, but her shoulders never dipped. "Or stuck in traffic."

Or simply not coming. Wes checked the tropical-themed monthly calendar tacked on the wall next to the delivery schedule. Today was the second Saturday of the month. The Roots and Shoots Garden Club was meeting this afternoon. They started promptly at one o'clock. But like a tailgate for a national-championship football game, people started gathering for Roots and Shoots in the morning.

Lynette Kinney was hosting today's club meeting and unveiling her newly renovated backyard, complete with a koi pond and an elaborate catio designed exclusively for her six cats. Lynette's extravagant backyard had been the talk of the town for the past few months.

"I'll be right back." Wes pushed through the swinging door into the kitchen. He nodded to Boone and Nolan Davis, his head chef, who were discussing the day's specials. He pulled out his cell phone and stepped inside his office.

Frieda Hall answered on the first ring. "Martin, dearest, tell me you found the extra jars of homemade maple syrup and will be here within five minutes. The waffles are drying out as I look at them."

"Frieda." Wes rubbed his cheek. "It's Wes Tanner, not your husband Martin."

"Wes. Oh, well, where are you, then?" Frieda laughed. "The waffles are hot, and the fish are swimming. You'll want to see this. It's quite something. A bit more than I would've done, but that's our Lynette…"

"I'm at the bar." Wes closed the door to his office. "With Abby James."

Frieda sucked in a breath. "Wes, you were supposed to set her straight about today. It's what you do best."

"Exactly what do I do best?" He stared at the ceiling, suddenly certain he didn't want to know the answer.

"You tell it like it is." Frieda rushed on. "You should consider it a gift, not a curse, by the way."

And yet somehow it sounded more like an unfortunate trait of his. "What exactly am I supposed to tell Abby?"

"I liked Abby too much after our first encounter to tell her that no one would show up for her meeting. She was so endearing and so very excited. But everyone's social calendar is already booked. You know how it is." A shuffling of sorts echoed over the speaker. Frieda's voice became a muffled yet urgent whisper. "The truth hurts sometimes, Wes. And I don't like to be the one to burst bubbles. It's not nice and hardly my style."

Abby was hurting now. A fact Wes didn't much care for. And apparently Wes was the town's bubble-buster and now tasked with letting Abby down gently. "I'll take care of it."

"Abby has such a lovely spirit about her, Wes. Such a sincere sweetness." Frieda sighed. "The world needs more kindness like hers."

"Should I suggest Abby reschedule her town meeting?" Wes asked.

"Heavens, no." Frieda's voice lifted as if she clutched the phone closer to her mouth. "Between several milestone-birthday parties, a fiftieth wedding anniversary to celebrate and kickoff meetings for the kids' football and soccer seasons, we can't squeeze much more in."

"Yet you want Abby to plan a big town event without the town's input." Wes frowned.

"That's different." Frieda laughed again and called out a greeting to a new arrival at the club gathering. "Wes, I must go. Let Abby know we trust her to put on a spectacular event. That's why we hired her. Make sure to bring her over here. She'll want to see this too. *Koi.* I never knew what those were. Quite pretty, really. And the covered patio for cats so they can be outside, but still inside. Who would've thought of such a thing?"

The line went dead. What was he supposed to do now?

He shoved his phone into the back pocket of his jeans and returned to the bar.

Abby clutched the wireless microphone looking like a lost songbird without a song. "No one is coming, are they?"

Wes winced. Some bubble-buster he was. "You already know the answer."

Even Tess had slipped out earlier to meet a delivery truck at her store.

"Can't you lie to me to make me feel better?" Abby aimed the microphone at him.

"It won't help." Neither would drawing her into his embrace and holding her tight. That was definitely a complication he didn't want. Yet the urge to do just that wouldn't fade. He opened the condiment tray, then grabbed a bamboo cutting board and a paring knife to slice fruit. If his hands remained busy, he wouldn't accidently reach for her.

"It's not helping to face the facts either." She

opened the carrying case and repacked the microphone.

"What facts are those?" Besides the fact that he had no business considering Abby as more than a passing acquaintance. More than a customer, despite not charging her for her daily cups of decaf coffee. Her bubble was already burst. His responsibility to her was over.

"The fact that you were right." She snapped the lid closed and locked the microphone case. Her words snapped out next. "The town doesn't want an event. Progress. Or more business."

The sneer she had made her almost unrecognizable to him. He focused on what mattered to her. "The locals don't know what they want. Maybe you need to show them."

She flung her arm toward the stage and the blank screen she'd set up earlier. "What do you think was in the presentation?"

He hadn't given it much thought. Not that she'd want to hear that. Or that he'd given way more thought to how she'd feel inside his arms.

What was wrong with him?

Bubble-busters like him weren't supposed to deal in emotions and sentiment. He cut a lime in half, then sliced it neatly and quickly into wedges. "Pick something and just do that."

"What if it's the wrong thing?" she countered.

"No one will show up." There. His bubble-busting ways had returned. Still, he shrugged to cover his flinch and protect his insensitive facade.

"I don't want to repeat today's disaster." Her stale tone was flat and dull.

"Tell me your ideas." Wes picked up another lime and tossed it from one hand to the other as if that would shake loose his insistent urge to make things better for her. "I know the town. The people. I can help you pick the right one."

"You don't even want an event." Abby pressed her palm against her forehead as if trying to rid herself of a headache. "You'll pick the simplest, easiest, no-fuss option. The one-and-done event."

Now who was telling it like it was? And there was nothing inherently wrong with one and done. Except it wasn't what Abby wanted. Wes caught the lime and clenched the fruit in his fist. "Just show me your ideas."

"Fine." Abby walked to the small stage, rummaged through her oversize bag and yanked out a folder. She placed the folder on the bar top and set her palm against her head again.

Wes left the folder untouched and eyed her distress. "We can discuss this later."

"There's no time." Abby inhaled and exhaled loudly for several seconds. "In terms of planning, Labor Day weekend's right around the corner."

"Lynette Kinney's place is right around the corner too." Boone stepped through the swinging door and reached for a pint glass. "Just heard the woman filled her pond with koi. That's the wrong fish for fishing."

"It's a decorative backyard pond." Wes set the lime on the cutting board.

Boone gaped at Wes. The soda sprayer poised over the pint glass but nothing coming out. "That's nonsense."

"People like the serenity." Wes grabbed the sprayer and filled Boone's glass with his favorite soda—a blend of vanilla cola and root beer.

"Give me a fishing pole. Good pair of waders, and I'll show you true serenity." Boone cackled and waggled his eyebrows at Abby. "What do you say, Abby? Want to join me for an afternoon of fishing? It'll help you put this entire morning in the rearview mirror."

Wes glanced at Abby. "Abby. You okay?"

"Sorry." Abby rubbed her temples and gave her head a slight shake. "I'm feeling a little lightheaded."

"You need something to restore your spirits." Boone set his soda glass down. "It's been one heck of a morning."

Wes rounded the bar and guided a very pale-looking Abby onto a stool.

"Sit tight." Boone headed into the kitchen. "I've got just the cure."

Wes rested his arm on the back of Abby's stool and kept his gaze locked on her, ready to catch her if she listed sideways. "Can I get you something? Water? Ginger ale?"

"Just need a moment." She rested her elbows on the bar and dropped her head into her palms.

He listened to her inhale and exhale in a series of deep-breathing exercises. His fingers twitched against the stool. He wanted to rub her back. Return the color to her cheeks and the fighting spirit to her attitude. He wanted her angry at the morning's fallout, not sick from it. "Does this happen often?"

"I'm back." Boone's boisterous return scrambled Abby's reply. Boone set a bowl of his triple-spiced chicken tortilla soup on the bar and slid it right under Abby's nose.

She gasped and jerked away like she'd inhaled toxic fumes. Her hand instantly slapped over her mouth. She stumbled off the stool, swayed against Wes's chest, then sprinted for the bathroom.

Wes lowered his arms and watched Abby's erratic departure.

"Never seen anyone revive like that from

one small whiff of my soup." Boone tapped his cheek and sniffed the steam rising from the bowl. "Usually takes most people eatin' two helpings to come back around to themselves again."

Wes frowned. "That's because you usually give your soup to people who've had a little too much to drink when we've announced last call."

"I've served it in the morning with coffee. It truly is a cure-all." Boone picked up a spoon and eyed the soup bowl as if he wanted to ensure the recipe hadn't been altered. "Besides, Abby hasn't been drinking."

Exactly, Wes thought. He went down the hallway toward the bathrooms.

"Think she'll mind if I eat the soup?" Boone called after Wes. "Don't seem right to waste a perfectly good bowl."

"Help yourself." Wes knocked on the women's bathroom door, announced himself and peered inside. Only silence greeted him. He called Abby's name.

She finally appeared, one hand pressed against the shiplap wall. More color had left her cheeks and lips. Her gaze skipped past him, refusing to settle.

He held the door open. "I'm thinking fresh air on the patio."

Her head bobbed in agreement. She shuddered and made for the wide back doors.

Wes remained within hand-holding distance. Alert and aware of her every move. Her every uneven breath. Her unsteady gait.

She dropped into one of the closest lounge chairs and rested her head on the thick cushion. Her eyes closed. Her voice was sandpaper-rough. "I skipped breakfast today."

He didn't doubt that. He'd only ever seen her with a coffee cup in hand since her arrival five days ago. Never a bagel, a pastry or even a sugarcoated doughnut. Surely, she ate during the day. Surely, it wasn't his concern. "Breakfast is the most important meal of the day."

"I was too busy preparing my meeting presentation to eat." She barely opened her eyes to peer at him. "You'll see how good it is when you read it."

"I'm sure I will." But first he wanted to see her looking like herself again. He adjusted the other chairs around the glass-topped wicker table.

"I used to skip breakfast all the time. No problems." She squeezed her eyes closed again. The color drained from her face. Even her grimace paled. "But that was before…"

Wes stilled and waited.

"Before I got pregnant." She touched her

stomach. "It seems babies, even eight-week-old ones, require their moms to eat regularly."

Pregnant. Abby was pregnant. As in having a baby. And seemingly surviving on a continuous supply of his decaf coffee. She had to take better care of herself. She had to know that. Someone had to remind her. Not him, but someone. Then that same someone needed to look after her to make sure she listened. Again, not him, but clearly, the woman needed someone.

"I didn't want you to think failing at my job made me sick." She rolled her head on the cushion and eyed him. The rasp in her voice seemed to diminish her conviction. "I'm not that weak."

He'd never once considered Abby weak. A complication—definitely. But not weak. "Do you really think you failed today?"

"Well, this was a setback." She waved toward the patio doors leading into the bar. "However, I'm not done trying, not by a long shot."

He appreciated her resilience. Boone would call it *grit*. Then remind Wes there was nothing wrong with that. But grit wasn't enough to explain her appeal. Or his continued interest in her well-being as if he was invested. Certainly, this would pass. She was pregnant and deserved someone who would stick by her side. That wasn't him, even if a tiny part of him wished otherwise. "I've got hot tea and crackers in the kitchen. Sit here until I get back."

"That sounds like an order." Her eyebrows wrinkled as her frown deepened.

"It is." He'd look after her for now. Like he would any one of his customers. But that was all. She was on her own once she stepped outside the Owl. As it should be. "You can't take on the town if you aren't taking care of yourself."

She conceded by removing her flowery sandals, tucking her bare feet onto the chair and curling deeper into the cushions. Wes grinned and accepted his victory.

He walked inside the Owl and paused to watch the trio huddled at the other end of the bar. His favorite cowboy duo, Sam Sloan and Boone, were seated on their usual bar stools. And Ilene Bishop, his favorite bartender and mom of his friend, Evan Bishop, stood on the other side of the bar.

Ilene had retired from the Bishop family cattle ranch, leaving the work to her only son, Evan. But the widow had quickly discovered she had too much free time and had applied to work at the Feisty Owl. That had been a month after Wes had arrived in town. Ilene had become an essential part of the staff.

And an instant coconspirator with Sam and Boone.

Not that Wes minded. Until the trio looked like they did now: intent, serious and clearly up to no good.

Wes walked behind the bar and kept his voice casual. "What are you three chatting about?"

Ilene straightened and reached for the apron she always kept on the hook near the swinging door. "Just catching up."

"You saw each other only yesterday." Wes shifted his gaze from one to the other.

Ilene turned around to fiddle with her apron ties. Boone studied his soup as if he'd lost his contacts in the bottom of the bowl. And Sam busied himself choosing a package of crackers from the basket despite the crackers all being the same brand and flavor. Yup—they were up to something. Wes rubbed his chin. "You all were even in this exact spot. Yesterday."

"Doesn't mean we don't have new things to discuss." Sam crumbled several crackers into his soup bowl.

"I watched the news last night." Wes's voice was as bland and dry as Sam's crackers. The last time these three had looked like this, they'd assisted the runaway bride and reunited her with her groom. "Other than the cow running loose on the interstate and the new weather reporter, it was more of the same." Just as Wes preferred it: predictable and quiet.

His entire military career had been anything but predictable. And the only time it was quiet was during the dead silence of a mission, and his heartbeat had echoed inside him, and adrenaline had surged. He craved a different lifestyle now, and he refused to apologize. Or let anyone, including this trio, disrupt that.

Ilene set a basket of crackers on a tray, next to a steaming teapot and empty mug. "It's ginger and lemon tea. It's good for settling stomachs quickly."

Wes glanced at Boone. "What exactly did you tell them?"

Ilene shoved the tray into Wes's hands and nudged him around the bar. "We can talk later. Abby needs you."

Wes planted his boots and resisted.

Ilene nudged him harder, adding a poke into his ribs. "She's alone and pregnant, Wes. You have to help her right now."

Wes waited a breath, then finally nodded. Clearly, Boone hadn't wasted any time getting Ilene and Sam fully up to speed. Now he needed to figure out just what they were planning next. "I'm going. I'm going."

Wes closed the patio door and set the tray on the glass-topped table. He sat in a chair across from Abby, filled her mug and handed it to her.

Abby sipped the tea. "Don't you have a bar to go manage?"

"Ilene Bishop came in early for her shift." Wes linked his hands behind his head and leaned back in the chair. "She runs the bar and the staff better than I do most days."

"Then, you intend to sit out here and watch me drink this tea." The discontent in her voice gave away her annoyance.

Wes muted his laughter. "And I'm going to watch you eat the crackers. Don't forget those."

She picked up a package of crackers and looked at him. "Is this the part where you ask me about my pregnancy?"

"I believe people's personal business should remain personal." He added a slight warning to his tone. He wouldn't pry into her life the same as he expected her to remain out of his. They weren't building anything here. He was simply following orders from Ilene and looking after Abby. For now.

She nodded and bit into a cracker. "Have you always worked at the Feisty Owl? Did you start your career busing tables, then eventually step into the manager's role?"

He tilted his head and studied her.

She laughed, drawing much-needed color back into her cheeks, and motioned between them with her half-eaten cracker. "This is what two people do, Wes. Friends talk."

"Is that what we are now?" They'd graduated from acquaintances to friends. Nothing he couldn't manage.

Her voice softened. "I'd like to think so."

He watched her. And turned the idea of them being friends over in his mind. "Do you always pry into your friends' personal business?"

"I haven't had many friends." She shrugged one shoulder. "That's not exactly true. It's more that there hasn't been anyone I've wanted to talk to and get to know in a long time." She paused, sipped her tea and added, "Does that make sense?"

Unfortunately, it made too much sense.

CHAPTER EIGHT

ABBY STOOD, raised her arms over her head and lowered into a squat. All the while she kept her gaze fixed on the dark alcove. The one Tess had disappeared into minutes after ordering Abby to remain seated.

For the past hour that they'd been in the general store, Tess had been carrying boxes from the alcove into the main room. And Abby had been secretly stretching every time her cousin disappeared into the alcove. Neither one of the alcoves nor the storeroom had working lights. Abby couldn't see Tess, but she heard her mutters and muffled groans. The scrape of wooden crates across the floor alerted Abby that she had more time to move and bend. She rolled onto the balls of her feet and called out, "You know I can help you clear out that space."

Tess stepped over the velvet rope blocking the alcove and adjusted a dented box in her arms. "You know, you can also keep your feet up and not have a repeat of yesterday. I love you, Abby, but you gotta love yourself."

Abby plopped back onto the stool. She crossed one ankle over the other on the crates Tess had stacked up for a foot stool. Her foot tapped an irritated beat.

There were several things she'd rather not repeat from yesterday.

Her morning sickness was only one of them. It had woken her at sunrise like an unpleasant alarm and appeared to be sticking around, even as their Sunday morning edged toward the noon hour. Also sticking around was her suddenly all-too-consuming interest in Wes. She'd fallen asleep thinking about Wes. Dreamed about him. And, worse, followed his instructions to try toast for breakfast. *Keep it simple. Keep it plain, Abby, but make sure you eat in the morning.*

As if he knew the first thing about being pregnant and suffering morning sickness. But he had known exactly how to make her feel better yesterday. And that's what kept her thinking about him. He was stubborn, infuriating and kind. He'd been attentive without hovering. He'd been present without acting judgmental. She could've stayed in that chair beside him for hours, talking or silent. It wouldn't have mattered.

And that was what stuck with her the most. And tangled her insides like the dense cobwebs covering every corner of the storeroom and the alcoves inside the Silver Penny.

Abby followed her cousin's path through the uneven aisles. Wes had filled Tess in when he'd walked Abby back to the store yesterday. Abby hadn't needed the escort. But she'd liked it.

His tattletale ways she very much disliked. It had only made Tess worry more. Not helpful.

Abby had finally convinced Tess they could get some work done if she promised to sit while doing it. Abby swallowed her sigh and smiled at her cousin. "I meant I can do more. I ate breakfast this morning, so there won't be a repeat of yesterday's dizzy spell."

At least, she hoped. To be safe, she'd already planned to avoid spicy food the entire day. Possibly forever.

"Sorting through these boxes is hard work." Tess dropped the dented box beside the other boxes already lining the long counter. "We might have priceless antiques or valuable family heirlooms inside these."

Abby opened the box and stared at a collection of tarnished vintage spoons thrown in on top of various wooden boxes. Their grandparents had no filing system. No organization. Not one box had been labeled. In one of his last letters to Abby, her Grandpa Harlan had explained the store had been in transition when they'd closed it to move north to help Paige and Tess's newly widowed mom.

Grandpa Harlan had written that the general store only needed to find its identity and then it would be successful again. He'd believed the same for Abby, encouraging her after every job loss and every life transition. *It's like the butterfly, sweet Abigail: if it stayed a caterpillar, it'd never become a butterfly.* Maybe Abby was simply destined to remain a caterpillar. "Or everything inside these boxes could be rubbish."

"Are you okay, Abs?" Tess touched Abby's arm. Concern radiated from her voice to her grip.

Abby wanted to be. She'd intended to be. She'd even put on her favorite yellow sunflower sandals, white jean shorts, pale green tank top and her whisper-soft, frayed-hem kimono—the outfit that always made her feel happy. Then she'd added her macramé necklace with the teardrop peridot pendant and her sun dangle earrings. All for more positive energy. Yet her smile refused to surface. "Sorry. I'm worried about this town event."

Tess nodded. Understanding tempered her usually sharp green eyes.

On the flip side, Abby was worried about her cousin and the grief that shaded Tess like a storm cloud. Add in the pregnancy and failing to secure a full-time job, and her well over-flowed with so many uncertainties and fears.

In the past, Abby had simply floated from one career to the next, certain she'd find her fit eventually. But a baby needed stability. A child needed their single parent to be strong and fo-cused. Reliable and secure. How was she sup-posed to prove she was all that if she couldn't keep any job? But those were her concerns, not her cousin's.

She patted Tess's hand, then tugged the dented spoon box closer. "I'll figure everything out, but first I'm going on a treasure hunt."

"Treasure hunt." Boone's voice bounced through the store, overwhelming the chime of the shopkeeper's bell and pulling Abby's smile free. *Finally.*

Seeing Boone Bradley was like finding a let-ter from her grandparents in her mailbox. A letter from her grandparents had always bright-ened her day. Much like Boone's arrival now.

Sam and Ilene followed Boone inside. Abby's smile expanded. She'd met the pair only yes-terday at the bar but felt like she was greeting longtime friends. Perhaps she was, in a way. Her Grandpa Harlan's stories had often featured his childhood friends, Boone and Sam. A wicker basket swung from Ilene's arm as she moved to pull the double doors closed.

"There's rumored to be a treasure buried in Silent Rise Canyon." Boone made his way to the counter. Interest and mischief in his shrewd gaze.

"One of the McKenzie sisters buried the Herring Gang's loot in a cave in the canyon. Victoria McKenzie had declared the loot to be cursed." Sam lifted his cowboy hat and scratched his fingers through his thick white hair as if pulling the details of the legend loose. "The Herrings had been on quite a successful robbery spree. Amassed a large loot of gold and silver coins, jewels and countless other valuables."

Tess scooted another box onto the counter. "Is this a real treasure or merely legend?"

"As real as the silver on my belt buckle." Sam hitched his thumbs in his jeans and lifted his chin.

"Of course it's real. Harlan had a map guiding him to the buried treasure, didn't he?" Boone set his hands on the counter and leaned toward the box in front of Abby like an eager kid. "He always claimed this store held countless secrets."

Abby sorted through the box and pulled out the different-sized vintage spoons in all kinds of metals. "This looks like silverware, not a treasure map."

"Harlan was smarter than to drop a treasure map in with the utensils." Sam's full beard covered his frown, but his voice remained hopeful. "Keep looking, Abby. It's certain to show up."

Ilene laughed. "You two have been arguing over that map's existence since before my oldest was born."

"Longer than that." Boone nudged his elbow into Sam's side. "We argued with Harlan in grade school. Always boasted to anyone who'd listen that we'd discover that missing treasure together."

Abby pictured the trio of boys, devising their treasure-hunt adventure. That one Christmas she'd spent in Wisconsin, she'd had an adventure with her cousins. She touched her stomach. She wanted her child to have as many backyard adventures as could be imagined. And the same deep friendships and connections shared as her grandparents had had. "Did you look for the treasure?"

Her own fingers tingled. The urge to tear through the boxes for an old treasure map was very tempting. The dreamer inside her stirred. But she'd vowed to keep her feet on the ground and her head out of the clouds. She'd leave the dreaming to her baby. And, for now, let herself be enchanted by the story and another link to her grandfather.

"More than one summer we set up camp at

Eagle Run River and searched." Sam chuckled. "Never did find any gold or silver coins."

"But we did discover all the places you can get poison ivy. Some aren't pleasant." Boone plucked up a spoon from the box and tapped it against his palm, recalling more memories. "We also found the best rocks for skipping across the lake. And located the best hidden fishing spots within county lines."

"Grandpa Harlan told me Sam skipped the rocks the farthest." Abby smiled, picturing her grandfather detailing one of their excursions. "Boone caught the biggest fish. And Grandpa made the biggest fires."

Boone chuckled. "That was because he made the best s'mores."

"And cooked the fish to perfection over that same fire." Sam's voice was wistful.

"You boys did all that without a treasure map?" Ilene wrapped her arm around Boone's waist. "Sounds like you got sidetracked being boys."

"The map isn't essential." Boone pointed the spoon to his forehead. "What we need for a proper treasure hunt is already up here."

Sam held a large serving spoon up to the light. "Our grandparents and the ones before them passed on the tale of how the McKenzie sisters bested the Herring Gang outlaws."

"Grandpa Harlan never mentioned the McKenzie sisters or the Herring Gang." Tess glanced at Abby. Her forehead creased.

Abby nodded. She and her grandparents had been pen pals since Abby had learned to write. She had their letters in several shoeboxes in her room upstairs. She'd have remembered tales about a buried treasure, sisters and outlaws.

Tess asked Sam, "Can you tell us?"

Abby stilled. There was nothing wrong with hearing the full story. She was curious. But it hardly meant she would launch her own treasure hunt or imagine being the one to discover it. Same as she was drawn to Wes. She wasn't imagining there was anything more between them than what they had. Friendship. Abby clenched several spoons as if they were responsible for stirring her feelings into a jumbled mess.

"Tess is a librarian. If there's a record of the robberies or any written information about the Herring Gang, she'll locate it." Abby grinned at her cousin. "She's the best there is at historical research."

Both Boone and Sam considered Tess.

"Is that so?" Boone said. "Then, we'll definitely want to tell you this tale."

"But it's best told around the fire." Sam held up his hands and slanted his gaze toward Ilene.

"With Boone's smoked brisket and my famous baked beans."

Boone nodded. "And bourbon cherry cobbler for dessert."

"I suppose you'll be wanting homemade ice cream too." Ilene's put-upon tone crumbled when she affectionately squeezed Boone's shoulder.

"If it isn't too much trouble." Sam's teeth appeared, hinting at his wide smile. "We sure do like how the warm cobbler melts the ice cream to the right temperature."

"And where might we be having this fireside chat?" Ilene asked.

"My place. Tomorrow night. The bar is closed, anyway." Boone chuckled. "You can meet our new arrivals. A pretty American paint mare and her foal. They're settling in nicely with Wes's guidance."

Wes worked with horse rescues? Another layer. Another glimpse at the good guy within. Another reason he unsettled her. But only if she continued to let him.

Sam rubbed his hands together. "Now that we've settled tomorrow's evening plans, let's discuss today's work."

Abby shot a questioning look at Tess. Her cousin shrugged and asked the others. "What did you have in mind?"

"We're here to help you." Sam inspected the storefront, then leaned toward Boone. "They certainly do need us, don't they?"

"Desperately." Boone's whisper was more like an attention-grabbing alarm.

"We thought we'd clear out the alcoves and start with a completely clean slate." Tess's hands fluttered in front of her as if she'd lost their plan. "Then build the inventory from there."

Boone rubbed his chin. Sam stroked his fingers through his beard.

Ilene nudged a box aside and set her basket on the counter. "It's a start, as you say. And you have to start somewhere."

Tess exhaled, and her shoulders relaxed.

"I'm in charge of deciding what to keep and what can be sold." Abby waved to the lineup of boxes. "With help from the internet."

"I can sort and identify." Ilene walked around to Abby's side of the counter. "My aunt loved antiquing. And I loved tagging along. I miss those weekends we spent together scouting out new towns and new finds."

"That leaves the alcoves for us." Boone motioned in their direction. "Lead the way, Tess."

"There's one slight problem." Tess hesitated. "We have no lights in either of the alcoves. And the windows are blocked by furniture and boxes."

"That's a hazard for sure." Boone hooked his fingers on his belt. "Can't fix the lights without an extra-tall ladder."

"We don't have one," Abby said.

"The Owl does." Boone grinned. "Won't take but a minute to get it."

"Then, that's our first task." Sam slid a small bottle across the counter toward Abby and stage-whispered, "Take this. Make yourself a hot toddy this evening. It's a cure for every ailment."

"Abby can't have that." Ilene snatched the bottle from Sam. "She's pregnant."

"My great-nana had fourteen babies, and she's the one taught who me how to blend the whiskey for her special toddy recipe." Affection and admiration softened Sam's words. He set his finger on his nose. "Nana taught me only patience and a very practiced nose would produce the most flavorful, most pure of whiskeys."

"And how did that work out?" Abby asked.

"My grandson, Carter, took my basement-blended whiskey and turned it into a respectable distillery." So much pride shone in Sam's gaze that his eyes sparkled. "Our award-winning whiskeys are sold in stores around the country."

Abby wanted her parents to mention her accomplishments with the same approval. She'd only ever wanted to make them proud. Her parents were leaving their mark on the world every day at excavations and historical sites. Abby couldn't claim the same. At least not yet. Putting Three Springs on the map could change all that.

"It's ginger and lemon tea for Abby." Ilene slipped Sam's miniature whiskey bottle in her purse and motioned to her wicker basket. "With homemade bagels, oatmeal banana muffins and glazed apple crumb bread."

"That all sounds delicious." Abby lifted the blue-checkered linen towel covering the baked goods. "I don't know what to try first."

"Can't go wrong with one of these." Sam grabbed a cinnamon raisin bagel from the basket. "Best kept secret in town—Ilene's baked goods. And for everything else, it'll all work itself out like whiskey aging in a barrel. It happens in its own good time."

Abby didn't have time to wait. She had only weeks to create and organize her event. And she still had no direction for what type. She picked up a banana muffin and peeled off the wrapper, searching for inspiration.

Sam and Boone left to retrieve the ladder. Tess and Ilene sampled everything in the basket. Minutes later, Boone shouted again from the entrance. "Look who we found coming to see you, Abby!"

Wes. Abby touched her braids and quickly

wiped any crumbs from her face. Then reined herself in. She wasn't a teenage girl waiting on her crush to wander into the store. She was a soon-to-be single mom. With an entirely too-full plate. And no room for a crush, even a harmless one she had well under control.

A tall, lanky guy with striking red hair arrived at the entrance. The only resemblance between him and Wes was his worn, scuffed boots. Trey Ramsey introduced himself to Abby, then greeted Ilene and Tess. Despite his boyish face and charm, Trey's grip was firm and his voice deep.

Sam and Boone maneuvered the very tall ladder against the wall.

"Trey, son, you need to eat a muffin or slice of sweet bread." Sam pointed to the basket. "I've seen people at the cemetery looking less dire than you are now."

Ilene thrust a slice of apple bread at Trey.

Abby watched Trey shift from one foot to the other. He swallowed several times but never let his gaze settle on her.

"You should give it to her straight, son," Boone advised.

Her. That was Abby for sure. No one else had their cars at Trey's place. Abby straightened on the stool and waited.

Trey broke a piece of bread off, then set the

napkin with the uneaten bread on the counter. "I'm sorry, Abby. But I have bad news."

Abby reached for a piece of apple bread, needing something sweet to offset the sudden souring in her stomach. "How bad?"

Trey's pinched face made it look like he was chewing a bite of rotten apple. "You'll need to contact your insurance company to file a claim for a total loss on your convertible."

"It's a total loss…" Abby forgot the bread and gaped at Trey. There weren't enough apples in the orchards to sweeten that news. "But it was just a flat tire."

"Not just a flat tire." Trey popped the bread into his mouth as if sharing his bad news had made him immensely hungry. He spoke around the bite. "You hit the pothole and the wheel bent. That in turn caused the frame of the car to bend."

Boone stared at the muffin he held and shook his head. "There's no coming back from a bent frame."

"Now you can get a sensible car." Sam finished his slice of apple cake and brushed the crumbs from his denim button-down shirt. "Something reliable and built for our country roads."

"I need a new car." Abby's head spun. For the first time that morning she was glad she was sitting down. How was she supposed to afford so much new for herself and her baby?

"Trucks are good around here," Boone suggested. "Almost hit two hundred thousand miles on my pickup's odometer. Certainly made that to last."

How long was Abby going to last in town? She had no place else to go. Her head spun faster. She had to last too.

"You can use my car," Tess offered. "Anytime you need it."

"Wes has a good, solid truck." Boone polished off his muffin and wiped his hands together. "He can drive you wherever you have to go. That should solve everything."

Nothing was close to being solved.

"Who am I driving where?" Wes stood in the doorway. His arms crossed over his chest. His expression impassive.

Abby wanted to sprint into his arms. And shout at him to get out. Get out of her thoughts. Get out of her head. Just get out until she could rid herself of the sudden rush of feelings inside her.

And Wes had only barely walked into the store.

But he wasn't there to solve her problems. Or become her chauffeur. Or be her shoulder to lean on. Yet she wanted to slide her hand into

Wes's and ask him to reassure her. The last time someone had taken her hand like that, she'd been standing at her grandmother's gravesite. Grandpa Harlan had taken her hand and had promised her that they would both be okay. He had passed away one year later. Abby convinced herself she was okay. Then and now.

She just had to keep her heart protected. Keep her focus on practical things like her responsibilities and priorities. Wes didn't fit with either.

Wes crossed his arms over his chest and directed his frown at Boone and Sam. "Please don't tell me either of you plans to climb that ladder."

Boone grabbed the ladder. "Never you mind what I plan to do."

"Dr. McCall told you to stay off ladders," Wes warned.

"Dr. McCall suggested I stay off ladders." Boone tipped his chin up and never released his hold on the ladder. "And I'm not on the ladder."

"Yet," Wes said.

Trey stepped between Boone and Sam, took the ladder from the gentlemen and leaned it against the opposite wall. Ilene thanked Trey, then pointed at Wes. "The ladder can wait. Wes, you'll drive Abby wherever she needs to go."

"I never said I needed to go anyplace," Abby protested. Let alone with Wes. Besides, she refused to go anywhere with him until she could better manage her reaction to him. Once she found her inner discipline, all would be fine.

Wes's composed voice drifted through the store like a cold breeze. "What happened?"

"Simple." Boone tipped his head toward the auto mechanic. "Trey declared Abby's car a total loss."

"She needs a new one," Sam chimed in. "Until she gets one, we need to drive her."

"But Dr. McCall told me I can only drive during daylight." Boone eyed Wes. "And I have to stay in town."

Wes opened his mouth.

Sam cut him off. "That leaves you, Wes, to drive her."

"Abby, let me know when you've talked to your insurance company. If you want to locate a new car, I've got people who can assist." Trey grabbed a bagel and thanked Ilene. Then he buddy-punched Wes's shoulder on his way out. "I'm getting back to my shop before Boone and Sam convince me to add taxi to my list of services."

"It's not a bad idea," Sam shouted to Trey. "You should consider it."

Wes glanced at Abby. "Is there someplace you need to go?"

Not unless it was with the Wes from the bar

yesterday. No, not even him. Then she'd forget her self-restraint and discover another layer. And then she'd want to learn even more about the man. And if she started to like Wes—really like him—her heart would start to want more. Her heart couldn't be trusted. When it got swept away, she lost sight of what else was important. And she couldn't afford to be anything but clear-eyed and levelheaded.

"Abby has a doctor's appointment in Belleridge tomorrow morning," Tess offered.

Boone pointed at Wes. "Didn't you mention you needed to pick up supplies from there?"

Wes's nod was the slightest shift of his head. As if he disliked the idea of driving Abby as much as she disliked riding with him.

Sam's smile lifted his handlebar mustache. "Looks like Wes can drive you, Abby."

"That's not necessary." Really not necessary. Abby's gaze locked on her cousin's. "Tess said I could use her car."

"Trey has it scheduled for maintenance tomorrow." Tess tucked her hair behind her ear. "The engine was making a strange knocking noise before you got here. You should probably ride with Wes."

No, she probably should not. "I can change my doctor's appointment."

"Not after the incident yesterday in the bar." Boone shook his head.

"I agree with Boone," Tess said. "You shouldn't wait to see the doctor."

Even Ilene stopped sorting through the spoons to nod in Abby's direction.

"That wasn't an incident." Abby looked to Wes for backup.

He stepped over to the counter and peered inside Ilene's bakery basket. "What time is your appointment?"

Abby blinked. "Nine o'clock."

"I'll pick you up at eight fifteen." He chose a muffin and twisted off the top.

"That's settled." Boone removed his cowboy hat, ruffled his hair, then resettled the hat on his head. "Now, let's get going in here. We've a lot to do."

Wes intercepted Boone before the older man could reach for the ladder. He glanced at Tess. "What are we doing with this?"

"You don't have to help." Abby skirted around the counter toward Wes and the ladder. "I'm sure you have other business to tend to."

"If you tell me what to do, I can get it done and move on with what I need to do." Wes had moved quickly and stealthily into Abby's personal space.

"We're changing out the light bulbs in the

back room and the alcoves." Abby set her hands on her hips and stared at Wes. Denying that she wanted to move closer. Arguing that she was in full control of her feelings. "We can't see very well, and it's a hazard."

Wes picked up the ladder and headed into the storeroom. Abby followed, close enough that she winced when he banged his elbow on a shelf. He remained silent and opened the ladder beneath one of the overhead lights.

"Now that you've set up the ladder, I'm sure we can handle it from here." Surely, she could handle light bulbs more efficiently than she was handling her being around Wes.

Wes rested an arm on the ladder and eyed her. His gaze was shadowed, but his tone was blunt. "How many 1940s-era electrical boxes have you seen, let alone repaired?"

Abby crossed her arms over her chest. It was darker, more intimate in the storeroom, despite the dust and those pesky cobwebs. "How many have you repaired?"

"On this street, almost every single one," Wes said.

"So you're an electrician too?" What wasn't the man capable of? And when would she stop wanting to know his weaknesses? Stop wanting to learn about everything that made him, well, him?

"Wes was an engineering and advanced demolitions specialist in his SEAL platoon." Boone's voice drifted from the doorway. The pride in his tone more than obvious.

"Wait." Abby held up her hand. "You were a SEAL? Like a Navy SEAL? In the military." She didn't know much about them, but she knew the SEALs were an elite group. Some of the best trained forces in the world. Another level of hero.

Wes eased around Abby. "Tess, where is your main electrical panel?"

Tess cleared her throat. "I believe it's on the back wall. But I think the main panel is in the basement. There's a flashlight hanging by the door if you go down there."

Wes headed deeper into the storeroom. Abby trailed after him.

"We'll leave you two to deal with the lights," Boone hollered. "Shout if you need us."

Abby followed Wes down the wooden stairs into the basement. She kept her gaze trained on Wes's hand and the wide beam of the flashlight. "How long were you a SEAL?"

Wes stopped at the base of the stairs and opened the metal cover on the out-of-date electrical panel. He glanced at Abby. "Is this another one of your friend conversation starters?"

"I haven't met anyone as resistant to talking

about themselves as you." Abby laughed and gripped the railing.

"I'm not resistant." Resolve hardened his tone. "I'm private."

Abby wasn't trusted enough to be included in his private world. She should be satisfied with that. She shouldn't want to be included.

He unscrewed a fuse, aimed the flashlight at it and frowned. "My mom used to tell me I could talk about my problems or fix them. And if I was talking, I wasn't fixing."

Abby pressed her lips together, surprised he'd revealed something personal. "Was being a SEAL a problem?"

"Those were some of the best years of my life, also the most challenging." He pulled another fuse from the box and inspected it.

Another confession. Another personal insight. Abby didn't want to push her luck. "Those burned wires don't look promising."

"It's really not good." Wes replaced the fuse and examined the next one. "If the others are like this, then the entire space needs to be rewired inside and out."

"And if this space needs to be rewired, I'm betting the rest of the building is the same." Abby searched for her positive energy.

"That seems to be how it is in these historic buildings," Wes said.

"But we can't afford that."

"I can take care of it," Wes offered. "Frieda's husband is a general contractor. He can pull the permits, and I can do the work."

"Why would you do that?" Abby asked. Her voice came out more charged than she'd intended. He barely knew her or Tess. Running new electrical in a building wasn't an offer made to acquaintances. And, personal insights aside, that's all they really were.

"It's the right thing to do." He closed the breaker box and faced her.

"Do you always do the right thing?" She searched his dark gaze. Because the right thing was to cut off her unwise attraction to this man. Right now. Sever it like the broken wires in the electrical box.

"Neighbors look after neighbors." He lifted his hand and tucked a strand of her hair behind her ear.

His touch was there and gone. Her nerves fired. Though nothing about her attraction to him short-circuited. Right became cross-wired with wrong. Abby kept her gaze locked on his. "I'll pay for the supplies."

He whispered, "It's not a problem. Consider us friends."

CHAPTER NINE

WES STOPPED OUTSIDE the Silver Penny General Store and put his truck in Park. He reached to adjust the AC vents to better cool Abby's side but pulled back. He was giving her a ride to her doctor's appointment. Only because he happened to be going to the same town for his own reasons that morning. He hadn't rearranged his schedule for her. Or agreed to make any special trip just for her.

As for looking after her, Abby seemed capable enough of doing that on her own.

He had plenty to focus on in his own life. Most important was finding his brother, the missing money and helping Boone.

Abby appeared. One hand braced against the slate wall of the general store and the other clutching a stainless-steel travel mug. The bun on top of her head loosened with every step, as if preparing to collapse around her shoulders. Her face was an odd gray cast, not exactly snowy-white like the crocheted sweater she wore, but not sickly-green either.

Wes jumped out of the truck and opened the passenger door. He locked his gaze on Abby, fully prepared to catch her if she swayed into a faint.

Steps away from the truck, he took her travel mug, then gripped her elbow to guide her into the passenger seat.

"Sorry. The toast is not cutting it this morning." She settled into the seat with what seemed like a full-body sigh. Her voice was a faint rattle, lacking its usual resilience.

"Hang on." Wes sprinted across the street and convinced himself he'd do the same for any of his passengers. Abby wasn't special. He rushed inside the Owl, located what he wanted in the kitchen and hurried back to the truck. He set the cracker basket on the console between them. "Maybe these will work."

"Thanks." Abby placed the metal wire basket on her lap and wrapped her hands around it as if cradling a priceless crystal bowl.

Wes's phone vibrated in the drink holder. "Do you mind if I take this call? One of our farms changed our delivery order late last night. We need to fix the menu for tomorrow."

There. That proved Abby wasn't special. If she meant more to him than a simple travel companion, he wouldn't consider answering his chef's call.

"Go ahead." Abby slipped on a pair of over-size sunglasses and leaned her head back on the headrest. "I'm going to keep my eyes closed and think happy thoughts."

"It's one straight road from here to Belle-ridge." All the better for Wes to keep an eye on the road and on Abby. He checked her once more.

She was calm, her elbows tucked into her sides, as if she was mentally holding herself to-gether. The bold turquoise frames of her sun-glasses the only color on her face. He added, "There won't be any hairpin curves. No coun-try back roads. No potholes."

The smallest smile flickered across her mouth.

Wes pulled out onto the street and answered his phone. He greeted his head chef, Nolan Davis, and explained Abby was in the truck too. Nolan offered a quick hello to Abby. Wes said, "So what do we have arriving tomorrow?"

"Too much zucchini. Broccoli. Cauliflower." The chop of Nolan's knife knocked across the speaker. "Limited tomatoes and spinach. No asparagus. No artichokes."

Wes tapped the steering wheel. The fried as-paragus and artichoke-spinach dip typically sold out on Tuesdays. The dip was an original menu item: the recipe, passed down through Boone's family, hadn't changed since the bar had opened more than fifty years ago.

"Zucchini corn fritters," Abby offered. "And buffalo fried cauliflower."

Wes glanced at her and aimed the AC vent in her direction. Uncertain if the glare from the sun was responsible for the color creeping into her cheeks, he figured more air wouldn't hurt. "Nolan, did you get that?"

"Yeah." There was a shuffling noise across the line. "Abby, what else you got?"

"Broccoli beer cheese soup. A grown-up grilled cheese with avocado, tomatoes and bacon." Abby shifted in the seat, picked up a package of crackers and ripped the wrapper open. "And bacon-wrapped onion rings."

Nolan's laughter burst across the line. "Are you a chef too, Abby?"

"Not at all." Abby broke the cracker and stared at it as if wishing she held one of those onion rings. "Just offering a few of my favorite menu items."

"Abby, what's your favorite appetizer not on our menu?" Nolan asked.

"Soft pretzel bites and dip." Abby chewed on her cracker, then sipped her tea. "It's all about the dip too. It makes it or breaks it."

"Challenge accepted." Nolan's animated voice

bounced around the truck cab. "I'll make you a believer."

"I look forward to sampling your creations." Abby chuckled. More color tinged her cheeks before quickly receding.

Wes ended the call. "Thanks for the menu ideas. They were good."

"You sound surprised." She opened another cracker package.

He was. Wes knew what he liked. What he could cook without burning. But for the bar and grill he leaned heavily on Nolan for menu guidance. "Are you one of those really skilled home cooks?"

"That was my Grandma Opal. She created her own recipes." Abby broke the cracker into small pieces as if her stomach could only tolerate the tiniest of bites at a time. "I worked as a hostess at a popular local diner. Then became a waitress and finally had a short stint as an assistant to the manager."

"What happened?"

"Diner closed." Confusion and sadness tinged her words. "Overnight, without any notice to the employees. One day the diner was open and seating customers. We all had jobs. And the next morning we had nothing."

He knew that feeling. One day he had a brother, a home on the family ranch to return to and a plan for his life after the military. Within twenty-four hours, he'd lost his inheritance, his family and his future. "What did you do?"

He'd spent an evening in a dive bar before staggering over to a dingy motel room to sleep it off. Not one of his finer moments. And the last time he'd turned to alcohol for answers to his problems. But he couldn't picture Abby wallowing. She was too positive. Too upbeat.

Abby straightened the cracker packages inside the metal basket. "I decided I needed something more reliable and took a job at a matchmaking company."

That must have been a fit for her. With her optimism and enthusiasm, she most likely believed in soul mates and true love. Happily-ever-afters and story-book romances. Nothing he subscribed to these days. "Were you good at the matchmaking?"

"Awful." Abby shook her head, spilling her soft laughter toward him.

He liked the sound: light and appealing. It filled him, sweeping into those restless places inside him. He wanted more of her like this. But that would mean a course correction. Altering the lifestyle he'd built and the one he intended to maintain even after he left town.

She added, "I did like planning the events and bringing people together for a fun evening."

And Wes did like Abby. For the first time in years, he wished he was someone else. Someone she deserved. But he'd lost too much to ever risk like that again. He cleared his throat. "Isn't that what a matchmaker does?"

"I wanted people to find each other organically. I created the space and the moment." Abby finished her cracker and brushed the crumbs off her denim sundress. "I assumed the couples who were meant to be together would discover each other on their own."

"And they didn't?" Wes kept his gaze fixed on the road and not on Abby. She wasn't his destination.

"Not to my boss's expectations," she said. "Two to three matches in a crowd of thirty potential matches was not good enough. And definitely not worth the expense of the event."

"What happened to the couples you matched?" he asked.

"They are still together." Abby crumpled the empty plastic wrapper. "I lost my job. Left my boyfriend. Then came straight to Texas for a fresh start."

Wes flexed his fingers around the steering wheel and tried not to release the questions backing up in his throat. Diving deeper and learning more about Abby wasn't necessary.

Served no purpose. He already liked her as she was. That was enough.

Getting to know her better might make him reconsider his path. Whereas he had to remain focused and find his brother. His entire future hinged on that. And now, so did Boone's. Wes's future wasn't a woman who'd swept into town one morning with nothing more than her suitcases and a pocketful of hope. Besides, foundations that lasted weren't built on wishes.

Yet whenever he looked at Abby, a twinge of hope stirred inside him.

He pulled into the parking lot for the medical offices of Dr. Cynthia Carrillo and stopped near the entrance. "We're here."

Now he was off the hook. No more getting personal with Abby. Or even considering it. Her business she could keep to herself. Like he wanted.

"You don't have to come inside with me." She stuffed several cracker packages into her purse and opened her door. "I'll be fine."

"The supply store isn't open for another hour." He tugged his keys from the ignition and reached for the baseball cap on his back seat. "And it's already too hot to wait in the truck, even with the windows down."

Abby lifted her face to the sky and frowned. "Texas does take hot to another level, doesn't it?"

Wes laughed, and followed Abby inside Dr. Carrillo's office and appreciated the welcome, cool air-conditioning.

Another couple was already seated in the waiting room. The woman was much further into her pregnancy than Abby and shifted every few minutes as if uncomfortable. She clutched the hand of the man seated next to her and kept her other hand protectively curved over her stomach. Water trickled from a large rock fountain in the opposite corner of the waiting room. And a dozen colorful fish swam in a large aquarium. The misty gray walls and navy-and-white floral print of the contemporary armchairs encouraged a Zen, spalike feel.

Wes sat in a chair beside the fountain, skipped his gaze over the baby and parenting magazines covering the coffee table and pulled out his cell phone. Nolan hadn't texted any more updates from their farm suppliers. And there was only one shift-change request from his wait staff. The day was unfolding slow and easy like he preferred.

Abby dropped into the chair beside him, a clipboard and pen in her hand. "Are you sure you want to wait in here?"

Wes glanced up from his phone.

"It's just…" Abby stopped writing and shifted

to face him. Her pen wobbled in her grip. "Doesn't all this make you uncomfortable?"

Uncomfortable was wearing one hundred pounds of gear and jumping out of a moving aircraft at over twelve thousand feet in the pitch dark to a blind landing on a snow-covered mountain. It was training through extreme sleep deprivation—the kind few could handle. And plunging into hypothermia-inducing waters in the middle of the night for an ambush. The SEALs had trained Wes to embrace uncomfortable, accept it and never falter.

He watched Abby, noted her teeth pull on her bottom lip. And the nerves tremble through her uneven breath. He tucked his phone away and kept his gaze on hers. His voice shifted into neutral; he wanted to sound composed. "I'm good. But it's not about me. How are you?"

She blinked. Then blinked again as if his question had stumped her. "I'm…"

"Ms. Abigail James." A nurse stood in an open doorway. Her purple scrubs and smile cheerful.

Abby rose, fumbled with the clipboard and adjusted her purse on her shoulder.

The nurse held open the door for Abby, then to Wes she said, "We'll be back to get you after her exam." Her bubbly voice did seem reassuring.

Wes gripped the armrests. "That's not necessary."

"Partners are always allowed back." The nurse meant to be encouraging. Helpful.

Abby spun around, wide-eyed and panicked. "He's not…"

And for the first time in years, Wes faltered. Words escaped him. Confidence drained from his voice. "I'm just the driver."

Abby disappeared. The nurse nodded, her smile dimmed several watts. She scribbled a note on her chart and turned away. The door clicked softly shut.

Yet something inside Wes banged like a drum. He was desperate to know what the nurse had written on Abby's chart: *Single mom. Alone. No father. Only her driver present.*

Driver.

That was the very best he could come up with? Not *neighbor? Support? Friend?*

Wes rose and tugged on the collar of his T-shirt. Had they turned off the air conditioner? The office was suddenly hot and stifling.

He retreated outside and headed toward the shade of a massive oak tree across the parking lot. He leaned against the thick tree trunk, lowered the brim of his baseball cap over his eyes and crossed his arms over his chest.

Had he ever pictured himself being the other

half of a couple like the one inside Dr. Carrillo's waiting room—terrified and excited about the arrival of a child? He'd vowed never to be like his own father: a leaver. But a wife and kids and a family of his own? Those hadn't been connections he'd wanted or even considered during his military career. But now…

He rubbed his chest. Those things required love and trust.

Yet he didn't trust in family anymore. A lesson his father's desertion had taught him and his brother's betrayal had followed on. Blood ties meant nothing. Even his mother's love for his father hadn't mattered. His father had still walked away.

Now Wes trusted in himself. As for love, he'd never trusted that. *Ever.*

So he would remain Abby's driver. Nothing more. Just as it should be.

The trip to Belleridge had never been about exploring his misplaced feelings for Abby. He had other priorities and bigger concerns. Like making sure that Boone could keep living on the ranch and that those horses wouldn't need to be rescued again.

The door to Dr. Carrillo's office opened. Abby stepped outside.

Wes pushed off the tree and started toward her as if she was and would ever be his only priority. His main concern. He forced himself to slow down. "Everything okay?"

"Good." Abby slid her sunglasses on and grinned. "Looks like I am having a March baby."

Wes was a March baby too. Inconsequential really. And not information his passenger required. "That's a good month."

Abby's eyebrow arched over her round sunglass lens. A smile twitched in the corner of her mouth. "Why is that?"

"It just is." Wes shoved his hands in his jeans pockets. The curls that had escaped her bun absorbed the sun and bounced against her neck. He'd never seen blond hair like hers, never been so very distracted by a woman either. He had to stop letting Abby sidetrack him. "March is not the harshest part of winter or the hottest part of summer. You won't have to worry about missing the age cutoff for kindergarten."

"All very good points," Abby said as she laughed and climbed into the truck.

Wes walked around the vehicle to the driver's side and shook off his awkwardness. What was wrong with him? Kindergarten cutoff. *Come on, man.* "Shouldn't take long at the restaurant-supply store, then we can have an early lunch before we head back."

"Lunch isn't necessary." Abby lifted the

cracker basket as if she had all she needed to sustain her.

But lunch was very necessary, both for her and for his own personal reason. He could've had the restaurant supplies delivered. Although, then he couldn't have followed a possible lead on his brother. He started the truck and backed out of the parking space. "Did Dr. Carrillo say anything about eating?"

Abby looked out her window and away from Wes. Her voice slightly disgruntled. "She told me that it's best to eat every few hours for morning sickness."

Wes silently thanked the good doctor. "The Four Fiddlers Tavern has the best soft pretzels with smoked cheddar-cheese sauce around."

"We'll see about that." She leaned on the console, closer to him. "I'm something of an expert on soft pretzels."

"Want to make a bet that these are the best you've tasted?" His words slipped out before he could pull them back. Drivers didn't make bets with their passengers. More like potential boyfriends made the kind of bet he wanted to make with Abby right now.

Retreat. This was not good. And not the direction he wanted to be heading.

She never hesitated. "I'll take that bet. If I win, then you have to let me help you rewire the general store. If you win and those are the best pretzels I've tasted, then I'll cook dinner for you."

Either way, he won. He got to spend more time with her. He should refuse to accept the bet. Tell Abby that he'd changed his mind and course-correct. "You told me you can't cook."

"I said I wasn't a chef." She drummed her fingers on the console. "But I can cook a few things. Grandma Opal shared her recipes, and I mastered a few."

No deal. "I have one condition."

Her fingers stilled.

"You can't rewire anything with me unless you have proper work shoes." He grinned. Practical was not part of Abby's wardrobe. Now she'd back out and save them both. "No sandals. No fancy half boots. No flip-flops."

"Fine." She settled into her seat. "I've been wanting to get real cowboy boots. You can take me shopping. I don't know where to find the best ones."

His grin fell. He'd gone from Abby's driver to her personal shopper in less than a block. If he wasn't more careful, he'd be more than her friend by the time they got back to Three Springs.

Wes parked at the restaurant-supply store,

jumped out and walked inside. His order was waiting at the pickup counter.

Minutes later, and certain his focus was back, Wes took a seat across from Abby at a square table near the front window of the Four Fiddlers Tavern. The waitress breezed by to take their orders and quickly moved on to the other tables filled with hungry patrons. It wasn't long before the waitress returned with their drinks and a large plate of soft pretzel bites with smoked cheddar-cheese sauce.

Abby picked up a pretzel. Wes stopped her before she dunked the pretzel into the melted cheese. "Wait. I never did ask what recipes of your grandmother's you mastered."

Abby pushed his hand aside and dipped her pretzel in the sauce. "Does it matter?"

"Not really. I was just curious." Something he had to stop being when he was around her. Her business wasn't his business.

Locating his younger brother was his business.

He popped a cheesy pretzel into his mouth and scanned the crowded bar. The tavern was the first substantial, albeit unexpected, lead in his search for his brother that he'd had in a long while. One more scan of the patrons for a familiar horseshoe tattoo on the back of a neck and a six-foot-four-inch burly stature that was even harder to conceal, confirmed that his brother was not among the crowd. Wes put his disappointment aside.

He returned his attention to Abby. "Well, what do you think?"

"I'm still deciding." She picked up another pretzel and dipped it into the sauce. "But they're really good. You weren't wrong."

He watched her devour several more pretzels. Pleased the color had returned to her cheeks. And that the spark was back in her gaze. He couldn't remember when a woman had intrigued him like Abby did. Or made him so very interested in prying. Like now. "Where's the baby's father?"

Abby swallowed her pretzel and took a sip of her lemon water. All the while she watched him, assessing and probing.

He dipped a pretzel into the sauce and lifted one shoulder, keeping his voice mild and indifferent. "I'm just starting a conversation with a friend."

She wiped her hands on her napkin, then wiped off her mouth. "I'll tell you about my ex if you tell me why we're really here."

Her challenge was clear. He picked up another pretzel and held it between them. "You don't like the tavern's buttery take on soft pretzels?"

"These are a delicious bonus." Abby snatched

the pretzel from his fingers. "And you aren't stalking the chef for the secret ingredient to replicate them at the Owl. We aren't here for these. Or for you to win our bet."

Interesting turnabout. She seemed as in tune to him as he was to her. Now he had to decide how much to reveal. How much would satisfy her curiosity. How much would satisfy his. He wasn't certain he'd ever want to stop learning about her. He shouldn't have started this. Shouldn't have stepped into the water. Suddenly he wasn't interested in backing out either. "My brother. I thought he might be here. He isn't, by the way."

She lowered the pretzel. Concern automatically showed in her expression. "When was the last time you spoke to him?"

"Almost three years ago." Wes stirred his straw around in his soda, disturbing the ice the same way the anger and hurt stirred inside him. It'd been a brief text exchange about a month prior to Wes's return home. Nothing specific. Only his arrival date and a quick inquiry about their mom. Not even a real conversation. "I haven't seen or spoken to him since."

"Yet you've been looking for him all this time." Questions swirled through her probing gaze. Yet she held herself back.

Wes nodded and stopped himself from revealing his other failed search attempts for his little brother. What was it about Abby that made him want to confess more than he'd ever revealed to anyone, even Boone? That made him think Abby was someone he could lean on. That she would want to become his ally.

But he'd never invited anyone into his confidence. He wasn't about to start now. He couldn't trust his own family. How was he supposed to trust a stranger?

"What about your parents?" Abby asked. "Have they talked to your brother?"

"My mom passed away." Exactly one day after Wes had returned stateside. As if she'd been waiting for him. For that one last look. She'd been unable to speak, but she'd touched his cheek, held his gaze: hers peaceful, his tormented. Wes brushed off the salt stuck to his fingers, but not the grief fused in his throat. He still missed his mom every single day. Still had so much he wanted to tell her. So much he should have told her. "I never really knew my father."

"Your brother is the last of your family." Abby crumpled the paper napkin in her fist. Determination was clear in everything she said. "You must find him."

The search for his brother was about much

more than a lost family connection. Those were details he refused to share.

Wes tipped his thumb toward a group of men gathered around the tall bar tables. The branded labels on their hats and shirts indicating their long-standing and deeply established affiliation with their motocross sport. Their helmets, riding gloves and other gear resting on the benches were even more proof. "My brother, Dylan, competed in motocross since middle school. He lived for it. It was his only passion. There's a three-night motocross tour happening here on the outskirts of town this weekend."

"You should ask if anyone knows your brother." Abby studied the crowd. "Maybe they've seen him on rides in other towns."

Wes was convinced his brother's friends might lie to protect him. Wes had been careful not to make his search for Dylan public, afraid his brother's allies would alert him and his brother would move even further off the grid. As it was, Dylan's disappearance was hard to trace. "It was a long shot, but thanks for humoring me."

"I'm sorry." Abby reached across the table and held his hand.

Wes stared at their joined hands. Took in her sincerity and the steadiness of her touch. How simple it would be to link his fingers around hers. Hold on tighter. For much longer. But she wasn't his. Wouldn't ever be his. He pulled his hand away and picked up his soda glass to have something else to hold. But all he really wanted was her hand back in his. "I'm not done searching for him."

Abby nodded. She picked up her fork and dunked a pretzel crumb to the bottom of the dipping sauce bowl. "My ex, Clint Rhodes, is in Santa Cruz, most likely with his girlfriend."

Wes forgot about his own worries and focused fully on Abby. "Even though you are having his child."

"Clint had another girlfriend while I was also his girlfriend." Abby dropped her fork and pushed the pretzel platter away. "I think it's called double-dipping and is frowned upon by most people."

It was more than frowned upon. A different kind of anger stirred inside Wes. On Abby's behalf. He had words for her ex—words not for polite company. Words his mother would most likely frown upon. But appropriate all the same.

"I found out I was pregnant the same day I saw Clint making out with this other woman on our front porch." A flush of resentment washed over her face and through her voice.

"And he knows about the baby?" Wes asked.

Aware he was repeating himself. But he kept tripping over that one boulder-size detail.

"Clint knows about the baby." Her voice was matter-of-fact. Straightforward. Clear-cut. She added, "Clint also has my cell number and address in case he changes his mind about being a parent."

"Or if he wants you back." Her ex had let his child go. And he'd also let Abby go. What kind of man was he? Not the kind Abby deserved.

Wes knew that like he knew exactly how many seconds he could hold his breath without releasing any bubbles—a hundred and forty-four—and that he'd struggle to walk away from Abby if she loved him. Given the lingering anguish on her face, she'd loved her ex-boyfriend.

"Taking Clint back is not, nor will it ever be, an option." Abby sipped her water and lifted her chin. "But I would like my child to know his or her father."

"Agreed." Wes worked to keep the bitterness from his own tone.

He hated that Abby's child might end up making the same useless and wasted wishes Wes had as a kid. He'd always wished for his dad to change his mind and come home. For his dad to want to know his own sons. Wes had wanted to believe if his father had simply met Wes and Dylan, surely then, he wouldn't ever want to leave again. That old, bitter hurt knotted inside his chest. "But you can't make someone be a parent."

Abby spread her napkin over her lap. "That's why I'm going to be everything my child ever needs."

Like his own mother had been to Wes and his brother. He couldn't understand why Dylan had rejected that loyalty and left his mother when she'd become too sick and had walked away when it got too hard. Dylan had sold off the house, the land and every connection to his mom and brother. Even after all their mother had done for them growing up. Okay, their childhood hadn't been perfect. Rarely easy. But their mom had done her best to provide a home for her boys. In turn, Wes had gone into the military after high-school graduation to help provide for their family, leaving what little money his mother had saved for his brother to use for his own college career. Wes continued to send money home to keep the ranch running and the bills paid. He'd tried though failed to accept what had happened.

Old hurts. New hurts. He just hurt most days. Except sitting here with Abby, he hurt a little less.

The waitress brought their lunch orders: a

bacon cheeseburger for Wes, a turkey club sandwich for Abby.

Abby waited for the woman to leave, then asked, "Did you ever look for your father?"

Wes shook his head and pressed the top half of the bun onto his hamburger. "He gave my mother his parents' ranch and some money. In return, she promised not to bother him again. I honored her word and never contacted him."

"Your father never came back?" He was sure it was shock that had Abby's mouth dropping open and her lunch remaining untouched. "Not one time?"

"Not once, no matter how many stars I wished on." And there had been countless for many years straight.

"When did you stop wishing?" She slipped a piece of crispy bacon from her sandwich and took a bite.

Wes stretched against the tall back of his chair. The solid wood spindles pressed against his spine as firm and unyielding as that tangle of complicated emotions inside him. But he'd been well trained in compartmentalizing. And he quickly and precisely sealed the door on the past. Lingering along memory lane accomplished nothing.

He set his burger on the plate and considered Abby. "I stopped wishing around the time

I learned Santa Claus wasn't real. Wishes were useless. My mom was the one person I could always rely on."

"Her love was all you needed." Her voice cracked on the last words.

Wes wiped his hands on his napkin and reached across the table. He wrapped her hand in his own. "You're going to be enough for your child too."

"I really want to be." She curved her fingers around his and held on. One extra beat. One extra breath. "I'm going to do my best."

Wes squeezed her hand, ignored the warmth of her touch spreading through him, then quickly moved on. There would be no more like this. No more sharing and impromptu hand-holding. It served no purpose. She was not looking for a replacement father for her child. Even if she was, he wasn't that guy. Good fathers stayed for the long haul. And as soon as Wes located his brother and his inheritance, he would be gone. He ignored the tiny frisson of regret skimming over him and dipped his chin toward Abby's sandwich. "That can't be your best effort with your lunch. Especially if you'd like your own miniature salted-caramel pecan pie or dark chocolate pecan toffee, you'll need to feed junior more than that."

"I never saw pecan anything on the menu."

She reached for the plastic-coated menu in the stand with the condiments.

"It's not here." He lifted his burger and tipped his head toward the window. "It's around the corner at the Second Cake Bakery."

"I want that toffee." Abby picked up half of her sandwich. "And Tess's favorite is pecan pie."

Their lunch plates cleared and the bill paid, Wes held open the door of the tavern for Abby. She slipped on her sunglasses, and they walked side by side around the corner. Then she paused and frowned.

"What's wrong?" Wes stopped and faced her, checking her coloring and posture, worried her morning sickness had returned. "Do you need to sit down? Are you light-headed? Queasy?"

"I'm annoyed." Abby pointed over his shoulder, her frown dipped into a grimace.

Wes shifted and noticed the massive banner stretched across the main street of Belleridge. "I didn't realize this weekend was also their annual craft fair. It's quite large and well attended if you like craft fairs."

"It's their *fifty-fourth year* for their annual craft show," Abby grumbled.

Wes glanced back at her.

She raised her arms out to her sides. "I can't compete with that."

"You were thinking about holding a craft fair over Labor Day weekend in Three Springs."

"I was considering it. You can scale and grow a good craft show. Draw in people from all over the state." She motioned to the crowded sidewalk and dozens of people erecting booths and tents. "Case in point. This craft show and the motocross event most likely infuse the local businesses with profits to help sustain them through the slow-tourism months. I must have an event like this."

"This is fifty years in the making," Wes argued. "It's okay to start slow and small."

"Not if I want to make a mark and secure this job." She crossed her arms over her chest. "The event needs to be a big success."

Wes rubbed his chin. "What's next on your idea list?"

"Fortunately, I have several." Abby reached for the door of the Second Cake Bakery. "And a meeting with Corine Bauer tomorrow morning to run through the budget and my presentation."

"You're sure it has to be a big, splashy, take-the-town-by-storm idea?" Wes kept his eye on the glass-covered display of chocolate truffles, three-layered cakes and other decadent treats inside the colorful bakery.

"Definitely." Abby leaned closer to the display case and bumped against his shoulder.

"How else am I supposed to make a lasting impression?"

Wes feared Abby had already made more than a lasting impression on him. "But will working on such a big event make you happy?"

Right now, she looked worried. Tension filled the creases around her eyes.

"It doesn't matter if I'm happy." Abby accepted a sample of a white chocolate truffle from the cheerful woman behind the counter and stared at it. "It's about providing properly for my child. That only happens if I get this job."

There was a reserve to her now as if she'd accepted some sort of trade-off where her feelings were inconsequential. As if she believed she couldn't have everything.

And there he stood, wanting to give her everything.

And he wasn't sure he was happy about that revelation.

Perhaps she was correct.

Happiness had nothing to do with anything, and as for giving her everything, he'd never believed in the impossible.

CHAPTER TEN

"DINNER WAS REALLY AMAZING." Abby tugged on a pair of Boone's blue silicone oven mitts and clapped her hands together. "But I'm ready for dessert."

"You're only interested in the fireside chat Boone promised would happen over dessert." As for himself, Wes seemed to be only interested in Abby.

Boone's signature smoked brisket was tender and delicious as usual, and one of Wes's favorite meals. However, spending the evening with Abby was proving even better. He frowned as he considered the best way to proceed.

"Is it that obvious I want to hear the legend?" Abby grinned.

Wes only hoped his interest in her wasn't that obvious. Sure, he liked Abby. She was kind, funny and considerate. It was easy to like her. But his feelings should stop there.

Surely, his fascination was a side effect of their spending so much time together. All he had to do was withdraw from Abby, retreat to his apartment, and then his feelings would vanish.

"Abby, you even pleaded with Boone to have dessert first." Her cousin laughed. Tess was at the kitchen island and turned the mixer up to its highest speed to create Ilene's deluxe whipping cream.

Ilene returned from the garage with her double vanilla ice cream that she'd stashed in Boone's second freezer and nodded toward Wes. "How are they looking?"

Wes turned, cracked the oven door open and peered at the cherry cobblers inside. The thick cherry juice bubbled and oozed over the sides of the six individual-size cast-iron skillets. The desserts were ready.

Yet Wes wasn't quite ready to return to the firepit and the padded bench he'd shared with Abby the entire night. They'd been seated close to each other, but it hadn't felt close enough. He'd found himself smiling every time she'd smiled. And laughing with her, sharing her amusement.

He had to find an out before he returned to sit beside Abby and did the unthinkable, like wrap his arm around her waist and tug her to his side. *Very dangerous thoughts*.

Those thoughts should come with a warning label. And caution tape.

Abby bumped her hip against Wes's and bumped that connection he felt back to the forefront.

"Hurry up and hand me those cobblers." Abby laughed. "We've got a legend waiting to be told and a treasure waiting to be found."

If he tended toward sentimental and starry-eyed, he might argue that the real treasure was Abby herself. Good thing he was too sensible for that. Wes adjusted his own oven mitts, scooped the first skillet from the oven and settled it on Abby's waiting oven-mitt palms.

"Ilene, this smells divine." Abby inhaled the cherry cobbler aroma and smacked her lips as if she already had a missing treasure.

Wes wanted to hold her. Right now. In Boone's kitchen. He tapped the oven mitt against his forehead, wanting to realign his thoughts. He really needed to be sent home. Until he remembered that Abby was a friend only. And long embraces, hand-holding and deeper connections were not included in the friend clause.

"Is it too early to claim this as the best night ever?" Tess dropped the creamy beaters in the sink, then grabbed a wooden spoon from the holder near the stove.

This could not be the best night ever. Wes hadn't located his brother. He was no closer to helping Boone. He remained at a standstill, unable to rebuild his life in Colorado like he'd always envisioned.

The entire day should've been a total loss.

But it wasn't. And that, he supposed, was due to the Abby effect. Being around her seemed to make everything better.

He should've been running down other leads on his brother after he'd dropped Abby off at the general store. Instead, he'd gone straight to Boone's to help him prepare for tonight. They'd repaired a fence in the pasture, worked with the horses and weeded the garden. Side by side in an easy rhythm with few words exchanged as was their long-standing preference.

Except in the quiet, Wes's mind had wandered. Every time his thoughts had circled right back to Abby. The same way his gaze had settled on her tonight over and over. Again and again.

As if Abby had been what he'd been looking for all this time.

Abby spun toward the kitchen island while cradling the cobbler, drawing his gaze. Her black-and-white floral dress swirled around her bare knees. The crystals in the clips securing her braids around her head sparkled. Every part of her radiated joy.

And urged Wes closer.

Wes gripped the oven door and anchored himself in place.

Tomorrow, the charm of the evening would have faded. And with it, Abby's allure. Then surely, everything would return to normal.

He only had to make it through the rest of the evening. Keep his attraction to Abby in check.

Ilene scooped a dollop of ice cream onto the cobbler Abby held. Tess plunked a heaping spoonful of whipping cream on top. Abby declared it ready to eat and slipped it onto a wooden trivet before turning to accept the next one from Wes. Once all the cobblers were cooling on the island, Wes turned the oven off.

Ilene returned the ice cream to the freezer, then picked up two trivets. Tess carried two more, and together, the women disappeared outside.

Abby picked up the last two cobblers. "Can you grab extra napkins and that bowl of whipping cream?"

"I'll share the napkins." Wes switched the main kitchen lights off and waved the napkins at her. "But not the whipping cream."

"Be very careful what you say." Abby nudged the door open with her sandaled foot. "I'm holding your cherry cobbler too."

"Good point." Wes followed her outside. "I'll

trade you a scoop of whipping cream for my cobbler."

"Two scoops." Abby peeked into the bowl of topping. "You can never have enough whipping cream."

"There's more whipping cream?" Sam called out from his rocking chair on the other side of the firepit. He angled his cobbler on his lap and waved Wes over. "Drop another scoop on mine, won't you?"

"Mine too." Boone sat beside Sam in his oversize, thick-cushioned chair and eased his boots off the matching footstool. He leaned toward Wes and held up his cobbler. "This side here was left out."

Ilene and Tess added their own requests. Wes dolloped more whipped topping onto everyone's cobblers and set the empty bowl on the table. He dropped onto the padded bench beside Abby. He shifted into the armrest as if he sat on an airplane beside a stranger and wanted to ensure they each had space.

"Now that we're all settled in, let's get started on the tale I promised you." Boone stirred his spoon in his cobbler and peered at Abby. His grin quick and wide. His voice slow and wisdom-filled like a storyteller from centuries past.

Abby bounced on the seat, narrowing the gap between Wes and her.

Wes concentrated on his cobbler.

"The turn of the century was only two years away." Boone's words were soft and airy as if dust-coated and timeworn. "It was 1798, and the Wild West that we know from the movies and history books was still decades away. There was a town called Hollow Brook, some fifty miles northeast of here."

"There's nothing left of it now. Not even a ghost town." Sam brushed his napkin along the length of his white beard. "Been fields of weeds and dirt for decades."

"It's not good land." Ilene spooned up a bite of whipping cream and shook her head. "I'm not certain why they settled there in the first place."

"Caravan broke down. Horses injured. Too tired to keep on going." Boone scratched his cheek. "Wasn't easy to traverse in those days, unlike today."

Wes nudged his shoulder against Abby's. "Our backcountry roads aren't all that easy to traverse even now. Isn't that right?"

Abby slanted him a sideways glance and pressed her finger against her lips to quiet him.

Sam set his rocking chair into motion. "The travelers had to make a go of it somewhere and decided the where was going to be Hollow Brook."

"That was their first mistake among many." Wes took a large bite of his cobbler and chewed.

He wasn't certain what his first mistake was concerning Abby. Sitting next to her on this bench. Driving her to Belleridge. Or perhaps it was earlier than that. He never should've taken Dan on that morning ride along Old Copper Mill Road. He should've gone a different direction and changed things up. Then, he wouldn't have run into Abby on that backcountry road. And she wouldn't be changing things up inside him right now.

"You can't judge them that easily," Abby countered.

"Sure, I can." Wes liked the spark of irritation growing in Abby's gaze. "They should've known better."

Boone eyed Wes as if Wes was in grade school and misbehaving in the back of the classroom.

"What if it was the middle of the night?" Abby argued. That spark ignited. "What if they were exhausted? You have no idea what they were leaving behind. Perhaps anything was better than the life they had, even Hollow Brook."

Wes froze. Abby believed she'd have a better life than the one she'd left behind in Santa Cruz. That's what he wanted for her. It's what she deserved. But she'd have to get that for herself. He had his own life to secure, and it didn't include Abby. A disquiet whispered through him. One he ignored.

Wes held up his spoon and waved it back and forth between Sam and Boone. "Neither of you can deny that that land in the Hollow Brook area is bad. It isn't farmable. Wasn't then, and it isn't now. And do not get me started on the lack of accessible water. They should've kept moving until they found water."

Boone finished off his cobbler as if wanting the sweetness to offset his exasperation at Wes's interruption.

Sam picked up the story. "We can't deny that Hollow Brook and its folks had made a hard go of it. Even harder when the Herring Gang crept in during the middle of a quiet summer's night and stole everything they could."

"The Herring Gang had been on a robbery spree, thieving from caravans, mail couriers and stagecoaches." Boone waved his hands around. His voice lifted, sounding secretive and dire. "But they'd just taken their largest loot yet from a train robbery when they arrived in Hollow Brook."

"Those poor people." Abby touched her chest.

Wes marveled at how invested Abby was. Her face was pinched as if she felt the travelers' pain and fear. Her depth of empathy awed him.

"How much did the robbers need?" Abby set her empty skillet on the table and peered into the bowl of whipping cream. "Surely, the goods from the train were enough."

Surely, one day with Abby was enough too. Yet Wes wanted more. More of everything when it came to Abby. That made him greedy. "It was greed. Each successful robbery made them bolder. More confident. So, they escalated their sprees to try for bigger and bigger rewards."

"Don't forget. Robbing and stealing was how all outlaws and bandits made their living." Tess stacked Ilene's empty skillet on top of hers. "It was their lifestyle. How they supported themselves and their families."

Wes's own brother had stolen from him. To support himself, not a wife or children. Maybe then Wes would've understood Dylan's actions. Excused his little brother's behavior because the money was for a good cause. But Dylan wasn't married. Had no children. And that left Wes to conclude that it was greed, and that Dylan wasn't the brother Wes had believed he was.

"They probably thought they should take what they could when they could," Ilene continued. "Because they didn't know if it would be the last loot they'd ever see."

Had that been Dylan's motive too? Take it all while he could? It still didn't make it right.

And why hadn't Dylan talked to Wes first? If he'd been too tired. Too exhausted. Too overwhelmed. Why hadn't he trusted Wes to help? Instead, Dylan had disappeared in the middle of the night. No forwarding address. No goodbye letter. No explanation.

They were supposed to be family. They'd been raised to look out for each other. And that betrayal cut the deepest. Wes's gaze fastened on Abby's hand. The one resting on the cushions between them. The one he wanted to take in his own and hold onto. Would she take his side? Understand? Mute the loneliness that silenced him? But she wasn't his. And he'd been leaning on himself too long to change now. "You can't be justifying the robberies."

"Not justifying." Tess stared into the flames of the firepit. Her voice thoughtful. "Simply adding context and possible motivation."

"Greed." Wes crossed his arms over his chest. He could handle any loneliness he might feel. The same as he could handle his own affairs. "The Herring Gang could've just been greedy." Same as his little brother.

Abby stood and grabbed the whipping cream bowl from the table and returned to their shared bench.

"Either way, there were three sisters, Victoria, Vera and Violet McKenzie, living in Hollow Brook at the time." Boone set his cobbler dish on his footrest and stirred the wood in the firepit. "And the McKenzie sisters didn't take kindly to being robbed."

Neither did Wes.

"I don't blame them." Abby ran her finger around the rim of the stainless-steel bowl, collecting the last of the whipping cream.

Sam's smile grew. "Well, the McKenzie sisters hatched quite the plan and stole back their loot from the Herring Gang the following night."

"It's said they snuck into the Herring Gang's camp like ghosts at midnight." Pride shifted through Boone's words. "Turns out the sisters were miles away before any of the Herrings realized what had happened."

"It's like Robin Hood but with women." Abby wiped her fingers on a napkin and set the now-cleaned bowl back on the table.

"This is definitely not that." Same as it was not something more, something bigger and more meaningful between Wes and Abby. Robin Hood was folklore. Same as the legend Boone told now. It was all myth. Anything Wes thought he felt for Abby was just part of the evening's illusion.

"The youngest sister, Violet, had left a note with her fiancé that they'd return with the goods." Ilene sighed as if she revealed a fairy tale for the ages. "But only when it was safe."

If Wes subscribed to the improbable, he'd have convinced himself of the same about Dylan. That his brother intended to return with Wes's inheritance when it was safe. When Wes had gotten over his anger. Was Dylan facing some kind of a threat like the sisters had? Was that why he'd taken off without telling anyone?

"Well, the gang took off in pursuit of the three women," Sam continued. His rocking chair slowly swaying back and forth. "Intent on recapturing their treasure, the gang also vowed revenge on the McKenzie sisters and their families."

But unlike the McKenzie sisters, Wes's brother had no enemies. No one other than Wes chasing him down. Wes wasn't interested in revenge. He only wanted what was rightfully his.

"The siblings made it here." Boone's delight lit his face and infused his words. He opened his arms as if welcoming the McKenzie sisters into his backyard at that very moment. "They stopped at Eagle Run River less than ten miles from this very spot. There the women realized they needed to split up if they wanted to evade the bandits and survive."

"They stood beside the river. There's a spot where three different springs flow into the river.

One from the east, two from the west." Sam used his fingers to demonstrate. "It's there that the sisters split up. Each one following a different spring."

"That was a good move." Abby nodded approvingly. "Staying together would've made them a larger target."

"But this isn't a fairy tale with a happy ending." Just as Wes's reunion with his little brother wouldn't be tearful and joy-filled. Forgiveness was hard to come by. He glanced at Abby and knew she'd be able to forgive. But he wasn't like her. And that definitely made him not right for her. He shifted into the armrest and paid attention to the story. "This is barren land in the late eighteenth century that we're talking about. There's nothing fairy-tale-like about any of it."

That included Wes's situation with his brother and, even more, his relationship with Abby. The facts had to be faced and accepted.

"What happened?" Tess rubbed her arms as if she was cold, despite the warmth from the fire and the comfortable sixty-five-degree night. "It's not good, is it?"

"Depends on how you look at it." Boone lifted one shoulder and shot a warning glance at Wes.

Wes preferred to look at things directly. He always took the straightforward, matter-of-fact approach.

"Let's hear the rest and then decide." Abby slipped off her sandals and tucked her bare feet up under her.

The fact was Wes wanted to hold her close, keep her warm and protect her. But he stood up instead. Determined to stretch his legs and simply walk off the restlessness inside him. Because there was nothing straightforward about his feelings. Whenever he looked at Abby, everything became a mess. Wes moved to the edge of the patio, remaining within earshot of the tale.

"Violet, one of the decoys, was killed by Otto Herring, the oldest of the cousins in the Herring Gang." Sam smoothed his fingers through his beard. But the rasp of regret in his voice remained. "Violet had barely made it a mile up the spring."

Abby gasped, once again drawing Wes's attention and his concern.

"Vera, the middle sister, was injured when she slipped on the rocks in a steep part of the stream." Boone touched his own leg, then his forehead. "Broke her leg and cut her temple open."

"But Vera managed to make it to the meeting spot, despite her serious injuries." Ilene clenched the armrests of her chair. "That's guts right there."

Abby nodded, once again very intent and fully invested.

Vera had pushed through her injuries to be with her sister. Wes had seen his SEAL teammates do the same over the years. Push through horrific situations and injuries to not let down the entire group. Wes had done the same—refusing to be the weakest link. Refusing to fail the others he'd served with. They weren't bonded by blood, but they were bonded all the same. He'd always assumed his connection with his brother was that strong.

Now he doubted he'd ever share a bond as intense with anyone ever again.

He looked away from Abby, concentrated on Sam and the unfolding story.

"The two eldest, Vera and Victoria, were given sanctuary with a group of neighboring Indigenous people."

Sam rested his head back against the rocking chair as if emotionally drained for the two sisters. "And the Herrings returned to Hollow Brook empty-handed and riled up something fierce."

"The Herring Gang took up residence in the town." Boone shook his head. "They claimed they weren't leaving until the sisters returned the loot."

"What about Vera and Victoria?" Tess asked. "What happened to them?"

"Unfortunately, Vera developed an infection and fever from her injuries. She died not long after they'd found sanctuary." Sadness spilled through Ilene's words.

"That left the oldest sister, Victoria, with all the money and no family," Sam added. His voice was grim. "It wasn't too long before she determined that the Herring gang's loot was cursed."

"At the same time, Victoria fell in love with an Indigenous man," Boone said. "They married, or made a union, and together buried the treasure in a cave. That cave is said to be located in Silent Rise Canyon. It's miles of a dried-up riverbed. Yet that cave has never been found."

"Victoria chose love and her new family over money and riches." Abby stretched her legs across the bench as if satisfied with the ending. As if love had conquered all.

Wes frowned. Love was not the answer. Not the hero.

Victoria had risked and lost so much. Wes felt he had done the same. It was why he had to buy back their family ranch. To honor his mother and her sacrifices.

Boone added another log to the firepit. "There's more to the story that deals with your very own Palmer ancestors."

Tess and Abby shared a look, then Abby shifted toward Boone. Her eyes wide and curious.

"Your ancestor, Virgil Palmer, found a silver coin in the riverbank at the fork where the three springs flow into Eagle Run River." Sam smiled. "Virgil claimed it was from the original treasure. A sign from the McKenzie sisters themselves."

Boone's eyebrows rose. "Virgil opened the Silver Penny General Store here that same month."

Ilene pressed her clasped hands against her chest. "And that was the beginning of our town, Three Springs."

"It's said that every other business started in Three Springs that year was by folks who'd originally been robbed by the Herring Gang," Sam said.

"The idea was that Victoria McKenzie could find her town easily when she was ready to come home," Boone explained.

"Wait." Tess held up her hand. "What happened to the Herring Gang back in Hollow Brook? Surely, the outlaws followed the people to Three Springs."

"No one knows for sure, except that the town rallied together and took care of them." Ilene grinned. "There are varying stories about whether they were chased from town with cattle prods or suffered entirely different fates at the hands of the miffed locals."

"Every family has a different telling of how their ancestors routed a member of the Herring Gang." Boone laughed.

"So it was more like love for family and neighbors conquered all." Abby eyed Wes and lifted an eyebrow as if challenging him to argue.

"Victoria McKenzie never returned the loot. How is that love for others?" Wes challenged. He stepped closer and braced his hand on the back of the bench. "The McKenzie sisters are as much thieves as the outlaws. They weren't heroes, yet they are always spoken about with reverence and admiration."

"They did try, and they did care about one another. In that sense, they were heroes." Abby's hand landed on Wes's arm.

Her gentle, warm touch stilled his words as effectively as a shout.

She quickly added, "Hear me out. My ancestor, Virgil, believed the silver coin he found was a sign. He believed so strongly it led to a community whose spirit has lasted and grown ever since. It all started with something so small. And that spirit of supporting each other, neighbors helping neighbors, continues even today."

There was nothing inconsequential about Abby's grip on his arm. Or his reaction to her.

"The McKenzies' legacy wasn't a treasure," Abby rushed on. Her smile stretched from cheek to cheek. "Their legacy was the sense of community they shared."

Wes pulled himself back before he fell into her persuasive argument and under the spell of her appealing eyes. Would she fight for him like that? Would she see the positive in him? He had to go before Abby had him believing his brother had a just cause and deserved his forgiveness.

"The McKenzies united folks, and those folks built a close-knit, caring community. One that still exists today." Sam nodded and rocked his chair. "That's powerful stuff."

"They're still thieves in my book." Wes tugged his arm free of Abby's grip and gathered the dirty dishes and his common sense. "I'm going to wash these and then check on the horses."

"Give me those." Ilene rose and intercepted him. "I can take care of them while you go see to the horses."

"You should take Abby and Tess to meet our new arrivals." Boone pushed himself out of his chair and stood next to Ilene. "We still need to give the pair proper names."

"You go ahead, Abby." Tess rose and held

open the door to the kitchen for Ilene. "I'll help Ilene and Boone get everything cleaned up."

"I'll meet you there, Wes." Abby slipped on her sandals, moved toward Sam's chair and took her time gathering stray spoons and the whipping cream bowl. "I'll help bring in the last of the dishes."

Wes watched Abby. Knew immediately the dishes weren't her focus. She lingered while Sam stood. Her gaze shifting from Sam to Boone and back as she made sure both men were steady on their feet and not requiring assistance. Wes appreciated her consideration and subtlety. Neither of the proud men would ever ask for help. Or admit they weren't as agile as they used to be.

Wes waited until the trio had disappeared inside, discussing the whereabouts of that cursed Herring Gang loot.

He shook his head and headed to the stables. The only thing he wanted to find was his inheritance. The only thing he wanted to start was his future.

CHAPTER ELEVEN

ABBY WENT WITH SAM and Boone into the kitchen. Plenty of energy flowed through her, loosening her steps and encouraging her good mood. The legend had mesmerized her. Even more so since she had a personal connection to the people involved. Perhaps for the first time ever, Abby felt a real link to her parents. Her mother always described the electric charge she experienced every time she arrived on a historic dig site. Abby felt the same now.

"That silver coin Virgil originally found used to be in the general store." Boone sat at the rectangular farmhouse table and took a deck of cards from a small drawer in the table. "It was framed and hung on the wall behind the checkout counter ever since I can remember."

"I always snuck behind the counter to get a better view when we were kids." Sam dropped onto the chair across from Boone. "Mrs. Palmer would tell me 'Look, but don't touch, Samuel.' I was convinced it was magic. It practically glowed in that frame."

"Harlan kept it polished and looking newer than the day it was found." Boone shuffled the cards.

"You mean the silver coin really exists?" Abby dropped the last of the dessert dishes beside the kitchen sink and leaned against the counter. That charge sparked more excitement inside her.

Of course she'd wanted to believe. But centuries-old tales were often more folklore and legend than fact. And she'd promised herself she'd stop getting swept up in the fantasy. She'd fallen for an illusion with her ex, fallen in love with the idea of what they could be. It hadn't been genuine. When she'd collided with reality, the fallout had been splintering. Daydreams weren't for the practical-minded woman she was determined to become.

But the coin existed. And most likely the Herring loot too. A thrill rushed along her nerves, igniting her imagination and the possibilities. Discovering the missing antique treasure would be an extraordinary triumph. It would be a coup, really. An undeniable success.

Her parents would finally see Abby as more than a drifter through life. Her ex would finally understand she would've been worth fighting for.

"Obviously, there's a silver coin." Boone paused midshuffle and frowned at Abby as if she'd disappointed him. "Everything we told you is real. It all happened."

"Why didn't Grandpa Harlan ever tell us about it?" Abby tapped her fingers on the counter. So many lives—generations of her family—had been influenced by the discovery of a single coin. She couldn't help but be inspired. And very tempted. "Or the legend."

Boone dealt two cards to Sam. "Maybe Harlan thought if you weren't interested in this town, you wouldn't be interested in all that came with it."

Tess turned on the water, picked up the scrub brush and cleaned one of the skillets. "Maybe Grandpa thought it would all be here when we were ready to connect with our history."

Abby wanted to do more than connect. Finding the lost Herring Gang treasure would guarantee their future and the town's. "What if the missing treasure map is inside the silver-coin frame?"

Sam's eyebrows ratcheted up his forehead. "Abby could be onto something."

Abby held her breath. With Boone and Sam beside her, no one would accuse her of chasing another one of her castles in the sky.

This is a collections department, Abby. Getting to know customers personally and writing off their debt, however kind, cannot be a long-term strategy.

Journalists must remain impartial, Abby. You report the facts only. You aren't responsible for mending the feud.

If the client wants flat beige walls, we paint the walls flat beige, Abby. We don't add texture. Or murals. Or accent colors, even if it transforms the space.

Abby, we welcome visionaries, but we appreciate those who produce results more. Perhaps you'd be better suited for...

Abby still hadn't found her fit. Or that place she was better suited for.

Treasure hunter was perhaps not the most prudent career choice. But then again, her sensible job picks over the years had left her with a lengthy list of terminations on her work record. She shouldn't even entertain the outrageous thought. Let alone consider it. The old Abby would've already been racing back to the general store to begin the hunt. The new Abby forced herself to remain in Boone's kitchen and not get carried away.

"We must find that silver coin." Boone leaned

back in his chair and tapped his cards against the table. "It's the best place to start."

Abby exhaled and flexed her toes in her sandals. Her feet were still grounded. This was simply about locating a piece of Palmer-family history. That hardly stalled her enthusiasm or stopped her from imagining the next steps.

"I've always liked a good mystery." Tess scrubbed the last of the skillets, added the silverware to the dishwasher and turned off the faucet.

Abby studied her cousin. Certainly, Tess was not getting swept up in the romance of the legend. She was a librarian, trained to rely on hard evidence and proof. Practical was part of her DNA. Pragmatic was her lifestyle. Tess would rein Abby in any minute now.

"I'm with Boone. We must find the silver coin." Tess dried her hands on a towel and glanced at Abby. "Right?"

Abby agreed. "When was the last time anyone saw the frame?"

"Now, that's testing my memory bank." Sam tapped his finger against his forehead.

Boone nodded and rubbed his chin. "Mine too."

"Let's play a few rounds and see if our memories return." Ilene dropped into a chair beside

Boone and picked up the deck of cards. "Tess, come be my partner."

Boone motioned toward the back door. "Abby, you should go meet the horses, then you and Wes can join us."

"We won't make any real bets until you two get back." Ilene laughed and dealt the cards. "Here are the rules…"

Abby stepped outside and strolled the lit gravel pathway to the stables. Wes hadn't considered the McKenzie sisters heroes for their actions. Would he consider Abby foolish for wanting to find the missing treasure and return it to the people of Three Springs?

Abby opened the stable door and stepped inside. She found Wes in the last and largest stall in the barn. He held a brush and stood beside a beautiful but too-thin white-and-chestnut horse.

The horse's bones were pronounced, yet she stood still and proud as if, despite her struggles, her spirit remained strong and intact.

Abby wanted to believe the same about herself. *Sweet Abigail, if you're on a road without obstacles, pick a new one. A well-lived life isn't ever smooth. But joy can be found in every bump.* Grandpa Harlan would tell Abby she'd chosen the right road. It hadn't been smooth. Then he'd nudge her to find that joy. Her gaze tracked to Wes and stuck.

Wes never glanced her way. "I figured you'd be devising your treasure hunt with Sam and Boone."

The gentle sweep of the brush across the mare's slim chest matched Wes's calm, quiet tone. Abby set her arms on the stall gate, followed his lead, and spoke softly. "We decided on the first lead."

"What's that?" He swept the brush toward the mare's belly. Slow and steady as if he had all the time in the world for the horse.

"We've decided we need to find the original silver coin first." Abby kept herself in the mare's line of sight, not wanting to startle the new mom, and shifted slowly along the stall. Searching for a glimpse of the mare's baby. "The silver coin is real."

"I don't doubt that."

Abby stopped and switched her focus to Wes. "What do you doubt?"

He seemed to be trying to hide a grin. "I doubt that anything I say will change your mind about the legend and the missing loot."

He was right. Abby smiled. Her shoulders relaxed. She'd been ready to stand her ground with Wes. To convince him to believe the same as her. But this was a start.

A movement in the straw caught her attention. A tiny horse, her pink tongue darting in and out, tucked her lanky legs awkwardly under her, and flicked her tail back and forth. "The others want us to join them for a card game. But I've never been this close to a baby horse."

Wes continued to brush the mare. "This is our newest arrival and first-time mother and her filly, who at present do not have names."

"We need to fix that." Abby folded her arms on the gate and rested her chin on them. The filly's markings were as striking as her mother's: a patchwork of pure white and deep brown. A perfectly straight strip of white ran from between the filly's eyes all the way to her nose. The white as pristine and dazzling as untouched snow. "What about Snow Raven? Cinnamon. Snickerdoodle."

"It needs to be an easy name to call." Wes worked his way to the head of the mare and leaned around her to look at the foal. "The longer names make training harder."

"Amber. Spirit. Poppy." The filly shook her head. Abby grinned. "I think she likes Poppy."

"Maybe," Wes hedged.

"Now, what about this beauty?" Abby studied the mare.

Wes took Abby's hand and extended her arm over the stall door toward the mare. "Horses rely on their sense of smell to detect threats and friends."

"You're stunning. And a fighter." Abby spoke to the horse while the mare sniffed her hand. "Protective of your little one too." She caught a sideways glimpse of Wes. "She keeps checking on Poppy."

"She's a good mother." Wes remained beside the mare and the gate, watching over both Abby and the horse.

"We should call her Queen Vee. In honor of the McKenzie sisters, who were also fighters." The sniff check concluded, the horse bowed her head, and Abby stroked her hand along the mare's neck. "Besides, there's something very regal about her. You don't agree?"

"I don't think it fits her." Doubt covered Wes's dry words like dust.

"Don't listen to him." Abby gave her full attention to the mare. "You are a queen."

Wes chuckled, stepped out of the stall, and latched the gate closed.

"Will she sleep now?" Abby asked.

"She'll take power naps." Wes checked the latch on the gate. "She'll keep a close eye on her baby."

"But she's safe now." Abby turned back to the mare and repeated her words to the horse. She glanced at a too-quiet Wes. "What? I thought she should know."

"That was kind." He started toward the main doors.

"So you talk to your horses."

"Every day." Wes held open the door for Abby. "As often as I can. It's for them as much as for me."

There was nothing flippant or offhand about his words. And it was a detail that gave her more insight into the man. "Was rescuing horses always your plan?"

"Never," he said. "Three Springs was never the plan either."

Surprise shifted through her. Wes seemed as if he was part of the fabric of the town itself. "What was?"

"Retire from the Navy and return to our family's ranch." Wes stopped beside the pasture fence and whistled. A familiar, robust horse pulled away from the herd and trotted toward him and Abby. "I retired. But then my mom passed. And the ranch no longer belonged to our family. I took it for granted that it'd always be there."

She'd taken for granted her relationship with her ex. She'd bought so fully into what she had believed they'd shared, she'd missed the truth. Opposites might attract at first, but relationships built to last needed more than chemistry. Clint and Abby were two different people with entirely different values. They had fit an image, but not each other's core beliefs.

Abby had been in love with the idea of *being* in love. She understood that now. Understood also that she couldn't trust herself to recognize love. And that joy her grandpa wanted her to find shouldn't be confused with her misguided feelings for Wes. "So you moved here when you retired from the Navy?"

"I came to tell Boone about his grandson's life and sacrifice." Wes straddled the fence and greeted Dan. Or, rather, the horse placed his massive muzzle in Wes's face and exhaled through his nostrils all over him. Wes never flinched and returned the greeting with a rub along Dan's neck. "Jake Bradley was my best friend. We met in basic, survived SEAL training together, then served on the same platoon for over a dozen missions."

"I'm sorry." Abby ached. For the grief shading Wes's face. For Boone and his loss. She'd seen the folded flag in a wooden frame on Boone's fireplace mantel in his family room earlier. Her response seemed too lacking. Not nearly enough. Taking his hand would give her comfort. But would he accept it in return? She curved her fingers around the fence post.

"Jake was my brother. Family, really." Dan worked himself closer to Wes and rested his head on his shoulder as if even the horse understood Wes's pain. Wes never lost his balance. But the sadness in his voice tapered off. "I had to come here for Boone. As it was, I felt like I already knew him from the letters he'd sent to Jake and the stories Jake had told. I admired their bond. Respected both men more than I can say."

And Wes had honored both men with his actions. He could've sent a card to Boone; instead he came in person. "What made you stay in town?"

"Boone gave me the apartment behind the bar and a job until I decided what I wanted to do next." Wes rubbed Dan's thick neck again. "I'll repay him one day soon for his kindness."

Abby opened and closed her mouth. Wes had repaid Boone. He continued to do so every day from the work he took care of on the ranch and at the bar. Wes had given Boone a link to his grandson and, no doubt, someone to share his grief with. But that had clearly evolved into a deep friendship between the two men who looked out for each other now as if they were family. She saw the respect and love each one had for the other every time they were together. And they were often together. Abby eased closer to Wes and reached to stroke Dan behind his tall ears. "How did Dan find his way here?"

"About six months after I arrived, a couple came into the bar. They had rescued Dan and four other horses. Their truck had broken down outside of town." Dan lifted his head and nickered. Wes continued. "The stables here were empty at the time. Boone offered them a place to board their rescues for the night. Even starved and neglected, Dan was still the largest and most stubborn."

Abby said teasingly, "There's nothing wrong with being tenacious and determined, Dan."

"I was the only one able to coax Dan off the trailer," Wes added. "I stayed with him that night."

"You slept in the stall?" Abby couldn't keep the disbelief from her tone. Dan wasn't a miniature poodle. He could've hurt Wes by accident during the night if he'd been startled or scared. Yet Wes had put himself in that position anyway. For a frightened and confused horse. Abby wasn't certain she wanted to know any more. Wes had layers and depth she'd only guessed at. Qualities that drew her to him even more.

But a relationship wasn't a road she wanted to take. She had a child to put first. A life and a job to establish. She couldn't afford to be distracted by one more of her illusions. And love was nothing more than that.

"I've slept in worse conditions than a clean,

dry horse stall. It's rare I even sleep through the night." Wes shrugged as if unconcerned by his admission. As if it was a fact of his life, not a problem. "The next morning, Dan wanted nothing to do with the trailer. I knew what Dan needed and how to provide for him, so I told the couple he could stay."

"You gave him a safe place to live." Abby pressed a kiss on Dan's muzzle. "Everyone needs that, don't they, Dan? To feel safe and cared for."

Wes cleared his throat. "Well, now Dan is the ambassador here. He looks after the herd."

But who looks after you? Who cares about you? Not that Abby was raising her hand for the part. "You gave him a purpose."

"We gave each other one." Wes pointed at a gray mare in the pasture. "I took in Cinder from the same couple last year. She'll be having her foal in September."

"How do you decide which horses to take in?" *And if you can let a horse into your life, could you let me in too?* That was the wrong direction. Entirely, utterly wrong. Abby blinked and concentrated on redirecting her thoughts.

"Their condition. Their story." Wes rubbed his chin and watched the herd. "A feeling that I can help. That I can make a difference in a particular horse's life in that moment."

He'd been making a difference in her life since she'd arrived. "Do you keep them?"

"Not always. I've found new homes for seven." Wes tipped his head and smiled. "Before you ask, yes, I keep in touch with the owners about the horses' progress."

There was so much affection in his face. He had a passion for the horses that was clear. He had joy too. So much, whether he was talking about the animals or working with them. It'd been wrapped around him inside the stable, woven through every movement. She hadn't recognized it before. She did now.

It was the joy Grandpa Harlan always spoke of. "This is enough for you."

He shifted toward her. "What is?"

"The horses. The bar. The apartment." Abby moved her hand around like she was waving a magic wand. "Your life is enough for you."

"Yeah. I'm content." Wes climbed off the fence and dropped into her space, facing her fully. "What more should I want—could I want, really?"

Me. You could want me too. Abby shook her head and adjusted her stance before she face-planted in that pothole. "I get it."

"How do you define *content*?" He leaned against the fence, one boot crossed over the other, and considered her.

"I'm still working that out." She reached up and curled her fingers around the ocean-colored jasper stone in her necklace. The grounding stone was worn for stability and confidence. "I thought I was happy in Santa Cruz. But it wasn't real."

"What did *content* look like in Santa Cruz?" he asked.

"It was a bungalow several blocks from the beach. A nine-to-five job. A newscaster boyfriend." They'd portrayed the ideal image of content. Abby flexed her fingers around the oval style stone. But feeling content inside, where it mattered, like Wes? Had she ever known that?

"And what does content mean now?" His quiet voice barely stirred the still evening air between them.

You. When I'm with you, I'm content. Safe. Seen. Abby settled her gaze on his and paused until her heart quieted. Her heart had fooled her before. She wouldn't put any faith in its whispers now. "Content means family and belonging. Being a part of something that's bigger than me."

"Searching for the McKenzie sisters' treasure won't make you content." Wes laughed. The sound wrapped around her. "It'll make you frustrated."

"It's not about a treasure hunt." Although it could be. That excitement simmered even now.

"It's about being connected to a place and the people who lived here."

"You're talking about roots?" Distaste twisted his grin into a frown.

"You don't like roots, do you?"

"It's not that, exactly," he said, hedging.

"What is it, exactly?" *Was it the idea of putting down roots with someone? Someone like me?*

"It's exactly time we return to the house and join that card game." He gestured beyond her. "Tess is coming to get us right now."

Abby spun around, waved to her cousin and called out, "We'll be right there."

"You guys are partners," Tess shouted back. "You have until you reach the house to come up with a good strategy to win."

The back door shut on Tess's laughter.

Abby and Wes walked to the patio. At the door, he rested his hand on the frame, preventing her from opening it. "Are you any good at cards?"

"Are you?" She faced him on the landing. "I like to win and don't want to have to carry every hand for my team."

"I can hold my own." Laughter swirled through his tone. He stepped onto the landing beside her.

She crossed her arms over her chest. It wasn't nearly enough distance between them. Oddly, it was as if she'd put herself even closer to him. "Care to make a side bet?"

"I would."

"If I win more points for our team, you have to tell me why you don't like roots."

His eyes widened, revealing interest and a warmth she hadn't seen before. "What if I score more points in this partnership?"

"I cook dinner for you."

"You already owe me dinner." The humor in his voice pushed one corner of his mouth up. "I'm not entirely sure how many of your Grandma Opal's recipes you've mastered."

"Then, you pick." Her words held no more weight than a whisper.

"If I win, you answer a question of my choice." That warmth in his gaze glinted from the challenge in his voice.

"Any question?"

He nodded.

She had questions she wanted to put to him. Too many in fact. Could she pick the right one to ask? Could he?

"Deal."

CHAPTER TWELVE

ABBY PARKED IN Corine Bauer's driveway and brushed dust from her arms. The dirt smudged on her off-white lace dress was going to require laundry detergent and a washing machine. She grabbed her bandanna-print knee-length cardi from the passenger seat of Tess's car and adjusted the thin red cotton wrap until it hid most of the dirt stains. Then she rubbed at her hands again.

She was meeting her boss. For the first time. Dirty fingernails and a wrinkled, smudged dress wasn't the look she'd been going for. But she'd gotten caught up in the impromptu search at the general store.

One that had begun with a vigorous knocking on their apartment door not an hour past sunrise. Abby had greeted Boone and Sam, both wearing eager grins and clutching coffee cups and flashlights. The foursome had descended the stairs and had spent the past three hours searching shelves, drawers and cabinets for the framed silver coin.

Boone had unearthed a cuckoo clock from a hutch in the front alcove. Tess had discovered a doorstop collection inside a stuck bottom drawer behind the counter. Sam and Abby had encountered more dust and cobwebs than anything in the second alcove. Dozens of boxes, assorted chairs and two vintage chests had to be moved before they could even properly search. Still, the conversation had flowed easily, and each discovery had fueled their enthusiasm. Despite the missing penny not turning up.

When Abby had finally checked her watch, she had just enough time to drive to Corine's house. Changing would've made her late. She'd chosen punctuality over a spotless appearance. And now could only hope Corine agreed.

A man, wearing a plaid shirt and serious-looking tool belt, opened the Bauer front door. He introduced himself as Keith Bauer, welcomed Abby inside and guided her around stacks of wooden floor planks. "Sorry about the mess. It started as new hardwood flooring for the office. Just this morning, my wife declared she likes it so much, she wants to extend it to the entire downstairs."

Sawdust fell from Keith's work boots with every step he took. Abby relaxed. "It's a lovely honey-colored floor. It will add a warmth to your rooms."

Keith slowed and glanced at her. "Have you been talking to my wife too?"

Abby laughed and shook her head.

"I've got a list of projects to finish quickly." Keith opened a bedroom door on the first floor and motioned Abby inside. "At this rate I'm not ever going to get the nursery completed on time."

Corine Bauer sat propped up by pillows in a queen-size bed. Her thick brown hair twisted into a haystack bun on top of her head. She threw her arms wide and accepted a hug and kiss from her husband. "I'm not adding to the project list. I'm improving it."

"Either way, it's getting longer each day." Keith ruined his put-out gruffness by giving his wife a big smile and fixing the covers around her. He then set his palm gently on her stomach. As if he was checking on his twins. Or perhaps just letting them know he was there.

Something snagged inside Abby's chest. From the reverence on Keith's face to the love glistening in Corine's brown eyes. Abby glanced away.

Photos filled one of the bedroom walls, detailing the couple's journey from their marriage proposal to their outdoor wedding. Abby had always envisioned herself following the same sort of traditional path. Proposal. Wedding. Children. She'd skipped a few steps. Jumped ahead to a child. Accepted her new road. Still, she couldn't deny that tiny sting of envy. And that pinch of regret.

But it wasn't for herself entirely. It was more for her child and the father he or she wouldn't know. Abby flattened her palm over her own tummy. Vowed again she would be all her child ever needed. Doubled down on her promise to provide a home. Stability. That started now. Here in the Bauer house by convincing this woman that Abby could handle the job.

"Okay, I have work, and so do you." Corine gave Keith another kiss and pushed him away. "Try not to make too much noise, please. I don't want Abby and I to have to shout at each other."

Keith pulled a pair of headphones from his tool belt and slipped them on. "That's what these are for."

"He got me a pair too." Corine picked up a pair of silver wireless headphones from the bed-side table. "They really come in handy. Now, Abby, come and sit. Just don't choose the rock-ing chair."

Abby veered away from the antique rocker and crossed to the tall-backed armchair between the bed and the window alcove. "Is there some-thing wrong with the rocking chair?"

"My husband's relatives claim their many-times-over-great-grandmother sat in that very rocking chair with a cattle prod and watched the Herring Gang be chased out of town for good." Corine's voice shifted from an awed whisper to distaste. "But it can't be true."

Another doubter. Like Wes. If Corine wasn't a believer, how would she convince her boss that her idea had merit? "You don't believe in the legend, then."

"Oh, that's true." Corine flicked her wrist at the rocker and grimaced. "It's the sitting in that particular rocking chair that I don't believe for a hot second."

"It's beautiful." Abby walked over to the chair and studied the intricately carved arms and the headrest. "What's wrong with it?"

"It's like sitting on a pile of sharp, crushed rocks." Corine eyed the piece as if waiting for it to transform. "Doesn't matter how many pillows you pile on it. Your bottom hurts something fierce in under a minute."

"It can't be that bad." Abby dropped into the chair. The spindles jammed between her spine like hard ice picks. And the seat. She jumped back out and studied the antique rocking chair. Barely refraining from rubbing her backside. "Okay. It is that bad."

"I thought my sister-in-law was a bit too giddy when they dropped off the chair," Corine explained. "All the Bauer women supposedly rock their newborns to sleep in that chair. It's tradition. But traditions are supposed to be enjoyable. Like a crown on your birthday. I still have the one my mom made me. Candles in your birthday doughnut stack. I'm stealing that one from my neighbor across the street. Traditions should be fun."

Like the birthday tins of homemade candy Tess used to send Abby every year. Abby backed away from the rocker and dropped into the armchair again. "What are you going to do with it?"

"I've been staring at it for days." Corine adjusted her pillows behind her. Her words were hopeful. "I'm open to suggestions."

"You could designate the rocker for your husband." Abby tiptoed around the swish of guilt. Keith had been very polite and nice. And adorably attentive to his wife. But Abby had to look out for her boss. If Corine was cranky or sleep-deprived that would surely make her less receptive to Abby's ideas. "Twins means you're going to need an extra set of arms."

"I could get this one I found online." Corine pulled a tablet from beneath the covers and tapped on the screen. Then she handed it to Abby.

"It's the perfect chair for a new mom." A navy glider rocker with matching footrest filled the screen, looking comfortable and functional. And exactly like the kind Abby would want. Except she didn't have her own home like Corine. She had a futon at her cousin's place. The reminder, however sobering, refocused her. She'd buy her own glider rocker one day for the home she'd have. But there were things she had to accomplish first. "Where should you and I begin?"

"I know the particulars. You're Tess's cousin. Harlan and Opal's granddaughter. They were good people. You came from Santa Cruz. Sorry about your car." Sympathy shone on Corine's face. She took the tablet from Abby and slipped it back under the blankets. "Our potholes do need to be addressed. And the town council tasked you with planning something special for Labor Day weekend. Why no one mentioned the Roots and Shoots Garden Club meeting to you is beyond me."

Abby waited a beat, making sure Corine was drawing a breath and not continuing. "Frieda invited Tess and me to the garden club meeting."

"But it's not just a meeting, and it's rarely about gardening. It's an all-day affair from early morning until evening. Everyone attends." Corine pulled a pair of knitting needles and a ball of pale yellow yarn from a drawer in the bedside table.

"Which is why no one came to my meeting last Saturday." Abby exhaled.

"It's a small town. We can turn the tiniest thing into a massive social gathering." Corine plucked at the yarn. "Which means we shouldn't have a problem for Labor Day weekend."

Except worry pinched Corine's eyebrows together. Abby asked, "Is there a problem?"

"The land developers add a definite wrinkle." Corine shifted her gaze to Abby. "Along with the town council's expectations."

Abby crossed her legs and pushed her shoulders back against her own unease. "I was told they want a big, successful event that will entice the land developers."

"But what's big and successful, really?" Corine tapped a knitting needle against her palm as her thoughts tapped out one after the other. In rapid succession. "A large crowd of locals. All we need is a Friday night high-school football game for that. Turning a large profit. That's trickier. We like to gather socially, but we're thrifty people. Don't be fooled by Lynette Kinney's catio and koi pond. Lynette harangued that poor contractor until he reduced the cost. Is it one or the other? Because I've seen the winner of a four-man poker game leave with a larger profit than the grocery store generates in one day. Call it a success, but not a big event."

Again, Abby waited and watched the woman. Corine's knitting-needle drumming slowed, and her mouth dipped into a frown. Abby reached for her courage. "This might be outside the box…"

"I like outside-the-box thinking. It's under-appreciated. Undervalued." Corine pointed the knitting needle at Abby. "How far outside of the box are you thinking of going? Not long ago, the town council hired an internet guy, Marshall Solis, to fix the internet infrastructure and check on the cell towers in the county. But the position quickly spiraled into Marshall becoming the entire town's help desk."

Abby held onto her grin, nodded and waited for Corine to get to the point as if she had all afternoon to visit with the pregnant woman. How quickly she'd adapted to Corine's running commentary and the town's slower pace.

"Folks called Marshall for things like broken alarm clocks and oven-temperature recalibrations. They wanted him to reset their passwords on their personal computers and cell phones. Don't get me started on the ones who'd installed their own home-alarm systems. Marshall's phone never stopped ringing." Corine sighed and pressed her hand against her stomach. "Marshall lasted one week. He called to tell me he quit because his job responsibilities had fallen too far outside the box, even for him. And that the town council wouldn't know internet infrastructure if they tripped over a wire."

Abby struggled to keep her chuckle in check.

"Last I heard, Mrs. Buckley was still blaming Marshall for her burned lasagna." Corine's lips twitched. "But she's been burning her lasagna for years now. It's not the oven."

Abby covered her mouth and caught her laughter against her palm.

Corine's own laugh spilled out and was charming and infectiously sweet, like the woman herself. Corine focused now on Abby. "So I ask again. How far outside the box are you willing to go?"

Abby leaped over the box. "I recently learned about the McKenzie sisters, the Herring Gang and the missing loot. I can't seem to get it out of my mind."

Corine's head bobbed up and down. "It has everything good legends are made of. Villains, heroes, romance and gold. What's not to like, really?"

Encouraged, Abby added, "I keep thinking about the missing treasure and how finding it would set Three Springs apart from other towns and make it a real destination spot."

"Have you been to the town hall?" Corine asked. "We have a small museum. And by small,

I mean closet-size tiny. The treasure wouldn't fit. Although, there's the Stagecoach Inn. Hasn't been opened for years. Out-of-towners usually stay with their family so I'm not sure that makes them visitors. Just returning locals."

"We'd have to find the treasure first," Abby said, pulling Corine back to her idea. "That would mean an organized treasure hunt."

"Treasure hunt." Corine sat up. Her bun bobbled on her head, then swayed to a stop. "That's brilliant."

Corine's enthusiasm took Abby aback. She'd expected more resistance. Asking the town to go on a treasure hunt in Silent Rise Canyon was, well, a big ask. Way outside the box. The town kept surprising her.

"There can be a scavenger hunt before the movie on Friday night," Corine rushed on.

Abby opened and closed her mouth.

"Friday night is our first annual family movie night in the town square. It was scheduled before the council decided they wanted a Labor Day weekend event too. That's two different weekends with two different events, but it'll work out." Corine tossed her knitting needles and pile of yarn onto the other side of the bed, then considered Abby. "No one told you about this weekend, did they?"

Abby shook her head.

"It's good we're meeting, then. Everything is already rented. The delivery and setup are confirmed for Friday." Corine smiled and lifted her shoulders in an easy shrug. "You just need to oversee the entire evening and now plan a scavenger hunt for the kids."

"You mean *treasure hunt*." Abby wanted to plan a whole-town treasure hunt. Get Three Springs some much-deserved attention. Secure her job and declare herself a success.

"Center the scavenger hunt around the businesses in downtown. Have the kids find scavenger hunt items inside the businesses with their parents as escorts," Corine continued. The woman had gone from knitting to hardcore strategizing in less than five minutes. It was remarkable, really. "It's a stretch, but a way to get the locals to revisit the stores and shops again. It would be great if they could support our local business owners more. We can add the Silver Penny when it's reopened."

Abby rubbed her forehead. Following Corine was exhausting. Good thing the woman was confined to her bed. Abby could only imagine what she'd be like on her feet. Probably a whirlwind. "What movie are we showing?"

"You'll have to choose." Corine pointed at the dresser on the far side of the room. "I started a binder for movie night before I was put on bedrest."

"What about the Labor Day event?" What about the treasure hunt in the canyon? Abby stood and retrieved the binder.

"If the first-ever movie night is a success, we can repeat it all on a larger scale during the holiday weekend." Corine pursed her lips. "Maybe that means food trucks. Two movie showings. More outdoor games. Crafts. But we keep the focus on family."

Abby didn't disagree. She had a child of her own coming. Having town-sponsored kid-friendly things happening only added to its appeal for those who were already here. But what about making Three Springs attractive to outsiders, like their land developer? Abby opened the binder and hid her wince. It contained two pages covered in handwritten scribbles and flowery doodles. More doodles than notes. A personal shopping list that reminded Abby she needed to make her own grocery list and also get a yellow highlighter.

"You're not convinced."

Was it really big enough to meet everyone's expectations? "We need to bring in more than locals."

"Right. We have to build up the businesses in downtown to show we're viable, open and thriving to newcomers, especially those willing to invest. Corine beamed at Abby. "That means promoting all this to the neighboring towns. We'll need signs and fliers and have the details advertised in the papers and online."

"Do you think the businesses are going to agree to be part of a scavenger hunt and remain open later on Friday?" Abby tried to recall the shops on Fortune Street. Yet all she could think of was the Feisty Owl.

"That'll be down to your powers of persuasion. This has been really productive." Corine linked her hands behind her head and leaned back as if her workday was finished. "I'm glad you're here, Abby. You just need to make this a success so we can work together on a permanent basis."

Permanent. Abby hadn't ever had that as a framework. Certainly not in her childhood. The most constant part of her life were her grandparents, who'd always been present through their letters. Letters that had arrived every month since Abby had been in grade school. Now her grandparents were gone, and nothing had been consistent in Abby's life since. "I'll bring you feedback about whether the stores noticed an uptick in sales and foot traffic, along with attendance numbers."

"You won't need to. I'll hear that evening.

Not even a decades-long drought could kill the gossip grapevine in Three Springs. It's truly indestructible." Corine laughed again. "Welcome to town!"

Abby was appreciating it more and more each day. "Thanks for giving me a chance."

"It's what Three Springs was founded on." Corine smiled. "Neighbors helping neighbors. Been that way for centuries, and it's just what we do."

A few hours later, outside the Five Star Grocery Depot, Abby had her list written and her movie-night poll almost complete. She'd been stopping shoppers heading into the store, introducing herself and asking them which one of three movies they'd come to see for Friday's family movie night in the town square. She'd polled thirty-two people, two of whom were Five Star baggers.

She headed into the store for her own groceries and walked out beside Mr. Bybee, whom she'd met in the spice aisle.

"Thank you, Mr. Bybee." Abby wrote another check on her clipboard and grinned at the gentleman. "Don't forget to add that fresh tarragon and strawberries to your chicken salad tonight. It'll bring out the flavor in the dish. At least, that's what my Grandma Opal always told me."

"Got fresh tarragon right here." Mr. Bybee

patted his reusable shopping bag. "It's the first thing I'm going to add. I'll let you know Friday night what I thought."

Abby grinned and walked to Tess's car. Groceries loaded, she stopped at the corner gas station, polled the two customers pumping gas, thanked them for their time and drove to the general store.

She searched through more boxes, uncovering plenty of antiques but no coin, before heading up to the apartment. She had one of Tess's casserole dishes, filled with homemade Swedish meatballs hot from the oven, and packed it into a cloth shopping bag. She was honoring her side of the bet she'd made with Wes.

When she entered the Feisty Owl to find Wes, she greeted several familiar couples and worked her way over to the bar. Wes added a cherry to a soda glass, set it on a waiting serving tray and skipped over a greeting. "You aren't polling my customers, Abby."

Abby set the cloth bag with the casserole dish on the bar. "What are you, Wes? The town spy? How is it possible that you know everything that's going on without leaving the bar?"

"I have a good network." He leaned forward and lifted the opening of the bag. "What's this?"

"None of your business." She slapped the top

of his hand. "Why can't I poll a few of your customers?"

"Because we have a no-soliciting policy," Wes said.

"I'm not soliciting," Abby said. "I'm polling. There's a difference."

"You're still interrupting their meal," Wes said. "And the Feisty Owl strives to give its customers a peaceful, undisturbed dining experience."

"You have a massive mechanical bull in the corner. Live music in the other corner." Abby ramped up the sarcasm. "And peanut shells scattered all over the floor, crunching under everyone's boots. And *I'm* the disruption?"

"That's all part of the ambience." Wes stretched his arms wide and braced himself against the bar. "Part of the draw."

He was part of the draw for her. Abby waved her hand, brushing aside her attraction and his words. "I already have overwhelming support for one movie in particular. You don't have enough customers in here to change the vote anyway."

Boone came by and greeted Abby with a welcoming hug. He leaned toward the fabric bag and drew a deep breath. He rubbed his stomach. "Is that what I think it is?"

Abby grinned. "If you're thinking Grandma

Opal's signature Swedish meatballs, then, yes, it is."

Wes crossed his arms over his chest and watched her. "You don't know anything about how bets work, do you?"

"Who cares about bets." Boone patted his hand against the bar top. "She's got meatballs and mashed potatoes. Opal never served them on anything else."

"*Potaytoes, potahtoes,* it still doesn't mean that she's paid up." Wes seemed to be smothering a smile, but she wasn't quite sure.

Ilene's smile was wide and warm as she came up beside Abby with a drink order.

"If it's Opal's recipe, you are in for a real treat," Boone added. "Never could get that recipe from her."

"No one could get any written recipes from her." Except Abby, who treated her grandmother's handwritten cookbook like the priceless first edition it truly was. "Grandma Opal never measured out any ingredients when she cooked. She told me it was because she thought her measuring spoons were too pretty to use."

Boone's voice sounded far away as if he'd stepped inside a memory. "Opal had quite the collection. Harlan would keep building display racks for her. Never once complained."

"Do you think those measuring spoons are

somewhere in the store?" Abby couldn't keep the wishful edge out of her words. She had taken extra care to find special measuring spoon sets in the countries she'd lived. Every time she sent one to her grandmother, it was like sending a part of her heart. She liked knowing she was connected to the collection. "I don't remember more than one display case in her house in Wisconsin."

"Can't see why not." Boone accepted a full soda glass from Wes and moved to his usual stool. "We locked that place up the day they left, and everything still seems to be where we left it. Always assumed they'd be back to sort it proper like and take what they meant to keep."

"Did they ever mention moving back?" Ilene rinsed off some cutlery in the sink.

"They went to help my aunt Katherine with Tess and Paige after my uncle Neal passed. Then they stayed to care for my aunt during her long struggle with breast cancer." A ten-year battle her aunt had ultimately lost when Abby was in college. It still didn't seem fair. "Then there was a knee replacement for Grandpa. Hip replacement for Grandma. Moving back here, or anywhere, became complicated."

"Seems the timing was never right." Boone sipped his soda. "Meanwhile, Sam and I watched over the building."

"Now Tess and I are here to pick up where our grandparents left off." Abby set her purse on the stool and rummaged inside the large bag. She pulled out a soft-backed book. "But first, that means new electrical so we can see what we're doing."

"You brought dinner, and you intend to help with the electrical at the store." Wes rubbed the back of his neck. "Seriously. Do I need to explain how bets work? You can't win and lose at the same time."

Abby set her book on the bar top and held Wes's gaze. "I thought we could have dinner and design your electrical plan for the store."

He filled a mug and added a ginger and lemon tea bag to the steaming water. "Uh, what are we going to do?"

Abby flashed the cover of her how-to electrical book for beginners at Wes. "Chapter one says we need an electrical-wiring diagram."

"I thought you were getting a book on pregnancy in the bookstore yesterday." Wes ignored the book.

"I got that too." Abby opened her DIY manual to chapter one. "And this one. Now I really can help you. How great is that?"

Wes looked less than thrilled. He sounded even less delighted. "You are not helping me run new wiring in the general store."

"Why not? I've read the book already." She'd skimmed it more than read it. Not even that, truthfully. She'd fallen asleep during chapter one. Her eyes had crossed on the page with all the wiring-diagram symbols and completely lost focus on the section about diodes and capacitors. But she would read it. Maybe.

"Yes. I want to know why Abby can't help too." Ilene edged closer.

"Is it because I'm not a guy?" Abby mirrored Wes's stubborn stance, tilting her chin upwards and censuring with her tone.

"It better not be," Ilene muttered. "His momma taught him better than that."

"Think before you speak, son," Boone hollered, then lifted his eyebrows at Abby. "I taught him that."

Wes set four tumbler glasses on the bar. He reached for a whiskey bottle on a top shelf and took his time adding the caramel-colored liquid to the glasses. As if he still had to master the perfect pour and hadn't been preparing the proper whiskey neat for years. He stretched the one word into his slow pour. "Because…"

Abby interrupted. "If you say because I'm pregnant, I'm going to come around the bar and kick you."

Boone's deep rumble of laughter spread across the bar.

"You are pregnant." Wes set the whiskey bottle back on the top shelf and faced her. Only the bar separated them. "There's absolutely nothing wrong with me wanting to make sure you're safe."

"I knew he'd get it right," Boone said.

Ilene smiled and patted Wes's shoulder in approval before slipping to the other end of the bar.

"Of course you'll keep me safe." Just as she wanted to look out for him. Nothing wrong with that. She didn't believe she could do the actual electrical work, anyway. But she could hand him tools, water. Whatever. She could just be there for him. If he'd only let her. "I can be helpful. Come on, Wes. I won't ask any friend questions. Promise."

He wiped the back of his hand across his mouth as if rubbing away his smile. The one that lingered in his gaze. "You're telling me that you're going to follow every instruction I give you. No argument. No pushback. Because you know it's for your own safety."

Obviously, she'd push back. He knew it too. His lips twitched. She stalled and flipped through the pages of her how-to book. "If it's different than the book explains, then what?"

"My way goes." He arched one eyebrow and angled toward her.

"What if it's wrong?" Abby challenged. She

leaned into the bar, appreciating that spark in his eyes. The one that kick-started her own pulse.

"It won't be."

"That's arrogant."

"That's experience." He finally closed the distance between them. "And experience trumps theory every time."

She wanted to experience his embrace. One time. A moment inside his arms to feel safe. Cared for. Wanted. Abby tried to backpedal, but she tripped over her errant thoughts. He unsettled her. She unsettled herself. "Looks like you have an electrical assistant. When do we start?"

And when exactly would her heart stop racing?

Because they'd started something, and she wasn't quite certain how to stop it. Or if she even wanted to.

"You can begin by getting out of this bar and enjoying Opal's meatballs." Ilene hung a dry towel over her shoulder and made a shooing motion with her hands. "Believe it or not, Nolan and I can handle this. And Boone's here to guide us."

"Don't be drawing any electrical diagram either," Boone ordered. "Just enjoy a good meal with good company."

"I feel like we're being kicked out." Abby worked to hold back her grin.

"I don't think I'll be sharing any leftovers

with anyone." Wes shot a frown at Boone, then picked up the casserole carrier and motioned to Abby. "Follow me. I know the perfect place to enjoy a good meal and good company."

CHAPTER THIRTEEN

"THOSE WERE THE BEST Swedish meatballs and mashed potatoes I've tasted." Wes put the container of leftovers in his refrigerator. "What other recipes are in your Grandmother Opal's personal cookbook?"

"Why?" Abby finished drying her hands and hung the towel on the handle of the oven. Wes's perfect place had been his apartment attached to the back of the bar. The two-bedroom unit was uncluttered, unfussy and very inviting. It had reclaimed woods and neutral colors mixed with modern appliances and high-tech gadgets. A blend of the past and the present. And the place he looked the most comfortable. "Do you want to steal my grandmother's recipes for the Owl?"

"I'm considering it." He refilled their wine glasses, his with red wine, hers with a sparkling cider, and handed hers to her.

She eyed him over the rim of her wine glass. "You're serious."

"If you give Nolan a sample, he'll want to add that dish to the menu." Wes picked up his glass and headed toward the staircase tucked behind the kitchen. "I'm not kidding. It's that good."

"Can we call it Opal's One-of-a-kind Swedish Meatballs?" Abby followed Wes up the staircase to the hidden gem of the apartment: the rooftop deck.

"If it means getting the recipe." Wes propped the door open with his foot, letting Abby step onto the patio.

"Let me ask Tess. But I think my grandmother would've loved the idea of her recipe on a restaurant menu." About as much as Abby loved the rooftop deck. Her view of the star-filled sky extended for miles in every direction. The bar wasn't visible. She wasn't even aware there was a bar next to her. Her feet weren't vibrating from the beat of the loud music. Nothing, not even the deep bass, thumped through the walls. It was as if they'd stepped into their own secluded slice of the night.

"Would Grandma Opal like it even though it's a bar-and-grill menu?" Wes set his wine glass on a side table and sat on one of two cushioned lounge chairs.

"Especially if it's the Owl." Abby cradled her glass in her palms. "It's like the heartbeat of the town, isn't it?"

"I think that's more Boone." Wes stretched out and stacked his boots one on top of the other. "And Sam. They're staples in the community. They know everyone, and everyone knows them."

"I want to be like them." Abby stared at the bubbles in her sparkling cider.

"Why?" Wes asked.

"They're a connection to the past." They'd known her grandparents. Could tell Abby if she had her grandmother's laugh. Or her grandfather's eyes. Or even better, if her child had her grandmother's dimples and her grandfather's mischievous side.

Wes tipped his head and eyed her. "It's those roots again, isn't it?"

She laughed. "It's not a bad thing."

"Why do you want roots?"

"I never had them. And yes, it's that simple." Abby set her glass on the table and paced along the railing of the cozy deck. There was just enough room for one couple to slow dance under the stars. "Growing up I wanted to be able to walk across the street to my grandparents' house. I wanted to have the same classmates in the same school. I wanted to have a home."

Wes sipped his wine. "What did you have?"

"A series of tents and cabins." She leaned back against the railing and faced him. "My mother is an archaeologist. My father is an English professor. I spent most of my childhood traveling from one of Mom's sites to another."

"That's not what I expected." A small smile curved across his mouth.

"It was different." No one else she knew had the same experiences she'd had. "And not all bad. I don't want it to sound that way. My parents love me, and I love them. We're just not the same kind of people."

"What are they like?" he asked.

"They love to travel and immerse themselves in new cultures while exploring ancient ones. They both knew in high school what they wanted to do and what they wanted their future to look like." Abby still didn't know. She ran her hand over her hair and rearranged the clips holding her braids together as if finding clarity was as simple as changing hairstyles. "Most days I feel like I'm still struggling to figure everything out."

The search was ongoing and constant. Abby feared she disappointed her parents more and more each day. With every job loss. Every false start. She stepped away from the railing and her looming melancholy. It wasn't the time or the place to voice her fears. Tonight was about a good meal with good company. She couldn't afford to blur the lines. Wes wasn't her safe place. She'd have to create that on her own.

Wes shifted in the lounge chair and changed the conversation as if he recognized those boundaries too. "Speaking of figuring things out, what have you come up with for Labor Day weekend?"

"That's still evolving for the holiday weekend." Abby claimed the other lounge chair and sat. "So far there's only the family movie night this Friday in the town square and a newly added scavenger hunt."

"That's a bad idea." His eyebrows pinched together.

"It's a scavenger hunt for the kids, Wes." Abby flopped back into the chair and crossed her arms over her chest. Of course he wasn't her safe place. He was too disagreeable. Too discouraging. Safe places weren't supposed to be so exasperating. "This is not a treasure hunt for centuries-old loot."

"It's still not a good idea." He looked up at the sky.

His words were all the more irritating framed by his calm and reasonable tone. "There's a storm coming."

Abby swallowed her huff of frustration and pulled her phone from the pocket in her dress. She opened her weather app and scanned the forecast for the next several days. The one showing a clear sky for Friday. "There's nothing on the weather app."

"Doesn't mean it isn't coming." No inflection. No hesitation. Just more of his flat-out certainty.

"You aren't a weatherman." Abby tapped her irritation out on the phone screen. She pulled up the local TV forecast and waved the screen toward him. "I don't see your picture on the local news channel under *Meteorologist*."

"It's the horses. They sense weather changes and let me know." He turned his head to look at her. Straight-faced, serious and entirely relaxed. "And if you really want to get into the details, it's also the honeybees."

She skipped completely over the honeybees and set out to set *him* straight. Someone had to. "I know you're a horse whisperer, but forecasting the weather is pushing it."

"You think I'm a horse whisperer." Appreciation swirled from his gaze to his half smile.

"I saw you with Poppy and Queen Vee. I watched how they responded to you inside the stall." She put her phone away. "There's Dan and the other rescues too."

"We never decided on Poppy and Queen Vee for their names." His smile disappeared.

"There was a consensus during cards." She nudged his shoulder in a playful push. "But that might have been when you were pouting about losing the hand."

"I wasn't pouting. Poppy can stay." He held up his hand, stalling her victory dance. "Queen Vee is still under consideration."

"I'll come up with more options." Or she'd wait him out and win him over. Queen Vee was the perfect name. He just refused to admit it. "Now, back to movie night in the park."

"That's going to be rained out." He relaxed into the chair again, setting his arms on the chair rests. "You really should have a contingency plan."

"I don't make those."

"Ever?" he pressed.

"I suppose you could say I wouldn't be here pregnant and fighting for this job if I had a backup plan." She tugged her dress over her knees and pressed her lips together. She had to stop blurring the lines. Stop confiding in him. Change her focus. "What about you? Do you have backup plans for your backup plans?"

"I make one plan and stick to it."

She believed that. Believed he finished whatever he started. Made goals and accomplished them. Abby stretched out on the chair and tilted her head toward the sky. "I have plans. It was the sticking to them that tripped me up. Not anymore, though. I vowed things would be different here."

"How's that working out?" he asked.

"Right in this moment, quite well." Abby crossed one foot over the other and gazed at the cloudless sky. "I can't remember the last time I sat and stared at the stars."

"Boone built this deck for his wife. He says it was his favorite place because it was her favorite place first."

"I can see why." Abby sank into the cushions, relaxing into the silence. "You could fall asleep up here, counting the stars."

"You never counted stars on the beach in Santa Cruz," he said.

"No." Not with Clint. Not even by herself. Abby traced the Big Dipper with her finger. "When I was a kid, my dad and I would make hammocks or bring our cots from our tents and watch the sky for shooting stars."

Sometimes it took only minutes, sometimes hours before they saw one. Sometimes she fell asleep before she'd even come up with her wish. But her father had always been beside her, encouraging her to never stop reaching for the stars. The memory warmed her. "What about you? How many nights do you spend up here, getting lost in the nighttime sky?"

"Most nights, actually." He shifted in his

chair. His voice deepened into mysterious and vague. "But tonight is somehow better."

"It was probably the good meal." She angled her head to look at him. "Never discount the power of good, homemade food."

"Maybe." He reached toward her, curved his fingers around hers. Gentle. Confident. Steady. Like his voice. Like his presence. "Still, I could look forward to more nights exactly like this."

Abby stared at their joined hands. Palm to palm. Fingers entwined. The perfect fit.

And suddenly, with her hand tucked securely inside Wes's, it became everything to the woman she was now.

CHAPTER FOURTEEN

WES PARKED THE UTV outside Boone's garage and tossed the keys to him. Water-pump repairs in the pasture troughs had taken longer to fix than Wes had anticipated. They'd had coffee and biscuits for breakfast on Boone's porch almost eight hours earlier. Hadn't stopped to consider lunch. Now, dinnertime was closing in quick. And Wes still had more work to finish.

"Are you joining us for poker tonight?" Boone climbed out of the ATV and stuffed a pair of leather work gloves in the back pockets of his faded jeans. "Carter is hosting."

Carter was Sam Sloan's oldest grandson and the master distiller of Misty Grove Whiskey. The former moonshine operation in his great-grandfather's basement on their working ranch had become a full-fledged, award-winning operation. Carter had also taken more money from Wes in their monthly poker games than Wes cared to admit. Wes had returned that favor by letting his friend buy more than one round at the bar whenever he came in.

"Gotta win big tonight." Boone took off his hat and knocked the dust off. His frown notched deep into his skin. "I got the appraisal on the property."

Wes leaned his arm against the UTV's steel frame and eyed the old cowboy. "And?"

"And I ain't got that kind of money lying around." Boone's hat settled against his thigh, his wisdom-aged gaze settled on Wes. An impatient defiance tightened into the wrinkles in his forehead. "And I'm too old for loans and banks and all that paperwork nonsense. So don't even be mentioning it."

"Poker is your plan, then?" Wes grabbed the toolbox from behind the passenger seat and dropped it into the bed of his truck.

"Until Abby finds that treasure map, poker is what I got." Boone dropped his hat back on his head, in a silent good-day-to-you gesture and headed toward the house. His cue to Wes that the discussion was finished.

Boone also had Wes. For now. Until Wes located his brother and his inheritance. Then, both men would have the homes they wanted.

Wes flexed his fingers around his truck keys, recalled Abby's hand inside his, and another sort of want resurfaced. But he belonged in Colorado, honoring his mother like he'd always intended. His mother had deserved to spend her final days in her family home. Not alone and scared in a hospital bed. He couldn't right that wrong. But he could turn their former ranch into something his mother would be proud of. Holding Abby's hand one night under the stars wouldn't alter his course.

Boone stopped on the porch steps, turned around and called out, "Don't forget about poker."

Wes opened his truck door. "I have to finalize a few last-minute orders for Saturday night's trivia league and check in with the staff, then I'll be out to Carter's place."

An hour later, his hair damp from the shower, Wes finished the last of the leftover meatballs and added the address of an upcoming motocross race into his phone. Looked like he had an errand to run in the morning. He'd gotten a message from the owner of a motocross repair shop just across the Oklahoma border about a customer fitting Dylan's description. The customer had paid in cash and mentioned entering the local race nearby.

Wes had been banking on his brother not being able to walk away from the one constant love in his life: motor cross racing. All Wes's research on successfully going off the grid had revealed one common requirement: a person had to walk away from everyone and everything they ever knew. No exceptions allowed. When exceptions were made, the person often tripped up. Wes was banking on his brother making an exception for motocross.

Wes washed the empty leftover container and glanced at the clock. He had time to check in on the staff, confirm the weekend schedule and get to Carter's before the first hand was dealt. Provided he didn't stop in at the general store and Abby didn't drop in at the bar for a refresher on her tea or decaf coffee. He seemed to lose track of time whenever Abby was around. Something he definitely couldn't let continue.

He grabbed a baseball cap from the rack in the entryway, slipped on his boots and walked to the bar. With Ilene's wish of good luck and the schedule fully staffed for Saturday's trivia night, one of their busiest evenings each month, Wes climbed into his truck and pulled out onto Fortune Street.

Less than a block later, he slowed outside Rivers Family Hardware and rolled down the passenger-side window. "Trouble, Gordon?"

"Engine won't turn over." Gordon tipped his gray fedora at Wes in greeting. "I suspect Trey is already at Carter's place. You wouldn't happen to be heading that way yourself, would you?"

Wes leaned across the truck and opened the

passenger door. "Hop in. I could use the company."

Gordon closed the hood on his blue truck that had seen the turn of its odometer years ago and still kept running. The gentleman climbed into the passenger seat and brushed his handkerchief across his forehead. "Air-conditioning sure feels nice. We need to pick up Keith and Martin. So we'll have even more company."

Wes made a quick U-turn and drove toward Keith and Corine Bauer's house. Keith was already on the sidewalk waiting. Wes barely had to slow down for the burly man to jump in.

Martin Hall came outside carrying a tin of homemade sweet-and-spicy candied nuts from his wife, Frieda, and a box of cigars taken from his personal collection.

"Thanks for the lift, Wes." Keith opened the container of mixed nuts and scooped out a handful. "Maybe you could give us a few hints for trivia night. I've got twins coming and could use a win Saturday."

"I'll raise my hand too." Gordon took Frieda's nut tin from Keith. "I've got my eye on a new truck. I could use a big win tonight or this weekend."

Everyone in town seemed to be in need of a big win and soon. Wes included. But his big win would come once he found his brother, not from cards or trivia night. "What about you, Martin?"

"I wouldn't turn down a list of the topics for trivia night." Martin met Wes's gaze in the rearview mirror and grinned. "Can't deny I have my eye on the jackpot for the trivia league."

Wes had started the trivia night soon after he'd started working at the bar. Within months, the night had become competitive as the town had divided into teams and created weekly prizes and finally a cash grand prize. The grand prize grew every month and would be awarded on Halloween night when the winner was finally drawn. Then the league would reset, and monthly trivia nights would start all over again. Wes glanced in the rearview. "Are you finally taking Frieda on that Caribbean cruise?"

Frieda had shown Wes the pamphlets for the cruise, declaring it was the perfect way to celebrate forty years of marriage to her one and only true love. There were so many things inside Frieda's claim that he wanted to sidestep. True love. Marriage. Things that hadn't ever been on his radar. Until one curly-haired blonde had crashed into his life. Wes concentrated on the road.

"I'm thinking about something more lasting. Frieda cooks for the kids, grandkids and neighbors and would even for strangers if she could." Martin chuckled and shook his head. "She never complains about the old oven or the tired stovetop or the cracked counters. She just keeps on singing and cooking."

He imagined Abby mostly likely hummed and danced in the kitchen while she cooked. She had a way of throwing herself into things that made her quite irresistible. And made him want to spend more time with her. He lowered the visor as if the setting sun, and not his own reckless thoughts, was blurring his view.

"Can't say I've ever heard a complaint about Frieda's cooking." Gordon shifted and took a handful of nuts from the container on the console. "This nut medley is one of her best."

Wes's only complaint about Abby's cooking was that he wanted more. He'd been inside Tess's apartment to fix her ceiling fans last month. If the moving boxes were still crowding the already-cramped space, Abby would've had her challenges cooking yesterday. Yet, she hadn't mentioned anything. And delivered one of the best meals Wes had ever eaten.

"Frieda wouldn't have to cook on a Caribbean cruise," Keith offered.

Wes wondered if Abby would want a fancy ten-day cruise. Or would she prefer something closer to home instead to celebrate an anniversary? He flexed his foot, wanting to slam on the breaks and slam some sense back into himself. Abby, anniversaries and long-term weren't part of his future. He focused on Martin in the rearview mirror—the man who had the future Wes had never wanted or even considered having. Until recently. "Are you remodeling your kitchen for Frieda?"

"She'll get her cruise and a kitchen." Martin nodded, his smile private and reserved as if he held back the best parts for Frieda. "I can't deny she deserves more than that after forty years of being married to me."

From all accounts, Frieda and Martin had a love story for the books. A love-at-first-sight encounter that had grown into four decades of marriage. And Martin was as much head over heels for Frieda as she was for him. Wes had heard on more than one occasion from his single staff and bar patrons that they aspired to be like the Halls when they finally settled down and wedded.

"What's your secret to a long marriage?" Keith asked.

Holding hands under the stars. Wes clamped his jaw.

"I'd like to say letting her win every argument. Letting her have her way," Martin said and chuckled. "But I think it really comes down to acceptance and friendship. We really like each other as we are."

Gordon nodded, slow and thoughtful. "And try to turn every moment with her into a date. Spending time together is so precious. Cherish it, even if it's just grocery shopping."

Or staring up at the stars. Or sharing a good meal. Wes parked behind Evan Bishop's dually silver truck in the Sloans' circular driveway, cut the engine and jumped out. As if he could outrun his connection to Abby. Or his wanting more time with her. Any time, really.

Keith shut the truck door and frowned. "With the babies coming, there doesn't seem to be time for more than house projects and bickering over the nursery decor."

Martin set his hand on Keith's shoulder. "You'll figure it out."

The men walked up the pathway to the two-story farmhouse and let themselves in. With five grandsons growing up in the house, Sam had declared the doorbell a nuisance and had removed it.

Carter Sloan and Evan Bishop intercepted Wes in the kitchen, blocking him from joining the others.

"You missed our last family poker night." Carter knocked his fist lightly against Wes's shoulder. "Then I hear you're rescuing women on horseback. Taking over chauffeur services. And polishing up your electrician skills."

"Wes has been too busy playing the knight in shining armor," Evan teased. "He's had no time for us."

Clearly Ilene had filled her oldest son in on Abby's arrival. The knight-in-shining-armor bit belonged to Evan. Wes could tell from his friend's self-satisfied grin. And Sam hadn't wasted any time giving full accounts to his grandson, Carter either. Wes determined his two friends knew more than enough.

"I'm here now." Wes patted his chest. "No armor tonight. Just money and luck. Unless you'd rather stand around and discuss my good deeds in more detail."

Carter rubbed his hands together then pointed to the massive outdoor patio on the other side of the open family room. "Grab a chair, boys. It's game on."

"If you start to miss Abby too much, let us know." Evan jabbed his elbow into Wes's side. "We're happy to let you talk about her while we take your money."

Wes returned Evan's jab with one of his own. "The only thing on my mind tonight is winning."

And not thinking about Abby. At least, not any more than he already had been.

CHAPTER FIFTEEN

"Is Mr. Wes your boyfriend?" Riley Bishop, Ilene's six-year-old granddaughter, bumped into Abby's side on the sidewalk. The little girl stuffed her Three Springs postcard, one of the scavenger-hunt items, into the cloth bag Abby had designed for the kids.

Abby had offered to escort Riley on the scavenger hunt while Ilene helped Trey's wife get set up at the hot-chocolate booth in the town square. Abby and Riley followed their scavenger-hunt team from the town hall toward the Rivers Family Hardware store.

Abby glanced at the sky and the clouds gathering over their heads. And hoped again that Wes's horses were wrong about the rain coming tonight.

She set her hand on Riley's thin shoulder, steadying her. The vibrant little red-haired girl was a bundle of energy, nonstop conversation and complete cuteness. Abby smiled. "Wes is just a friend."

"Harvey has just a friend too. Her name is

Misty." Riley bent down and tugged on the pink handle of her rainbow-colored polka-dot rain boots. "But Grandma Ilene says Misty and Harvey have to keep their distance."

"Why is that?" Abby had kept her distance from Wes the past two days. Determined to prove to herself she had no time for hand-holding, stargazing or romance. And what she shared with Wes was only friendship. That was all it could ever be. There was no room in her life for more.

"Harvey and Misty aren't married, so they can't be together." Riley switched her scavenger-hunt bag to her other shoulder and peered at Abby. "I haven't been to a wedding. Have you?"

"I have." Abby quickly adjusted to Riley's quick topic change. Abby and her ex had been invited to dozens of weddings. Clint had never wanted to attend, always citing a work conflict. Now Abby wondered if it had been more straightforward for her ex: Clint hadn't wanted to attend because he didn't believe in marriage. Something she should've recognized sooner. She had no idea where Wes stood on marriage, but as his friend, it certainly didn't matter. "I have to admit, eating the wedding cake is the best part."

"Maybe Harvey and Misty should have a wedding." Riley flipped one of her thick braids over her shoulder. "Then we can have cake too. My grandma's cakes are my favorite."

Could Wes be Abby's favorite? Abby picked up their pace as if she could outrun her thoughts. Keeping Wes out of sight had not kept him out of her mind. If anything, she'd thought about him even more.

She focused on Riley and the little girl's friends. "Do Harvey and Misty like each other? If they're going to get married, they should like each other."

"I think so." Riley slowed and lifted her round hazel eyes to Abby. "How did you know you *like* Mr. Wes?"

The little girl's stretching of the word *like* stretched the bonds of Abby's denial. Sure, she liked Wes. As a friend. But *like* Wes? No. Her denial snapped and deflated inside her like a popped balloon. She *liked* Wes. Really liked him. She accepted the truth. Resolved it changed nothing. Reminded herself that she was still in control.

Abby looked at Riley. Freckles sprinkled across her cheeks and nose. She was everything sweet and innocent, and she was waiting so patiently for an answer. Abby confessed the most simple reason. "Wes held my hand. That's how I knew I liked him."

Riley's nose wrinkled and her sunshine-filled

giggle spilled into the air. "Harvey and Misty can't hold hands. They're both Flemish giant rabbits."

Rabbits. Abby laughed. Now it all made sense. Even liking Wes made sense. He was a good friend, and she couldn't confuse her feelings of *like* with something more. Something stronger. "I can't say I've ever been to a wedding for rabbits before."

"But you think we should have one, right?" Riley skipped beside Abby. "Then, they won't be lonely in their own cages anymore. Same as Mr. Wes."

Abby stubbed her toe on a broken gap in the sidewalk. "What do you mean?"

"Grandma Ilene says Mr. Wes isn't lonely anymore 'cause he has you." Riley slipped her hand inside Abby's, swung their arms between them and continued to skip down the sidewalk. "You don't want him to be lonely, do you?"

Abby didn't want anyone to be lonely. That included Wes and herself. Riley's expectant gaze was nonnegotiable. Abby glanced at the clouds, then looked at Riley. "No, I don't want that. That's why it's good that Wes and I are friends."

Riley jumped over a crack in the sidewalk. "How come you keep watching the sky?"

"I'm worried there might be rain later."

And ruin the first family movie night in the town square. After the businesses had been so supportive and everyone so grateful Abby had agreed to put it on without Corine. To get washed out hardly seemed fair.

"It's gonna rain for sure. You know why?" Riley tugged on Abby's arm.

"The horses told you too?" Abby squeezed Riley's hand, finding the little girl irresistible.

"No." Riley's mouth thinned. Her voice hushed and pensive. "Macybelle laid down."

That hardly sounded good. Abby pulled up. Worry thickened her words. "Is Macybelle okay?"

"Macybelle is a cow." Riley tapped her neon-yellow fingernail against her chest and grinned. Pride lifted her voice. "She's my cow. Macybelle lays down in the same spot before the rain comes. You know why?"

Of course Macybelle was a cow. Abby shook her head.

"So her spot in the pasture is dry after the rain comes." Riley grinned. "She's really smart."

Abby couldn't argue. She wasn't familiar with cows or their rain-predicting behavior. One more quick peek at the clouds rolling in—the very dark-looking clouds. "That is quite smart."

"Macybelle is one of the smartest cows I know." Riley jumped over another crack in the sidewalk. "It's not the reason I got to keep her, though."

"Where was she supposed to go?" Abby asked.

"To the slaughter." Riley's voice was matter-of-fact and calm. "All Daddy's cows go there. He's got the best beef around. When he gets branding rights, everyone else will know it too."

Riley's father, Evan Bishop, ran a place called Crescent Canyon Ranch. Abby knew from Ilene that her son was dedicated to two things: his daughter and the ranch. Beyond that, Abby knew very little about what branding rights meant or even how cattle ranches worked. If she meant for Three Springs to be her home, she needed to change that. "Why did you keep Macybelle?"

"Because her momma rejected her." Riley rubbed her cheek. "We had to bottle-feed her and care for her all the time after that until she got strong and could eat on her own."

Abby's chest squeezed. She wasn't certain where Riley's mom was or what had happened. Ilene never mentioned Riley's mom, and Abby hadn't wanted to pry. But Riley's watery eyes and the sadness in their depths made Abby sense the little girl felt like her poor, abandoned cow. All Abby wanted to do was wrap the adorable child in her embrace and promise her the world. Promise no one would hurt her again. But Wes's caution about promises swirled through Abby. She tightened her hold on Riley's hand and vowed to look out for the little girl as much as she could.

"And I kept Annabelle too." Riley rubbed her cheek with her free hand, and that sadness drifted from her gaze. "Her momma did the same thing, and Daddy doesn't know why. Now Macybelle and Annabelle are friends and keep each other company in the pasture."

Having friends was extremely important to Riley. Abby liked having friends too. Now she just had to keep Wes as a friend only, and everything would be fine. "Was Annabelle lying down too when you left this evening?"

"Right next to Macybelle," Riley announced.

Abby frowned. That wasn't welcome news. She was starting to believe horse whisperers and cow rescuers were more accurate forecasters of the weather than the news. "Well, we should hurry and finish this scavenger hunt to get your prize. Hopefully, the clouds decide to keep their rain a little while longer."

With the scavenger hunt concluded and prizes given to every child, the first raindrop plopped on Abby's bare arm like a silent shout. The second raindrop landed on her shoulder like a soft reminder. And the third unplugged the clouds.

The downpour drenched Abby in seconds. Those folks who'd listened to their horses and cows fared better under their already-opened umbrellas, zipped-up raincoats and tall rain boots.

Abby wiggled her bare toes in the puddle building around her feet. She really had to invest in those cowboy boots. Or something other than summer sandals.

Ilene and Frieda, each bundled inside a long raincoat and huddled under their own wide, colorful umbrellas, made their way toward Abby.

Frieda pushed her dry bangs off her forehead and frowned. "It doesn't look like this is going to let up anytime soon."

Ilene shook her head and adjusted her grip on her umbrella handle. "We need the rain. Just not right now."

Riley jumped from one puddle to the next and pushed her rain hat lower on her head. "Does that mean it's over already? Before we even got to watch the movie?"

The disappointment on Riley's damp face made Abby's shoulders collapse. The same gloomy look tracked across the faces of the other kids. This was one of those moments like the stargazing nights Abby had shared with her dad. These were memory-building moments for these kids. And Abby wasn't going to see the first one on her watch washed out. Her gaze locked on the Feisty Owl's illuminated sign on the side of the bar down the street. "No, it's not over. We just need a venue change."

The kids cheered. The parents knocked rain from their umbrellas and grinned.

Abby curled her fingers into her palms, straightened her shoulders and marched toward the Feisty Owl. She had two blocks to figure out how to convince Wes to agree to her new idea. She had the town behind her, literally.

She wished on a star she couldn't see.

Prepared herself for a little fast talking.

And a whole lot of luck.

CHAPTER SIXTEEN

ABBY STEPPED INSIDE the Feisty Owl and shook the rainwater off her bare arms. Wes met her right away and blocked her entry into the bar. He looked dry, warm and unwelcoming. Well, she was soaking wet, slightly chilled and determined. He wanted a standoff? She stepped forward into his space to give him one. What he didn't know was she fully intended to win.

Wes reached out and wrapped one of her curls around his finger. One corner of his mouth tipped up. "The longer you stand here, the curlier your hair gets."

"It's raining outside. You can gloat later." Abby tugged her wet hair free from his grip and stomped on the delight firing across her nerves at seeing him again. Surely, she possessed more control. She reined in her reaction and refocused. "Right now, we need an immediate venue change."

Wes shook his head, crossed his arms over his chest and widened his stance. "This is a commercial enterprise, Abby."

"I know what it is." She knew what he was to her too: a friend only. Perhaps if she reminded herself of that fact enough, her heart would stand down. And she'd stop stumbling over her misplaced feelings. "What it is is perfect for a movie night."

"No." Wes's voice was flat and entirely too inflexible. "This place is perfect for adults who like to drink too much, sing too loud and test their skills too many times on the mechanical bull."

"I forgot about the bull." Abby rubbed her hands over her arms and rocked on her damp sandals. "The kids will love that."

"You're not listening, Abby." Wes tugged the dry towel he kept in his back pocket and ran it over her wet shoulders.

"Neither are you." Abby snatched the towel from Wes's grip. His gentle touch distracted her. She had to keep herself centered only on what mattered. If that meant she remained rain-soaked and chilled, so be it. "I can't disappoint these kids, Wes. The kids of the adults who like to come here and spend their hard-earned money to do all the things you just mentioned."

Wes crossed his arms over his chest again and settled into his closed-off stance.

Abby leaned toward him, rose up on the balls of her feet to peer into the dining room.

Then she leaned the other way to look into the bar. "Rain must have kept most of the out-of-towners away. You're not too busy."

Wes remained silent and still.

"Please." Abby set her hand on his arm, ignored the jolt of warmth against her palm and the heat that pulled her closer to him. "Please, Wes. I won't ask ever again."

"Is that a promise?" he asked.

His voice was rough, from unreleased laughter or something else Abby wasn't certain. She pulled back and set her hands on her hips. "I wouldn't dare promise you anything. You've made your feelings more than clear about them."

Wes opened and closed his mouth, rubbed his fingers across his jaw as if working the right words free.

Boone peered around Wes's shoulder to greet Abby. A mood for mischief brightened his gaze. "Is your movie night coming indoors, then?"

Abby frowned and hitched her thumb toward Wes. "If we can get past the big bad bouncer right here."

"We got a blank back wall in the dining room." Boone tipped his hat to her and then rubbed his palms together. "Seems like just the right size for a movie screen."

"This isn't a theater." Wes's voice deepened into a low rumble.

"When you buy me out and own the Owl, you can make it whatever you want." Boone slapped his hand on Wes's shoulder. His words stiffened into a challenge. "Until then, it's what I say it is. And tonight, it's Abby's call. If she wants the dining room to be a theater, then a theater it will become."

Abby spun around, hiding her victory smile, and waved everyone inside. "Movie will be showing in the dining room. The games will be to the right. Just give me a few minutes to get everything set up."

"Games." Wes's low voice was too close.

Spine-tingling, nerve-awakening close. Abby swayed. He settled one hand on her waist. She opted for bubbly and upbeat, trying to override her suddenly racing pulse. "Don't worry, everyone can play these games. I'm thinking horseshoes and pin the tail on the bull. Limbo, dance party chairs and dance hat on the dance floor."

Wes glanced at Boone. His steady grip on her waist never wavered. "I think she's serious. I'm not running a carnival. It's a bar."

"It's also one night." It was one night. Tomorrow she would remember her control. Tomorrow she would lock down her heart and rein in her feelings. Tonight, she gave in and faced him. Pressed a kiss on Wes's cheek, lingered longer than she should have and discovered it wasn't enough. She framed his face in her hands and kissed him. Quick and straight on. One press of her lips against his. The smallest of memory makers. More than she'd ever dared before. Or would dare again.

She retreated and pulled the breathless catch from her words. "Thank you. I owe you."

Boone took over the transformation of the dining room into a suitable theater space. He directed the staff to move tables and pointed to the wall where he wanted several white tablecloths hung to create a movie screen.

Abby greeted the incoming families and directed traffic. Wes returned to his position behind the bar as if he was completely content to stay there and observe for the rest of the evening. Abby preferred the distance. Needed it until she could completely collect herself.

She'd kissed her friend. Kissed Wes. Crossed boundaries that never should've been breached. Now all she could think about was kissing Wes again. Only the real kind this time. Not a surprise ambush. But an embrace pursued by both parties.

Abby shoved her damp hair over her shoulder and exhaled her frustration. She had games to organize and kids to entertain. Kissing Wes was not part of her job description. She stepped around a cornhole platform and grabbed one of the last tall round tables to be moved out of the way. The table didn't budge, much like her growing attraction to Wes.

Abby checked to make sure the table wasn't bolted to the ground. No bolts. Her heart needed to be bolted in place. Only a thick steel post and legs made up the rest of the table, contributing to its considerable weight. Perhaps she should invest in steel-toe boots instead. Then maybe her feet would remain grounded. One fleeting, barely there kiss and she was already feeling herself being swept away. She grabbed the table like her personal anchor and yanked. It wouldn't move.

Behind her, an overblown sigh reached her from the bar. Abby ignored the sound and faced off with the table. As if it was to blame for her reckless behavior.

Seconds later, Wes nudged her aside and clasped the table. "Where do you want this?"

"I can do it." She pushed at the table but couldn't take her eyes off him. She was in deep, *deep* trouble now. And that spark in his gaze hinted that he knew it too. She lashed out at him. "Go pour your customers a drink. Or better yet a double shot of something for yourself, because I'm going to be here all night."

He wrestled the table out of her grasp. "Just tell me where you want this."

Abby set her hands on her hips and frowned. "I didn't ask for your help, so don't get short with me."

He laughed.

Laughed! Galling man. She smiled, aware there was nothing sweet about her teeth-revealing grin. "Fine. I want it over there in the far corner. Thank you."

Even more infuriating, he carried the table to the exact spot she'd wanted without breaking a sweat or losing his breath. Entirely unfair. But now that she had him, she fully intended to make use of his strength. She held onto her grin and pointed at the second table. "This one needs to move too. It's blocking the cornhole game."

He picked up the table and eyed her. He wasn't breaking a sweat or gasping from the effort. But a fire burned in his gaze. Good. He frustrated her too. And they were far from even.

He placed the table in the corner beside the other and returned to her. "Anything else?"

Yes. One real kiss, if you please. She blinked and wanted to slap her hand over her mouth. Or kick herself. Anything to shake loose her fixation on Wes. Anything to save her from herself. "I need a long pole that can be used for limbo. And chairs lining the entire perimeter of the dance floor for dance party musical chairs."

"Is that all?" He tipped his head and considered her.

Not even close. But you're not ready, cowboy. And Abby had vowed not to let her heart play with fire again. After all, chemistry burned out, and it was what was left that mattered. That ensured a lifetime match. Sure, she wanted to experience a real kiss with Wes. But the risk wasn't worth the fallout that would certainly follow. It was only an illusion. Otherwise, hearts had to be bartered, and love had to be trusted. And she'd vowed she'd never make that mistake again. She had more than her own heart to protect now. "Got any extra cowboy hats?"

"Maybe." His gaze simply remained on hers.

"I'll need those too."

He leaned toward her and whispered, "I know what you're doing."

He couldn't possibly know. Because Abby wasn't certain herself. All she understood was that she couldn't retreat. Couldn't walk away. She closed the distance between them. As if the only direction was toward Wes. "What's that, exactly?"

"Distracting me." He reached up and drew a curl between his fingers. The quickest of smiles curved across his mouth. There and gone. "But it won't work."

"Are you sure?" Now she was entirely too

distracted again. Her heartbeat rushed through her ears. Her lungs failed to fill. All because of this one man.

He nodded. "I know everything that's going on inside this place. From the kettle corn being popped in the kitchen to the hot-chocolate station being set up in the dining room to the tails being made for the mechanical bull."

Well, he didn't know everything. He didn't know all that was going on inside Abby. She exhaled her relief. Glad her feelings weren't transparent. "It's not all bad."

"It's also not happening again." He released her hair and brushed his hands together as if satisfied with his statement. "Family night, hosted by the Feisty Owl, will not be a recurring town event, so you can forget the idea right now."

But could Wes and Abby be a recurring thing? She opened her mouth.

He cut her off. "One night. That's all, Abby. You better enjoy it."

"Oh, I plan to." And she planned to make sure he did too.

CHAPTER SEVENTEEN

WES BLENDED ORANGE juice and lemonade, poured it into a small glass, then anchored several fruit slices to the rim. He set the kid-friendly concoction on the serving tray with the other four child-appropriate drinks. Abby's laughter, a mix of lightness and joy, caught his attention. Again. Like it had been doing since she'd arrived earlier, completely drenched and completely compelling. Despite the crowd, searching for Abby wasn't difficult. His gaze tracked to her like a compass always tracked north.

She stood next to the mechanical bull and awarded prizes to the children gathered around her. He was fairly certain they hadn't followed any rules for pin the tail on the bull. Bright-colored ribbons covered every inch of the mechanical bull from front to back and top to bottom, making it look like it had been attacked by a rainbow. And every child seemed to be getting a stuffed-animal prize. Hugs for everyone concluded the fun, and the kids raced back into the dining room to watch the movie.

Abby drifted over to the dance floor where she'd set up a revised version of musical chairs for the teenagers and younger adults. Tess had taken over as the emcee. The enthusiastic and rowdy group had leveled up the childhood game into a good-natured competition. Abby blended right in, cheering for the chair-takers and consoling the ones who'd missed out each round.

Abby hadn't missed a beat since she'd charged into the Owl, demanding a venue change and Wes's cooperation. Wes had been a step behind since she'd kissed him. He could've overlooked the blink-or-you'll-miss-it kiss she'd placed on his cheek. That had been as light as a moth's wings and just as fleeting.

But then she'd pivoted. And that second kiss was impossible to ignore. All too brief like the first. But it had left an impression on him, like being branded. He was even more aware of Abby now. And he wasn't at all certain what to do with that.

Abby worked her way toward the bar, pausing to check on every guest. Her happiness more than infectious. Even Wes couldn't restrain his own smile.

Abby flattened her palms on the bar top

and grinned at him. "You're having fun. Don't deny it."

He was having fun because of her. "It's a busy, busy night, and these times are good for the bottom line. That makes me happy."

"You aren't fooling me." She accepted the ice water with extra lime and lemon he handed her, then shifted to survey the crowd. "I think the mechanical bull should stay just like that."

Wes wanted Abby to stay just as she was: glowing from a successful evening and radiating confidence. And he wanted to stay right where he was: beside her.

One brief kiss had him bypassing everything he thought he'd wanted. Now it was time with Abby that he really wanted. He turned on the bar sink and washed his hands. As if his interest in Abby could be rinsed away with hot water and soap.

Frieda and Gordon stepped up to the bar and greeted Abby. Gordon tipped his hat at Wes, then shifted to introduce Paul Molina, the mayor of Three Springs, to Abby. Both Frieda and Gordon slipped away to rejoin their grandkids and families.

Abby set down her ice-water glass, wiped her fingers on a napkin, then shook Paul's hand. "It's nice to meet the mayor. I hope you're enjoying the evening."

Paul ran his hand through his salt-and-pepper hair and studied the crowd. "It's quite full in here. That's a plus."

Abby's smile wavered. The slightest wobble before she pressed more wattage into it. "There are a lot of families in town. They all seem to be having a good time."

"But it's only one evening, isn't it?" Paul ran his hand through his hair again and kept his gaze trained on the guests. "And not quite what the town council or myself were expecting."

Wes grabbed a towel to wipe down the bar top and moved himself closer to the mayor. It still wasn't close enough to Abby.

Paul Molina was a good guy. He still worked on his farm, had raised four kids and always listened to the people in the town. The Molina family also owned the former Stagecoach Inn. There were rumors of family disagreements, very heated ones, about what to do with the vacant inn and property. And even more gossip that the Molina family had fractured after the most recent argument. But that hardly gave him the leeway to tear down Abby's accomplishment tonight.

Besides, it was Wes who'd declared family fun at the Owl as one night only. Abby could replicate this. He was certain of it. Inside the

Owl or out in the square like she'd originally intended.

Wes glanced at the end of the bar. Sam and Boone had taken to their usual stools earlier. Yet their smiles and good cheer had been replaced by frowns. Both men kept their focus on the mayor.

Paul glanced at Abby. The pensive edge to his words only sharpened his veiled criticism. "Family movie night really isn't a conversation starter, is it? I believe we were clear that we required a conversation-starter kind of event."

Abby deflated. Just like that. The sparkle in her gaze dimmed. Her shoulders drooped.

Wes clenched the towel. He had several conversation starters. Specifically, one about Abby and her spontaneous kiss. As for the mayor, he'd like to set Paul straight about a few things. That wouldn't require a lengthy conversation. Only the mayor's superb listening skills.

"What if I recover the missing Herring Gang treasure?" Abby blurted.

What if she created her own miracle? Proved the impossible? She was already enough. Just as she was. Surely the mayor could see that.

"Recovering a centuries-old treasure would certainly be worth talking about, wouldn't it?" The mayor rubbed his chin and nodded. "And those conversations just might be heard by more than the citizens of this fair town."

"It would certainly secure Three Springs's place in history," Abby added. "If there was a museum to showcase the treasure, tourists would come to see it…"

Wes watched Abby. She was talking about the missing treasure, but her voice was too flat. Too remote. As if she recognized what she told the mayor was impossible. Impractical. And unlikely. She sounded like Wes, the cynic. He hated that. What had happened to her? Where was the risk-taking, daring woman who'd taken charge of the evening? He wanted her back. Wanted the upbeat, optimistic Abby he knew.

"Do you believe in curses, Abby?" the mayor asked.

"Do you?" she countered.

The mayor stuck his hands in the back pockets of his jeans and rocked on his heels. "A lot of folks around here put stock in that missing treasure being cursed."

"Are you one of them?" Abby's eyebrows knitted.

Even Wes struggled to hide his confusion. Where was the mayor going now?

"Could be that the entire town is cursed, not just the missing loot." The mayor's grin was more vacant than genuine. "Either way, I wouldn't put all your chips on a curse or a missing treasure, Ms. James."

With that parting advice, Paul headed for the exit and disappeared into the rain-filled night. Abby escaped into the dining room before Wes could stop her. And he was left holding more drink orders from his wait staff and an insistent urge to make Abby feel better.

The drink orders were finally slowing and Ilene was back behind the bar after watching most of the animated movie with her granddaughter, Riley, so Wes went in search of Abby. He found her leaning against the far wall, arms crossed over her chest and her gaze fixed on the movie screen. The mayor had been gone for more than thirty minutes, and Abby still hadn't recovered her enthusiasm.

Wes bumped his shoulder against hers and leaned against the wall. "You aren't crying, are you?"

Abby brushed at the corner of her eye. "Nothing wrong if I was."

There was something wrong if the mayor had caused her tears. And there was everything wrong about Wes's reaction to her tears. He wanted to yell at whoever made her sad. He wanted to pull her into his arms and protect her. He wanted to make promises he had no right to give her.

"It's this movie." Abby sniffed. "It gets me. There's something about one sister sacrificing herself to save the other and getting turned into ice. It's all about magic and family and love. And who wouldn't want a talking snowman as their best friend?"

He sighed and handed her the tissues he'd swiped from the box Ilene kept behind the bar.

She flicked her wrist at him. "Go away, and let me enjoy the rest of the movie on my own terms."

"It's making you cry." Wes couldn't stand it. He wanted to rub the tears from her cheeks. Kiss her until she forgot the mayor's criticism. Until she laughed again. Kiss her until he forgot all the reasons he shouldn't. "I'd hardly call that enjoyable."

"It's touching." She waved the tissue in her hand and sniffed again. "And heartfelt and re-affirming and uplifting. Magical."

There would be magic in their kiss. He knew it deep inside him. It wasn't the place or the time to test that theory. He grabbed her hand and tugged her along with him. "Come on."

"Where are we going?" She stumbled after him.

"To win this dance hat thing you organized." He swung her onto the middle of the dance floor and twirled her into his arms. Right where he'd wanted her the entire night. Since the moment she'd walked inside the bar, soaking wet, shivering and fearless.

"Wait." Her palms flattened against his chest. "You dance?"

"Can you keep up?" He grinned and finally relaxed. Everything suddenly seemed right in the world. "Or do I need to find another partner that won't step on my toes?"

Her arms curved up and linked around his neck. "Lead on."

He spun them around. She never faltered. The song changed, and the dance shifted into a Texas two-step. They danced as if they were one. As if they'd been dancing together for years, not minutes. In tune and in step. Their gazes remained locked on each other.

Her smile returned, growing wider and more brilliant with every turn. Every shuffle. No one else but Abby mattered. And Wes could've danced the rest of the evening with Abby. The song ended. Wes caught his breath and pulled Abby closer.

Just then—in the seconds before his lips captured hers—a cowboy hat landed on his head. Another dropped onto Abby's. She threw her head back and laughed. Tess declared Abby and Wes the King and Queen of the Dance Floor to the crowd's delight.

Wes took Abby's hand and led her to the bar. Ilene set a full water glass in front of each of them. Wes returned to his bartending duties. Once again safely distanced from Abby.

Abby dropped onto the bar stool beside Boone and patted her forehead. "I forgot what a workout dancing is."

"It's only good with the right partner." Boone tipped his soda glass toward Wes. "The right partner makes all the difference in life."

It was one dance. Not the start of a lifetime. Fortunately, those cowboy hats had arrived at the perfect time. Wes had almost kissed Abby. On the dance floor. In front of pretty much the entire town. She tempted him. Tempted him to reconsider everything he wanted. Tempted him to believe that she could be his. That he could be right for her. But he wasn't made for falling for someone. And one dance wouldn't fix that.

The movie ended, and the families headed home, carrying sleeping kids and encouraging tired teenagers. The dining room was set to rights and the screen dismantled. The bar crowd shifted to its twenty-one-and-older clientele. Wes kept to his duties and his promise to himself to keep his distance from Abby. Abby walked her cousin home only to return and insist she intended to stay until closing and help

Wes clean up. No amount of arguing changed her mind.

Well after midnight, Ilene finished the final tidying of the bar, and Nolan completed his check on the kitchen and the pair departed. Boone accepted Nolan's offer of a ride home, leaving Wes alone with Abby and one rainbow-ribbon-bedecked mechanical bull.

"I've never been inside a bar after it closes." Abby picked up several horseshoes, walked to the line and tossed one at the pole. "It's sort of nice."

"I don't mind it." He took a horseshoe from her and threw it underhand. And he really didn't mind finally having Abby all to himself. He should tell her to go home and get some sleep. He should do the same. He tossed another horseshoe instead.

"What did Boone mean when he told you that when you buy him out, you can make the decisions on what this place is?" Abby picked up the horseshoes and waited for him to join her.

"Exactly that." Wes took a horseshoe and tossed it. The horseshoe hit the metal stake in a perfect ringer. If only sticking to his plan to build his future and legacy in Colorado was as easy as a horseshoe throw. He knew what he wanted. Yet every time he looked at Abby, he lost his focus. "Boone wants me to buy him out of the Owl."

"You don't want it?" Abby held onto her horseshoes and studied him.

"It's not that." Wes's hands fumbled at his sides as he fumbled for an explanation. It had all been so simple before he met Abby. So straightforward. Now everything was complicated. "This bar was supposed to be his grandson's legacy, not mine."

"But Boone lost his grandson. And you're here now." Understanding and sympathy underlay Abby's words. "Boone is so proud of you. He loves you like his own. You see that, don't you?"

Wes was proud of what he'd done to build the bar and ensure its longevity. He'd done all that for Boone. He owed Boone for giving him a place to stay and a job. He cared about the man too. How could he not? But he had a duty to his family, to honor his mother.

Wes walked toward the opposite horseshoe stake. "There's more to it. I told you I want to find my brother, but not the why."

"He's your family." She joined him and stopped near the metal stake. "That seems reason enough to want to find him."

"He *was* family." Wes picked up the horseshoes and returned them to the storage bin. "Until Dylan sold the family ranch and the land it's on when he learned my mom's cancer was terminal."

"Did he need to pay your mother's medical bills?" Abby asked.

Always looking for the positive side. That was his Abby. Wes closed the lid on the bin and tried to close his jumbled emotions inside too. "No. Dylan disappeared with all the profits from the sale. Left my mother in an inpatient facility and me with the medical bills."

He glanced at Abby. Saw her searching for the good in the heavy silence. "There's no upside, Abby. Dylan stole my part of our inheritance and left our mother to suffer alone."

"There has to be a reason," Abby argued.

"Not one that I can find." Wes headed toward the dining room and cut the lights. "And believe me, I've been looking."

"What happens when you find him?" she asked.

"I get my inheritance back."

"But not your brother." Her tone was all the more sharp in the dim room.

"I'm not built like you, Abby." It was a reminder he needed. One he should heed. Abby deserved better than him. "I'm not made for forgiveness and happily-ever-afters."

"You can deal with all that once you find your brother." She grabbed his hand and linked her fingers with his. Natural and easy as if in that one simple connection she'd filled all the empty spaces inside him. She continued. "When the time is right, you'll know what to do."

It was time to tell Abby good-night. Time to go their separate ways. End the evening as friends. But he was selfish. He should've warned her. "Come on. I'll show you where I like to be on a rainy night after the bar closes."

He took her out onto the patio, turned on the gas fireplace and grabbed several blankets from the cabinet on the wall. He dropped the blankets on the nearest couch and motioned for her to sit. He joined her and stretched out his legs, setting his boots on the stone fireplace frame. Rain fell in a steady rhythm around them. The fire cast the softest glow.

Abby unbuckled her sandals and eased her bare feet under the blanket. "This is peaceful."

"I like the silence after a busy night." And he liked sharing it with Abby. Liked that with her, he felt less alone. "The quiet gives me a chance to collect my thoughts."

"I could fall asleep out here," Abby admitted. "Except my thoughts are going to keep me awake all night, I fear."

Wes dropped his arm across the back of the couch and shifted to face her. "The evening couldn't have been a bigger success. And you were responsible for it all."

"I'm also responsible for telling the mayor that I'd find the missing Herring Gang treasure." Abby pressed her face into the blanket and groaned. "It was the mayor, of all people."

"But you believe in the treasure." He liked that too. That she believed in the improbable. Made him want to believe too.

"Of course." Abby lifted her head. "It's real. I know that. And I also know it won't be found for Labor Day weekend. And the mayor knows that."

"And he made clear that another family movie night won't cut it." Wes scratched his cheek.

"Exactly." Abby smoothed her hand over the blanket and rested it on top of her stomach. "Wes, what if I can't come up with something? What if I fail at this job like all the others? Am I going to fail at being a mother too?"

The fear in her whispered words pierced Wes. The tears gathering in her eyes gutted him. He took her hand, half tugged her and half scooted himself until she was curled into his side. He wrapped his arm around her. "Abby, you should've seen yourself with those kids tonight. There wasn't a kid in the entire place who didn't want to be near you. You lit up the room, and they responded. Don't ever doubt what kind of mom you're going to be. You're going to be the kind every kid wants. The mom every kid wishes he had."

"How can you be so certain?" she asked. Her fingers tightened around his.

Because he'd seen her heart. Because she was the mom he'd want for his own children. He tucked those truths away and concentrated on her. "You just have to believe me."

She lifted her gaze to his. Tears trailed down her cheeks. "I just wanted to do something special. Something worth remembering."

The kids wouldn't soon forget the night. As for Wes, Abby was too special to ever forget. And that he'd have to deal with. But right now, he had her in his arms, and he had this one moment. "You did exactly that tonight. And you'll do it again for Labor Day weekend."

"You're not going to let me wallow in my fear, are you?" She sniffed.

"No." He reached up and brushed the tears from her cheek. He wasn't going to give in to his own fears either. "It's not the way to end a practically perfect night."

A sliver of a smile worked across her mouth. "Is there a right way to end this practically perfect night?"

"I can think of only one." He curved his hand

around to the back of her neck and leaned in. She met him halfway. He captured her lips beneath his own for one practically perfect kiss.

CHAPTER EIGHTEEN

WES TURNED ONTO the long dirt road leading to Boone's property. He'd intended a quick trip to Country Time Farm & Ranch Supply, but it had turned into something more leisurely. Wes had been stopped in each aisle of the supply store to chat about everything from last night's dance-off to the Owl's specials to newly learned watering techniques for pastures and farmland.

Mostly everyone, including the cashiers, had wanted to discuss possible topics for the evening's trivia night. The competition, it seemed, was on, and teams were deep into strategizing mode.

Wes checked the sun in the sky. Not a single cloud lingered from last night's storms. Not that he had any complaints. He'd spent most of the rainy night on the couch next to Abby. When the rain had finally slowed, he'd walked her back to her apartment, lingered over another good-night kiss and returned to his own bed alone. For the first time in years, he'd slept peacefully until sunrise.

Now, the Saturday lunch hour had passed, and Wes couldn't find his irritation at being behind schedule. He also couldn't remove his smile. That he blamed on Abby, and he grinned even more. She'd promised to come help host trivia night with him. He'd have to be quick repairing the broken gutters on the barn and repairing two pasture gates. Then Boone and he would be back on track and make it to the bar on time. Wes hummed in tune with the song on the radio.

His truck hit a rut in the road and disrupted his sing-along. The ruts were an aftereffect from last night's storms and one more thing to add to his to-do list. He rounded the corner, lost his smile and stepped on the gas. Dan stood outside the pasture gate. In the driveway. His large ears back. His head tossing from side to side. Boone's UTV was inside the pasture.

Wes slammed the truck into Park, cut the engine and jumped out. He checked Dan and sprinted toward the UTV. Boone was in the driver's seat, slumped over the steering wheel. Wes curbed his panicked shout and reined in his alarm. Allowed himself one touch to Boone's shoulder. "Boone. You okay?"

Boone clutched the steering wheel. Sweat beaded across his forehead. "Got some pain in my chest."

He had more than some pain. His skin was pale and damp. His words barely reached the level of a breathless pant. Wes pulled out his cell phone and dialed 9-1-1.

Boone shook his head and sagged backward in the seat. "Nothing to fuss over."

It was everything to fuss over. Wes greeted Margot McKee, the town's resident EMT, and requested an ambulance. Margot relayed instructions and told Wes to remain calm: help was on its way.

"Take me into the house," Boone whispered. "It'll pass."

The hospital was Boone's destination. Wes kept his hand on Boone's shoulder to reassure himself or the old cowboy, he wasn't sure. "Rest, Boone. Help is coming."

"I got you," Boone wheezed. "Don't need no one else."

And Wes needed Boone. More panic and fear rolled through Wes. He glanced at his watch. Time seemed to have stood still. It felt like hours since he'd talked to Margot, like days before he heard the siren racing up the dirt road to Boone's place.

Margot leaped from the passenger seat of the old-model ambulance and raced to Boone's side. "Kellie Pratt is driving us, Boone. She's the best there is."

That was the end of any conversation. The two women worked in tandem: kits were opened, vitals registered, medical jargon tossed out. Margot never glanced at Wes. And Wes knew, deep inside him, it was serious. It wasn't passing. And every minute mattered.

With the IV started and Boone secured on the gurney, the women loaded him into the ambulance. Margot climbed into the back with Boone. Kellie shut the door and rushed to the driver's seat, then hollered, "Follow us, Wes. Belleridge Regional Hospital."

The lights began flashing, and the ambulance headed out to the main road. Dan nickered in the quiet of the fading noise and snapped Wes into action. He pulled the UTV from the pasture, then guided Dan inside and offered the horse a few calming words. The pasture gate would need to be repaired, but he rigged a temporary lock and climbed back into his truck.

Phone in hand, he pressed Abby's name on his contact list. He didn't have time for a greeting and hurdled into his world-tilting news. "I'm headed to the hospital in Belleridge."

"The hospital." Abby's worry scratched across the speaker. "What happened?"

"It's Boone." Wes cleared his throat. He stepped on the gas as if it was the speed limit disturbing his equilibrium, not the worry spearing through him. "He's in the ambulance. I'm pretty sure it's his heart."

"What can I do?" Abby's voice was clear. Calm. Composed.

Everything he wanted to be. Everything he needed to be for Boone. Wes flexed his fingers around the steering wheel.

Abby, promise me Boone is going to be fine. Tell me I'll be fine. Wes couldn't lose Boone. Not like this. First Jake. Then his mom. Not Boone too.

"Wes." Abby's steady voice steadied him. "I'm here. I can meet you at the hospital. Whatever you need."

Yes. Can I lean on you? Just until I get my legs back under me. It won't be long. Maybe a moment. Maybe a lifetime. Wes worked his clenched jaw loose. "It's trivia night. We can't cancel."

Especially now. There would be medical bills to pay. Expenses they hadn't budgeted for. None of it mattered. Boone making it through mattered.

"I can run things for you." Abby never hesitated.

I can't ask you to. I shouldn't be relying on you. But I'm lonely. Lost. "Are you sure?" His words sounded as if they'd been scraped over rough rocks.

"Yes. I've got this." Again, no hesitation. And perhaps a hint of irritation at his needing her to repeat her answer. She added, "Concentrate on Boone."

Abby, I'm scared. "I owe you."

"No." Her resolve sounded so clear. "This is what friends do for each other."

And if we're more than friends, what happens then? "I'll call you when I know something."

"Wes," Abby said, "Boone is going to be okay."

No promise. No vow. Simple straightforward confidence as if there was no other option. But was Wes going to be okay? One last throat-clearing, and he pushed out a weak "Thanks."

Wes pressed the End Call button and white-knuckled the rest of the drive to Belleridge Regional Hospital. The emergency room was a series of blood draws, EKGs and IVs. Monitors beeped. Codes were announced over the PA system. And Wes paced. He paced every single inch of the waiting room.

Then Boone was loaded into a different, more robust ambulance for immediate transfer to the cardiac unit in the city hospital. Wes caught the words: *Major. Heart attack. Blockage. Arrhythmias. Surgery.*

He managed to shake the ER doctor's hand. Felt the physician's encouraging squeeze on his shoulder. Heard his assurance that the doctors at Northwest Plains Medical Center were some of the best in the state.

Numb, Wes drove to the next hospital. Found himself in another sterile waiting room. But his continuous pacing failed to burn the chill away. He was cold all the way to his core. Had he ever been this cold?

Boone wasn't supposed to leave Wes. Wes had been the one meant to leave. But the idea was that it would be fine. Boone living out his days on his ranch. Wes returning to Colorado to build his own legacy.

It was not supposed to be like this. Wes alone in a hospital. Hurting and helpless. He hadn't been able to give his mother her last wish: to spend her final days at her own home on their family ranch. But he could do right by Boone. Ensure Boone was cared for properly in his own home like he wanted. Like he deserved.

That meant asking for help. Revealing his private family affairs. Admitting he'd failed his mom and his brother. He should've been able to locate his brother—his blood relative. Their roots were supposed to have been deep and permanent, not shallow and fragile. Not so easily severed and spurned.

Boone needed Wes. Boone had taken him in when Wes had been at his lowest point. He couldn't fail the old cowboy now. Wes dropped into a chair and pulled out his cell phone. He scrolled through his contact list, hit the Call button for his former commander and pushed his pride aside.

Wes, after twenty minutes and having given his word to check in more often with his former commander, had a reliable reference: J&H Associates, based in San Francisco. He had even more than that: the name of the owner of the company, Brad Harrington, and his personal cell number. Brad was former FBI and now ran a private-investigation firm that operated worldwide. Wes's commander had worked with Brad on several undisclosed cases. His commanding officer trusted and believed in Brad Harrington's skills. He'd also dubbed Brad one of the good ones. That was enough for Wes.

Wes checked his watch, calculated the time on the West Coast and dialed Brad's number. Within the hour, Brad had returned his phone call. Wes had forwarded the information he had on his brother to Brad. And then there was nothing left to do but wait. Wait for Brad to locate Dylan. Wait for the surgeon to finish operating on Boone's heart.

Wes returned to his pacing. The only difference was that chill had finally receded to being almost bearable.

CHAPTER NINETEEN

ABBY CHECKED HER PHONE—for the hundredth time in the last hour—and tossed it on her bed. No texts from Wes. No missed calls. No update on Boone. The last text she'd received, several hours ago, had been brief and to the point, informing her Boone was headed into immediate surgery. Abby slipped on a pale yellow jumper, adjusted the straps on her bare shoulders and added her tigereye necklace for luck.

She walked into the kitchen, grinned at Riley and Tess. The pair was playing cards at the small island. Abby twirled around. "Well, do I look like a bartender?"

Riley giggled, revealing her adorable dimples. "You look too pretty."

"Thank you for the compliment." Abby touched her necklace. "What's wrong with looking pretty?"

"You might spill something on your nice clothes. That's what Dad always tells me." Riley picked up her cards and studied her hand like a seasoned card player. "But Grandma Ilene can wash your stuff like she does mine if you spill. I always do."

"Riley makes a good point about spills. Maybe jeans would be better." Tess glanced up from her cards, lifted her eyebrows at Riley and added, "Go fish."

Abby left the duo to their card game and headed to her room to change. Ilene had driven Sam to the hospital, and Tess had agreed to babysit Riley. And Abby had agreed to bartend. A job she knew nothing about. She was going to have to fake it and run the trivia competition. Abby tugged her jumper off and pulled her jeans from her suitcase. She could do this. For Boone and for Wes.

Besides, it was nothing compared to what Boone and Wes were going through. Abby buttoned her jeans and added an off-the-shoulder flowy chiffon top with billowy three-quarter sleeves and a swirl of colors. She twisted her braids around her head, secured them with shiny clips and tucked her phone in her pocket. Her outfit approved, she hugged Riley and Tess, then walked to the Owl.

Abby stepped inside, waved to one of the waitresses and rounded the corner. Only to stop. A tall dark-haired cowboy with electric-blue eyes that matched his vibrant-blue-plaid shirt stood behind the bar as if he had every right to be there.

"Who are you?" Abby blurted, then pressed her hands against her cheeks. "Sorry. That was quite rude."

"No offense taken. I'm Evan Bishop, Riley's dad." Evan grinned, revealing a twin set of dimples that matched his daughter's. "I'm also Ilene's only son and your assistant bartender tonight."

Relief skimmed over Abby, dulling one of her worries. She'd been concerned about how she was going to manage the bar alone. "Well, you're a welcome addition. Thanks for coming this evening."

"You say that now, but I should warn you. I'm not my mom. I know absolutely nothing about how to make the drinks I usually am drinking." Evan grabbed his mother's apron from the hook and slipped the strap over his head. He tugged the apron into place and flashed his dimples again. "And I spill things. A lot."

"Sounds like we're going to get along great." Abby laughed and stared at the stocked bar from the opposite side. There were multiple draft-beer handles and a soda sprayer with more buttons than a receptionist's phone console. A variety of stainless-steel bar tools, including long spoons, shakers and strainers in every shape and size.

All waited within easy reach. The bar mats were clean, and the rubber floor mats dry. Everything was ready, except Abby. Like Evan, she preferred to slide onto a stool, place her order and enjoy herself. "I think I might need a stool to reach most of these bottles."

Evan opened the swinging door, stuck his head into the kitchen and greeted Nolan.

Several minutes later, Nolan appeared holding a step stool and a wide grin. "Will this work?"

"It's perfect." Abby took the stool and set it near the shelves on the back wall. "Now I can reach the bottles on the top." There were a lot. She hadn't known tequila came in so many types and flavors. As well as rum, vodka and gin. She studied the labels, the brands and a worn recipe book she found buried in a bottom drawer of odds and ends.

A commotion in the entryway startled her out of her crash course on alcohol offerings. Abby spun around and gaped at the men filing into the bar. The five cowboys looked like ladders—each one taller and broader than the next. Her stool height hardly brought her to their eye level. "Evan, who are they?"

"Sam Sloan's grandsons." Evan reached over the bar top and shook hands with the tallest of the men. "Abby, meet Carter Sloan and his brothers, Ryan, Grant, and the identical twins are Josh and Caleb."

Each of the Sloan brothers stepped forward to shake Abby's hand and introduce himself with equal parts wit and graciousness. Josh was the eldest of the twins. Caleb was the youngest of all of them and motioned to his brothers to explain they were all test runs on the way to Sloan perfection. Abby connected to the Sloan men immediately, much like she had to their grandfather, Sam.

"Abby, we're yours for the night." Carter wore a half grin and spread his arms wide. "Tell us where you want us."

"Did your grandfather send you here because he didn't think I could handle things?" Abby set her hands on her hips. Her tone was playful but skirted around serious. "Wait. It was Wes, wasn't it?"

She'd assumed Wes's hesitation on the phone earlier had been from his concern for Boone. Not his concern that Abby couldn't manage the bar one night without him.

Carter laughed, a deep booming sound like his grandfather. And Abby liked him even more. "No one sent us down here, Abby. They didn't have to. It's just how things work in Three Springs."

"Neighbors look out for neighbors." Abby repeated Wes's reason for offering to replace the electrical wiring at the general store for free. The town was built on people helping each other.

"And family looks out for family," Carter explained. "And that's what Boone and Wes are. They're family."

So straightforward. And honest. Was it that simple? Claiming someone as family made it so. She had Tess, but she'd never considered she could have more in Three Springs. Until now.

"What's the plan?" Carter smacked his palms together. "Evan's already got the apron on. Nice look by the way."

"I need an emcee." Abby pointed to the stage where the wireless microphone and trivia-night box waited. "For the trivia session."

"Caleb and Josh, you guys are up." Carter pointed at his twin brothers. "Try to keep it clean up there. This is a family establishment."

The twins high-fived and headed toward the stage to test the wireless mic. Carter looked at his other brothers. "You guys get the mechanical bull. Stay off it until the customers have had a turn."

One brother shoved the other and claimed the first test ride, then twisted to smile at Abby. She remembered he'd introduced himself as Ryan, the best-looking of the Sloan brothers. His grin was mischievous, and laughter brightened his gaze. The brother Ryan pushed was Grant. He'd claimed to be the smartest of the Sloan men. And as a soon-to-be-graduate from medical school, Abby gave it to him.

Ryan tugged on his ear. "That's okay, isn't it, Abby? If we take a test ride."

"Sure." Abby eyed the two brothers. "Whoever stays on the longest gets a free order of chicken supreme nachos. But you only get one ride before the customers arrive. Better make it a good one."

Grant and Ryan walked to the mechanical bull ring. Carter considered Abby, then glanced at Evan. "I get it now."

Evan laughed. "Yeah, I've been here five minutes, and I get it too."

Abby stationed herself behind the bar. "Get what?"

"We get now why Wes has been avoiding our calls and declining our invites to fish, play poker and generally hang with the guys." Evan stuffed a towel in his back pocket and shrugged at Abby's arched brow. "It's what Wes does. I should at least try to look like him behind the bar."

Abby chuckled. "Why has Wes been avoiding you guys?"

"You." Carter drummed his fingers on the bar top. "You're the reason."

Abby stared at Wes's friend. Felt the heat splay from her neck to her cheeks. "I'm sure Wes has been busy with work and helping Boone at the ranch."

Carter made a noncommittal noise. His one-sided grin tipped up into his perceptive gaze. "Sure, we'll go with that."

The twins called Carter's name. He ambled off to check on his brothers.

Abby spun around, grabbed a cloth and scrubbed at the decades-old scratches and nicks no amount of polishing would ever remove. Carter was wrong. Wes hadn't chosen to spend time with Abby over his friends. That would imply Abby and Wes were something more than friends. She refused to jump ahead. To read into what they were. Sure, they'd shared more than one time-stopping, heart-turning kiss. But that wasn't enough to assume they were in a relationship.

Besides, this time she was focused. This time she wasn't falling for the idea of what a relationship could be. Not to mention, she had a baby on board. She was part of a package deal now, and she couldn't risk her baby getting hurt. If she fell in love and it wasn't real, hers wouldn't be the only heart broken.

Those kisses she'd shared with Wes were memories now. Moments stolen during a rain-soaked night. Nothing that would be repeated. Her heart put on notice, Abby wiped down the bar top and pulled out her cell phone. Wes hadn't sent an update. That persistent worry churned through her, pushing its way to the front.

Carter joined her and lifted his eyebrows up and down. "I guess I'll slip into Grandpa Sam's stool and enjoy the evening from the sidelines."

"I'm down a waitress tonight." Nolan propped open the swinging door to the kitchen with his boot. "Carter, I need you to cover the patio."

Carter ran his hand through his wavy dark brown hair that skimmed his collar. "I'm a master distiller now, Nolan. I've graduated."

"I can cover the patio," Abby offered. "Let Carter work behind the bar."

"No way." Nolan chuckled. "Carter and I bused these tables too many nights together in high school. Let him do the heavy lifting."

"Want to bet I'm still the fastest server in here?" Carter leaned forward on the bar.

"Carter Sloan, it's on tonight." Violet Myers, one of the Owl's most experienced waitresses stood at the end of the bar. She wore chunky platform boots and black-cat-frame eyeglasses and looked more than ready to take on anyone, including Carter, who towered over her by more than a foot.

"Violet, you still haven't paid me from losing our bet over that dart game from last month." Carter's grin ruined his hard-nosed tone.

"Well, it's double or nothing tonight." Violet tossed her blond hair over her shoulder. "Unless you're scared."

"Game on," Carter announced. "Nolan, I think we should sample the specials, since Wes and Boone aren't here to give their final approval."

"Wes already approved the menu." Nolan retreated to the kitchen.

"Then, think about the customers," Carter called to him. "When they ask about the food, I need to give them my honest opinion."

"Carter Sloan, you're relentless." Violet shoved him through the doorway.

"I believe in doing a job to the best of my ability." Carter tugged on Violet's hair. "I know not everyone has the same high standards as me."

"Do you hear yourself?" The door swung shut on their laughter.

The banter had distracted Abby. Muted her distress. She clasped her hands together and searched for a smile. Anything to prove she was confident and calm, not upset and nervous.

She wanted to know Boone was fine. Wanted to see Wes and know for herself he was fine. She wanted Wes there. Beside her. Where she could take his hand, offer him comfort or whatever he needed.

Sam and Ilene were with Wes. He wasn't alone. That should give her solace, not more anguish. She was where she was supposed to be. At the Owl. Helping Wes like a friend would. The same as any of his other friends.

She had to focus on the Owl. Not on soothing Wes or being his person—the one he turned to first no matter what. Because that implied stronger feelings. Like ones from the heart. Those involved trust and love and…

Abby cut herself off and tethered her unwise thoughts. Something in her chest clenched.

She ignored it and glanced at Evan. Her words tumbled out. "What should we be doing? I can cut up more fruit. Wes always seems to be doing that. Check the amount of ice. Polish bottles. Wash glasses." *I can be more than Wes's friend if he'll let me.* Abby clamped her teeth together.

Evan set his hand on her shoulder. His touch was gentle, his voice kind. "Boone's going to be okay. You know that?"

Abby's shoulders collapsed. She should be thinking about Boone. Not herself. Or her feelings for Wes. She could untangle those later. Or never. "Nothing stops the worry."

Evan pulled his phone from his back pocket. "Let's check. See if anyone texted an update yet."

Abby slipped her phone out and stared at the blank screen. "Nothing. You?"

"Nothing." Evan tapped her phone screen. "Text Wes."

"I don't want to bother him." Abby squeezed her phone. Wes had more to think about than her.

"Tell Wes the power is out here," Evan suggested. "He'll call you right back."

"That's just wrong." Abby frowned.

"But you want to hear his voice," Evan pressed.

Maybe she wasn't going to like having Evan behind the bar after all. She peered at Wes's friend. "Is it that obvious?"

"It's sweet." Evan squeezed her shoulder and held her gaze. "It's about time Wes had someone who cared about him."

She did care about Wes. Nothing wrong with that. "Thanks."

"You gonna text him or not?" Evan waved his phone in front of her. "Or I will."

"Fine." Except it wasn't fine. She wasn't certain what to say. What would be too much? Too revealing? Too heartfelt? She typed out a message and hit Send before she could rethink it.

"What'd you say?" Evan tried to grab her phone.

Abby jumped away and tucked her phone in her pocket. "That Evan is worried about you and Boone. And that he's harassing me for an update every minute to see if I've heard anything. So could he please text back to save me from his hovering, bag-of-nerves friend."

"Works for me." Evan grinned, then sobered. "You'll tell me when he texts back."

"Absolutely." The doors swung open, and Abby watched an excited crowd spill into the bar.

"Looks like the fun is about to begin." Evan rubbed his hands together.

Abby welcomed the distraction and hoped she'd work herself into exhaustion. Then she'd collapse in her bed and be able to fall fast asleep. Before the worry and second-guessing could overtake her. Before sleep became a wish and the hours slowly ticked by. And her heart rediscovered its voice.

Twenty minutes into the evening, Abby decided nothing about her current situation was fun. It was nerve-racking and stressful. Evan filled multiple drink orders from Carter and the other servers. A horde hovered on the other side of the bar, elbowing each other to get to the front and snag her attention. One overly eager and burly but jovial gentleman picked up his petite cousin as if she weighed no more than a dollar and set her out of his way. Anger rushed through Abby.

"This isn't working, Evan." Abby set her hands on her hips and raised her voice. "Not at all."

"What are you thinking?" Evan arranged three highball glasses on Violet's serving tray.

Abby grabbed the stool and set it next to the bar. Then held her hand out to Evan. "Give me a hand up, will you?"

Abby climbed onto the bar top and released a shrill whistle. The kind her father had taught her when she'd been a little kid. The kind that would startle whatever roamed the forest and alert her father to come get her.

The crowd quieted. Carter appeared in the patio doorways, a proud smile on his face. The other Sloan brothers grinned from ear to ear.

"Okay, listen up, everyone. We've got a few rules for the evening." Abby tugged on her puffy chiffon sleeves and secured her stance. "I'm not Ilene and definitely not Wes, but I'm who you have tonight. I can pour draft beers. Line up shot glasses. If you want a drink, you better know what it is when your turn to order comes. I'm serving ladies first. Not responding to shouts, rude comments or disrespectful behavior. If you have complaints, save them for Wes."

A round of applause and hollers of approval filled the bar. Abby shouted again. "And please put your tips in the Boone Bradley Medical Fund jar. Now, let's have fun like Boone wants us to."

Abby climbed off the bar with Evan's assistance.

Evan set a dry towel over her shoulder and gave her a high five. "Nice job. Now are you ready for this?"

"I bet it's going to be fun after all." Abby turned to fill her first drink order and work herself into that exhaustion.

The trivia contest turned into a highlight, followed closely by the mechanical-bull challenge won by Cassie Weaver, the town's farrier. The back-and-forth was good-natured, the rivalries spirited and lively, and the laughter all-consuming. Abby surprised herself and Evan when she'd answered the music-and-pop-culture trivia questions correctly. Evan, for his part, held his own on the unusual-sports and strange-habits-of-wildlife categories. Evan and she agreed that next year they were teaming up to win the grand prize.

The only argument came after closing. Evan left early to pick up Riley from Tess's place, and Carter insisted on walking Abby home after they'd cleaned up. Abby sighed. "Carter, I literally live across the street."

"Doesn't matter." Carter crossed his arms over his chest and stared at her. "I'm walking you home."

"I can make it by myself," Abby insisted.

"I'm sure you can," Carter said. "But I'm still coming with you."

The man was as frustrating as Wes. No wonder the two were friends. And he was thoughtful and considerate just like Wes. And like Wes, Abby recognized when she wasn't going to budge a cowboy. "Fine. I need to get something first."

Abby visited the patio, pulled the blanket she and Wes had shared the evening before from the cabinet and returned to the bar. Lights turned off and doors locked, Abby stepped outside, Carter right beside her. Thankfully, he never commented on the blanket she hugged against her chest and silently escorted her all the way to the apartment door.

"Abby." Carter's voice was low and quiet as if he didn't want to disturb nature's nighttime chorus.

She offered a small smile and looked at him.

"Don't let Wes push you away," he said. "He needs you, even if he doesn't know it yet."

With those parting words, Carter tipped his cowboy hat at Abby and started down the stairway.

Abby unlocked the door, went straight to her bedroom and crashed on the bed. She fell asleep wrapped in Wes's blanket with Carter's weighty words replaying in her mind: *He needs you*.

CHAPTER TWENTY

ABBY PULLED INTO a parking space at the North-west Plains Medical Center and dropped Tess's car keys in her purse. She'd left Tess, Sam and Riley at the general store. Riley had taken on the task of finding the missing silver coin. Ilene and Nolan were covering the Owl with bartending and staff relief from both Evan and Carter. Abby had filled in whenever she could. That had been the schedule for the past five days since Boone had been admitted to the hospital.

Boone had been moved from the intensive care unit to a private room yesterday. Today was the first day he could receive visitors other than Wes. Abby had been nominated as the first visitor. Sam would come down that evening and relieve Wes for the night.

Abby walked around to the passenger side and opened the car door. She hung the handles of a large cloth bag around her arm, then lifted the oversize care package Ilene and Tess had put together. She wrapped both arms around the gift basket and headed for the elevators. Inside the hospital, the cloth bag bounced against her hip. But every step closer to Boone's room and Wes tangled her nerves.

Wes had slept at the hospital every night. He'd returned every other day to check on the bar and grab new clothes. Abby had seen him only in passing. Long enough to note the exhaustion rimming his eyes and the tousled bend to his hair from his stress as if he'd spent too many hours pulling on it. There hadn't been time for lengthy conversations, cuddling on the outdoor couch or stolen kisses.

But they'd exchanged texts in the late-night hours. Some lighthearted and silly. Some simple updates on the staff and other happenings around Three Springs, like the town council's upcoming vote for another movie night next month. And the great cow escape at Mayor Paul Molina's farm.

Then there were other text threads that revealed more layers. Offered insight. And inevitably brought Abby and Wes even closer. She knew his favorite food: deep-dish pizza. His perfect-day activity: horseback riding. His hero: his mom. When he was little and got scared, he always sang to chase away the monsters. His mother often told him he had the voice of a talented singer. Abby had fallen asleep wondering what Wes sounded like when he sang. And if he'd ever trust her enough to sing for her.

Abby passed the nurses' station and paused to adjust the basket. There was no reason for her nerves. Yet that hardly stalled the jitters skating through her. She'd only kissed Wes that one night. Now, outside Boone's room, she felt more vulnerable and more exposed after sharing secrets over texts.

Abby rolled her shoulders back. She was there for Boone. She'd simply deal with all the rest later. She pushed the door open with her elbow and walked inside. Boone was in his bed, propped up with pillows, attached to monitors and IVs. He held the TV remote and flipped through the channels. Wes was sprawled in a recliner, his cowboy hat lowered over his eyes, his legs stretched out along the vinyl floor.

Boone pressed his finger against his lips and slanted his gaze toward Wes.

Abby carefully slid the care basket onto the cabinet between the bed and the recliner. Wes tapped his hat up and peered at her. "Tell me there's deep-dish pizza in that basket."

"No chance." Abby swatted at the rim of his hat. "It's not on Boone's diet. You can't eat pizza in front of him. That'd be rude."

Wes covered his yawn with his fist. "I could eat out in the hall."

We'll get some later. Together. Like a couple on a date. Abby blinked and swatted that thought away. Texting was not dating. Now wasn't the time to confuse things. Abby sorted through the items in the basket. "Boone, Tess and Ilene put this together. There's a robe, flannel pajamas, shampoo, soap and other essentials."

"That's very kind." Boone's words were lined with a frailness she'd not noticed before his surgery. "Give them my thanks."

Abby pointed to two tins tucked under the robe. "There are also a few nonessentials like your favorite fudge. And banana muffins."

Boone's grin removed the pallor from his face. "Now they're just spoiling me something good."

"Riley made you this blanket. There's no sewing. It's all hand-tied together." Abby pulled a horseshoe-print fleece blanket from the cloth bag. "Riley was worried you might get cold in here."

"Isn't that something special." Boone took the navy-and-brown blanket and spread it out over his legs. "I'm not cold so much as bored."

"I offered to bring him books or crossword puzzles." Wes rose from the recliner and stretched his arms over his head.

Abby took the opportunity to survey Wes.

He was obviously tired. There was a weariness around his mouth, covered now in a beard that had grown in thicker over the last few days. But his shoulders weren't stooped. And there was an inherent strength about him still. He was the kind of man she would want beside her. Steady. Solid. Reliable. He was the person she'd choose to be there at three in the morning or to help her on a back-country road. *Her person.* Abby touched her stomach, blamed the sudden flutters on the oatmeal she'd had for breakfast. She shouldn't have added that extra spoonful of brown sugar.

"The print is too tiny in them books, and my eyes are too old." Boone picked up the TV remote and shook it. "If you could find me a rodeo to watch on TV, I'd be more than satisfied."

"Boone has the Cowboy Channel at home." Wes ran his palm across his cheek, then pulled his arm away as if surprised to discover a beard covered his face.

That was nothing. Abby was still reeling from her surprise revelation. Wes could not be her person. She was supposed to be her baby's person. She didn't need said person. Or even want one. Still, she couldn't quite shake the idea. Or the feeling that something had shifted inside her.

"I can watch a rodeo anytime I please on that

channel." Boone tugged Riley's blanket up toward his chest and folded his arms lightly over his stomach. "It's the next best thing if I can't go to one in person."

Wes was not her person. Because then Abby would've fallen in… *No.* Love wasn't instant or quick. Chemistry wasn't love. Neither was friendship. Abby straightened Boone's blankets, but nothing rearranged the sudden hammering inside her chest. Or the warm reassurance she felt.

She focused on Boone. Anything to distract herself. Anything to deny the truth. "Did you compete in the rodeo?"

"Sure." Boone traced a horseshoe stamped on the blanket. A whisper of nostalgia came through in his words. "Can't think of anyone in town who didn't give it a try at least once."

That caught her attention. She sat on the end of Boone's bed, giving in to the wobble in her knees. "Even my grandpa?"

"Of course Harlan too. Your grandpa loved to compete." The wistfulness expanded into Boone's distant gaze as if he was back inside that rodeo ring. "Harlan was one of the fastest calf-ropers in the surrounding counties. We won a time or two, team-roping together. Have the belt buckles to prove it."

One more glimpse into her grandfather's life.

He hadn't mentioned he'd been a rodeo cowboy in his letters. She'd never thought to ask. But she remembered the polished belt buckles he always wore. "Did you guys travel the rodeo circuit?"

"Nah, nothing like that. We stuck to the local ones." Boone slipped his hand with the IV under the blanket. "Used to be a rodeo in town every year when we were young. Had it out at the arena just on the edge of the county line."

An idea started to form. Abby forced herself to slow down and gather the details first. Jumping too far ahead had always gotten her in trouble in the past. The same as jumping ahead in her relationships. Like right now with Wes. She'd let her heart get away from her. Only a brief blip. She wasn't in love. She was in like with him. The same as she liked Boone, Carter or Evan. That warmth flushed into her neck and face as if highlighting her lie. She just needed to concentrate on what mattered, then her heart would get in line. It'd be any minute now. "What happened to the property?"

"Can't say." Boone shrugged. "Shame too. That's where our kids got their start. Where they learned the rodeo ropes."

Wes dropped into the recliner and stacked one ankle over the other. "Now they come to the Owl when they turn twenty-one to ride our mechanical bull."

"Doesn't compare to riding a live one." Boone chuckled. "But it's still fun."

Abby recalled the line for the bull challenge last Saturday night. Those were adults. She supposed they might've had the same size line of teenagers wanting a turn. "Where do the kids in town compete?"

"Have to travel all around now." Boone frowned.

"Between the fees to enter the rodeos and the travel costs, how many young kids can afford to go these days?" Wes rested his elbows on the armrests and steepled his fingers under his chin.

"Not enough. That's for sure." Boone brought the blanket higher up his chest.

Abby's idea gained traction. A vision began to materialize. She allowed herself a small frog leap. "Do you remember the name of the rodeo in town? Or the owner of the property with the arena?"

"My heart had a bit of a blip, not my mind." Boone tapped his index finger against his forehead. "Besides, I got belt buckles to remind me if I forget. It was called Three Springs Reunion Rodeo Days. The Robles family had the arena. They hosted it every year."

"Is that the property out on the end of Old Copper Mill Road?" Wes asked.

"That's the back of the property. You have to

enter it from the north on the interstate side," Boone explained. "When the last of the Robles family passed, Arthur Jr. was his name, no heirs came to claim it. Been vacant for the past decade or so."

Abby was glad she'd taken small steps and hadn't shared anything further. Nothing could come of rebooting the rodeo without the right venue.

"The county must have auctioned the property off by now." Wes sat up straight. "They wouldn't have kept it. There has to be a record of the new owners."

Her interest zoomed again. Sure, it wasn't finding the missing Herring Gang loot like she'd pitched to Mayor Molina, but it was a solid, attainable idea. And if she was working on that, she wouldn't be falling harder for Wes. "Who would buy the land and not do anything with it?"

Wes eyed her. "Are you thinking of doing something with that property?"

"Yes." Abby leaped at the idea. Gave her idea a voice and shut down her heart. "I want to have a Labor Day weekend rodeo. Revive the Three Springs Reunion Rodeo Days."

"That would be something special." Boone pressed the button on his hospital remote control and raised the head of his bed. His gaze sharpened. His color improved. "The town would get behind it."

Even Wes appeared intrigued. He dropped his elbows onto his knees and leaned forward.

"I'm thinking a junior rodeo with a scholarship for the winners. Boys and girls." Abby's arms fluttered in front of her as if working her vision free. She channeled those jitters and butterfly flutters into something productive. "A rodeo for the adults, with a king and queen, if they have those. Food vendors. Booths for our local restaurants to showcase their specialties. A dance Sunday night in the town square."

"Gotta have belt buckles too." Boone touched his waist.

"Definitely." Abby slanted her gaze at Wes and tested the depth of his interest. "T-shirts with the Feisty Owl logo because the bar was a gold-level sponsor."

"Of the scholarship." Boone glanced at Wes. "Can we afford that?"

Wes nodded. He gripped the armrests and pushed himself out of the recliner. "But it needs to be the Jake Bradley Legacy Scholarship."

A catch snagged in Abby's throat. That was much more than she'd expected. But it was Wes. He'd been surprising her since she'd first met him. Her heart tumbled over, and she gave in to the inevitable fall. Accepted the truth. She'd fallen in love with Wes.

Still, she vowed nothing would change. Nothing would come of it. After all, she didn't have to share her truth. It'd be her secret.

"A scholarship in Jake's name would be real fine." Boone brushed at his eye. "Real fine, indeed."

"I can see it." Frustration rolled over Abby. Love was supposed to be shouted from the rooftops, not silenced and smothered. Love was supposed to feel good. Not like a bout of morning sickness. She pressed her fingers against her forehead. "How am I supposed to make a rodeo happen? I don't know anything about organizing one."

"It's good, then, that you live in a town that has some experience with all that," Boone offered.

"You need Ryan Sloan for starters." Wes pulled out his phone and tapped his screen. "He's a stunt rider for the movies now. But he used to compete on the circuit. He'll know people."

Ryan Sloan had won the free nachos on Saturday night after his test ride on the mechanical bull. Then he'd proceeded to share the double-size order with his brother Grant. The Sloan brothers had played her. She glanced at Wes.

Wanting to believe he'd played her too. Tricked her into falling in love with him. But she'd taken that trip all on her own. And the consequences were all hers to accept.

"Add Cassie Weaver too. Never seen anyone better at shoeing a horse than Cassie." Boone scratched his cheek. "She'll have solid connections."

"I need to call Frieda or Gordon." And get herself solidly working on securing her job. Get focused again on achieving her life goals like those podcasts had instructed her to do. "Maybe they can direct me to who owns the old Robles property. We can't have a rodeo without a venue."

"This is one event the Owl can't host," Wes said.

Boone brushed his hair into place with his fingers as if preparing for a meeting. "What else can I do?"

"Call Sam for me. Ask him if he can come by sooner than tonight." Wes dialed Sam's number on the hospital phone and handed it to Boone. He set the phone to his ear, and a new energy surrounded him. Wes added, "We can brainstorm here just as easily as anywhere else."

"Sam will have suggestions too." Abby sent a text message to Corine about her idea. Corine's response was immediate: one giant heart emoji. Followed by an offer to help from her bedroom. Abby requested her assistance on permits and belt-buckle design. Corine directed Abby to Lynette Kinney for information on the Robles farm.

Abby stepped into the hallway to call Lynette. She had barely mentioned the Robles' property when Lynette captured complete control of the conversation.

"The Robles place belongs to my cousin, Janette Cooley-Lane. We're twice removed, but we grew up together. And really, whose family tree isn't a little twisted these days?" Lynette's laugh shimmered like the tiny bells on a wind chime.

"Does your cousin still own it?" Abby tempered the hope in her words.

"Let me think," Lynette said. "Janette and her first husband bought it together. They'd planned to retire there and raise horses. Until her husband found a better offer in the Keys with another woman. Janette got sole ownership of the farm in the divorce, but she never dropped the *Lane* from her name. I can't imagine why not. Then Janette up and remarried not six months after her divorce papers had been signed. I told her not to rush, but Janette always was one to fall in love too far and too fast."

Abby knew something about falling too far

and too fast herself. "Is your cousin still married?"

"Heavens, no." Lynette now sounded secretive. "That's what happens when you fall like that. You lose sight of what's real. Had she not been lovesick, she would've seen her ex's gambling ways sooner. He emptied her bank account and retirement funds doing that online gambling. Shame too. He was a real charmer."

Abby squeezed the phone. What hadn't she seen about Wes? What had she missed? Lynette wasn't wrong. Love this fast couldn't be real. "What about the property?"

"Far as I know, the deed is in Janette's name." A rustling scratched over the line like Lynette stood outside in the breeze. "Janette has gone back to work as a nurse to rebuild her retirement account. Can't afford to pay her bills on her town house, let alone buy horses, restore the farmhouse and return the place to its former brilliance."

"Why doesn't she consider selling?" Abby asked.

"It's always been her dream." Lynette sighed. "Can't sell those, can you?"

"I guess not." Love hadn't been one of Abby's dreams. She hadn't thought she'd wanted love until she felt it. "Do you think I could have

Janette's phone number? I have a proposal she might be interested in."

Lynette rattled off her cousin's phone number, invited Abby and Tess out to her place for lunch, and reminded Abby of next month's Roots and Shoots meeting. Then the line went quiet.

Abby shook her arms out and walked in a circle outside the elevators. This was it. She had the idea. The event the town would get behind. The event that could become annual and grow every year. It would attract tourists and competitors alike. And secure her a full-time job.

She just needed the venue.

Abby inhaled and held her breath until her nerves settled. One call. One conversation to get Janette Cooley-Lane's buy-in. Abby dialed the number, exhaled on the first ring. At Janette's greeting, Abby chose a vibrant tone, introduced herself and slid into her best sales pitch.

Twenty minutes and a promise to save Janette a belt buckle later, Abby closed the door to Boone's hospital room and stepped to the end of his bed. Then she tossed her arms over her head. "We have a venue. The Three Springs Legacy Rodeo Days are a go."

Pride sparked into Boone's gaze. "Now I got a real good reason to get on outta here as fast as I can."

"There's so much to do. In ten days." Abby

pressed her palms against her cheeks. Her heart raced. Her mind raced. "Ten days. I only have ten days." It wasn't enough time. What had she been thinking? She'd set herself up for another failure. Stepped right into it.

Wes moved into her line of sight and took her hands. "You're not alone. Boone and I are here. There's more help on the way. You have a team."

A team. She'd never really had that before. People to rely on. People who could rely on her in turn. "Corine just texted me. We need a rodeo director."

"That's you," Boone announced. "It's a good, solid title. *Abby James, Rodeo Director.*"

"There's a job you never thought you'd have." Wes squeezed her fingers. Laughter sparked in his gaze. "Ready to show them exactly what you can do?"

Abby held onto Wes's hand. Held onto his confidence in her. And let the tiniest fear slip out. "You won't let me fall?"

"You don't need me this time. You can do this." He set his fingers under her chin and lifted her face until their gazes met. "It's going to be a success. You're going to be a success."

She stared at him. Hard. "Promise?"

"I don't need to." He ran his thumb over her cheek. His smile was genuine and private. "I already know it."

CHAPTER TWENTY-ONE

THE RODEO CLOWNS WERE in place, and tie-down roping, the first official event of Three Springs Reunion Rodeo Days, was set to begin.

The calf was being loaded into the chute and the rider was preparing himself and his horse in the roping box. Excitement and anticipation wound through the large crowd and ran through Wes. He sat beside Boone on the metal bleachers placed for optimal viewing of the entire rodeo arena. Tess, Ilene, and Riley filled in around the pair.

Everything was finally falling back into place. Boone had been home on the ranch and continuing to recover for the past five days. Between the home health nurse's visits and the town dropping in, Boone had round the clock care. And Wes had begun to let his guard down and settle into his old routine. With one exception. His gaze skipped to Abby.

A clipboard tucked under her arm, Abby stood beside the bleachers and surveyed everyone she'd assembled to make the rodeo weekend happen. She was in charge and overseeing an event that was already a big success. Wes couldn't have been happier for her.

She'd managed it all while conquering morning sickness and keeping an eye on Boone.

"Can we start looking for the silver coin again now that Mr. Boone is outta the hospital?" Riley swung her boots back and forth on the metal bleachers and dipped her corn dog into her honey mustard sauce on the paper plate resting on her lap.

"We have to find that silver coin if we ever want to hunt for the treasure." Boone accepted the waffle-cut French fry Riley handed him and grinned. "And I'm feeling more than ready to get searching again."

Wes slanted his gaze toward the older cowboy. He hadn't completely relaxed his guard. After all, he wanted Boone around for a long while to come. "You have to remember to take breaks and not push yourself too hard."

Boone stuffed another French fry in his mouth and frowned at Wes. "I'm following the doctor's orders. Don't you worry about me."

Wes did worry. Would always worry. He'd accepted that. "Fried foods aren't listed on your diet."

"Don't you have something you need to be

doing?" Boone asked, his voice gruff. "Checking on the Feisty Owl food stand maybe?"

"Nolan has everything covered." His chef had planned a special rodeo menu, organized the food stand, and manned it all day. Last Wes had checked in on Nolan, the chef was flirting with several customers and talking about a Feisty Owl food truck. Wes grinned at Boone. "I thought I'd enjoy the day with you guys."

"Got any carrots on that lunch plate, Riley?" Boone peered at the little girl. "I need to add veggies to my snacking."

"I got fried pickles." Riley studied her plate.

"Those will do." Boone opened his hand. Riley set a deep-fried pickle on his palm. The old cowboy arched an eyebrow at Wes. "Balanced diet. Check. Now back to the missing coin."

Wes shook his head and let the man have his moment. Tomorrow, he'd talk to Ilene about how to slip more vegetables into Boone's meals without him noticing.

Riley finished her corn dog and shifted to look at Tess, seated behind her. "Ms. Tess, will you help us look too?"

"As much as I can." Tess wiped a napkin across Riley's cheek. "The special-order requests have really picked up recently. And I have inventory coming to fill the empty shelves.

Customers will be able to shop inside the store now."

"We could help stock your shelves, so you could help us search." Boone nudged his elbow into Riley's side. "Right, Riley?"

Riley nodded. "What's stocking shelves?"

"Putting things away neatly and nicely." Ilene sat beside Tess and eyed her young granddaughter. "Like your dad and I ask you to do with your toys."

Riley's brows bunched together. "Mr. Boone, we might need to find me another job."

Boone chuckled.

Tess tipped her head, her smile soft. "I'll show you where to put everything. It'll be fun and easy. Then we can search the store some more."

The group hadn't given up on their search for the missing silver coin. Wes appreciated their tenacity. He wasn't certain the silver coin frame would have a missing treasure map tucked inside, but it was important to Abby and her cousin. And he wanted Abby to have another connection to her grandparents and her past. "Is it possible the silver coin was part of the things your grandparents took when they moved north?"

Tess shrugged. "It could be, but then we

would've gotten it eventually. It seems to have been an important piece of our family's history."

"And Harlan wouldn't have taken it from the store." Conviction strengthened Boone's words. "It belonged here. In Three Springs."

"It just seems like you've checked almost every part of the general store." Much like Wes felt in his search for Dylan. But then he was discovering there seemed to be an endless number of places for someone to disappear to. Yesterday, Brad had told Wes the search for Dylan had gone faster than anticipated and information would be coming soon. That had given Wes hope. "Maybe I can scour the basement for hidden alcoves and doors that might've been missed. Or that are blocked by boxes and things."

Boone nodded. "That's a good idea. Those old buildings hide many secrets."

"Like a secret tunnel maybe?" Riley asked, her eyes brightened. "Dad's reading me a book with castles and secret tunnels."

"Where is your dad?" Wes scanned the crowd looking for Evan.

"Evan and Carter are getting a tour of the bulls and meeting the riders. Thanks to Carter's younger brother who still has connections on the rodeo circuit." Tess grinned. "Hopefully, they aren't getting any ideas to start riding themselves."

"You don't think Carter could handle a bull?" Wes asked.

"I think Carter takes enough risks already." Tess crossed her arms over her chest. "That man definitely doesn't need to take any more."

Wes considered Abby's cousin, then shifted his gaze to Boone and Ilene. The pair had leaned in to hear Tess's comments about Carter and were now whispering. Wes should warn his best friend about the matchmakers possibly focusing on him. But he wasn't going to. It'd be entertaining to watch Carter try and outrun Cupid's arrows. And he was more than glad those arrows weren't aimed in his direction. "What about your dad, Riley? Will he get on a bull?"

"If he knows what's good for him, my son will keep his boots out of the arena." A splash of doubt crossed Ilene's face as if she wasn't certain Evan knew what was good for himself. Her gaze swept over the crowded bleachers. "The only bulls Evan needs to be concerned about are the ones that ensure the quality of his beef."

"Everything moving along with the branding program for the cattle?" Boone asked.

Ilene's shoulders relaxed, her smile slipped free. "I don't know how he's doing it, but yes. It looks like Crescent Canyon beef will be branded for sale in stores in the new year."

Wes knew exactly how Evan had accomplished that – hard-work, dedication, and perseverance. The same way Abby had pulled together the rodeo so quickly. Evan and she inspired Wes. He noticed Abby shaking hands with Mayor Molina and introducing him to two judges, who were heading to their spots in the arena.

"Looks like I got back just in time. They're almost ready to begin." Sam handed a water bottle and a bag of Kettle corn to Boone and squeezed into a spot on the bleachers. "What have I missed?"

"Riley and I are restarting the silver coin search." Boone tilted the popcorn bag toward Riley for her to scoop out a handful. Riley grinned and tossed the popcorn in her mouth.

"And Carter is about to take a run on a bull," Wes added.

Sam pointed at him. "We both know that ain't happening. Carter gave me his word and he knows full well a man's worth nothing if his word can't be trusted."

Wes glanced at Tess, who clearly looked relieved with Sam's words.

Abby stepped up and set her hand on Wes's leg. Her smile speared into him like sunshine. "I don't have much time, but you can't believe the number of people who've shared their version of the legend with me today."

"You have to tell us everything." Boone sounded anxious and intent. "Did they mention where the treasure is?"

"A few offered possible locations," Abby said. Her words likely rushed by her own enthusiasm. She glowed, too, whether it was from the pregnancy or her enthusiasm for the legend, he couldn't say. But it sure suited her.

Sam patted the pocket on his denim shirt. "I need a pen and paper. We have to write it all down. It could be nothing or it could be vital to our treasure hunt."

"You know, other towns have historical committees that collect this kind of information and they organize it," Tess explained.

"We already know everyone in town." Sam pointed to Boone and himself. "We can do that. We can be the town historical committee."

Wes rubbed his forehead. "Can you call it a committee with only two people?"

"It's our committee," Boone charged. "We can all it what we want."

"So moved," Sam nodded.

"Seconded," Boone echoed.

"I don't think that's how it works." Wes eyed the cowboy duo.

Abby patted Wes's hand. "Someone needs to visit folks, listen to the stories and take notes. Do you want to do that?"

Wes set his hand over hers and looked at the pair of buddies. "You should call your committee something official like Three Springs Historical Preservation Committee."

Boone preened. "That has a rather nice ring to it."

Sam shoved his shoulders back and tipped his chin up. "We could print that on business cards to handout. We could use the Owl's phone number for inquiries."

Wes squeezed her hand and worked his voice into mildly disinterested. "You both have cell phones. You can use those numbers on your business cards."

Abby's soft laughter circled around Wes.

Boone scoffed. "I don't want just anyone calling me any time of the day and night."

Wes couldn't imagine there would be that many phone calls about the missing treasure that they required a receptionist. But he didn't want to completely trample their excitement.

"You can use the general store phone number," Tess offered. "You're both at the store most days anyway."

"And it's the heartbeat of the community," Abby said. "Or it was. But it's going to be again. I know it. I can feel it."

And Wes knew he liked the feel of Abby's hand in his. He liked her beside him. He liked…

A horn blared in the arena. Abby gasped and clapped. "It's starting. It's really starting. I have to go and oversee things."

With that, she sprinted off and left Wes to wonder how quickly he could get her back.

CHAPTER TWENTY-TWO

NIGHT HAD FALLEN and the weekend was coming to a close. Wes scanned the square and the crowd gathering on the makeshift dance floor. His gaze landed on Abby on the other side of the dance floor, swaying under the tea lights she'd had strung in the trees. The soft glow shimmered off her hair. She looked like she'd been sprinkled with magic dust. He smiled. A contentment he'd never experienced before settled inside him. She was the reason he'd found his balance again. She was the reason for so many things.

Wes wanted her in his arms. All to himself. One dance under the stars. At least. He wanted to spend time with her. Their text-message exchanges and quick passing encounters weren't enough. He missed her. He started across the dance floor.

A tapping on the microphone echoed around the square followed by a blared *Test. Test. Test.*

Wes stopped and faced the stage. Frieda shouted into the mic, announcing it was on and working. Then she handed it to Mayor Molina. The mayor thanked everyone for coming out to support the rodeo and the town. Then went on to explain the entire weekend wouldn't have come together in such record time without one intrepid woman, who oversaw every detail and never faltered or lost her good cheer. He called Abby onto the stage amid resounding applause. The mayor quieted the crowd and handed Abby the keys to her new office at the municipal hall, welcoming her aboard as the town's assistant manager.

Another burst of applause filled the square. Abby accepted hugs and congratulations from the mayor and the council. Thanked all the locals who had helped her and vowed an even better rodeo next year.

Abby invited the Rodeo Queen and King onto the dance floor to kick off the evening. The fiddle player in the band began the intro bars of a lively country song. The couple lined up first and was then flanked by the entire group.

Abby moved off the stage, locked her gaze on Wes and waved. She started toward him. But Lynette Kinney took her hands and held her in place. Wes gave up and started toward Abby.

"Wes Tanner." A woman called out to him and approached. Her dark hair was swept back in a neat, low ponytail and her button-down shirt was tucked in a pair of dark jeans. She was of average height but had a very specific don't-mess-with-me vibe. The kind that had been earned from experience, Wes assumed. She held out her hand. "I'm Gwen Reyes, one of Brad Harrington's associates."

Wes shook her hand. "I was expecting a phone call or text with an update from Brad, not an actual visit from his team."

"Things took a bit of a turn." Gwen set her hands on her hips. Her gaze never settled and continued to scan the area. "Common side effect of my job, but this time it was a good turn. My partner, Thomas Cochran, is waiting over by the church."

"Did you locate my brother?" Wes gripped the back of his neck, trying to anticipate the next words that would come out of Gwen.

"We did more than that." She looked at him, the slightest smile disrupting her serious features. "We brought your brother to you."

"Dylan is here?" His palms dampened. Wes ran his hands over his jeans. He'd been dropped into active war zones, his very life at stake, and he'd never flinched. Never hesitated. Never trembled. Not one time. His brother waited somewhere nearby, and now Wes trembled. And hesitated.

Abby called his name. Reached for him and

curved her fingers around his, grounding him. Steadying him. Wes exhaled the breath he'd been holding.

"Everything okay?" Abby asked.

Wes introduced Gwen Reyes to Abby. "My brother is here." And time was up. Dread chilled him. What if Dylan wasn't sorry? What if he wasn't the same brother Wes had loved all those years ago? He wanted to see him, and he wanted to run in the other direction. He'd never run from anything. He held onto Abby instead. "Thanks to Gwen and her partner. They found Dylan."

"There are things you should know," warned Gwen. "Dylan has outstanding warrants against him in Oklahoma. This can't be an extended visit."

"But Wes can see him now?" Abby's voice was strong and unwavering.

Her grip on his hand tightened. Or maybe that was Wes, needing the connection. Requiring the certainty of Abby's touch. He'd never questioned her heart, but doubted family bonds, blood ties and loyalty. He wanted to believe. Believe like Abby. What if…

"Dylan is right this way." Gwen pointed toward the church.

The PI escorted Abby and Wes across the street and around the side of the historic church, then she melted into the background. Silently and effectively. His brother rose from sitting on an iron bench. His hair was longer, sun- and chemical-bleached. More tattoos covered his arms from his shoulders to his fingers, each one connected intricately to the next. A pair of tinted sunglasses blocked Wes from seeing what was happening in his brother's eyes. Still, Wes searched for a connection, one brother to the other, and worked through introductions. Dylan offered Abby no handshake, no personal welcome, only a barely there dip of his chin.

Wes recorded the slight. The anger—the bitterness—stirred inside him. "Dylan. You haven't been easy to find."

"You weren't looking in the right places." Resentment anchored Dylan's words and his deep frown.

Why did Wes feel as if he was on the defensive? He hadn't stolen from his brother. Betrayed him. Or abandoned him. "Where do you call home these days?"

"The road." Dylan stuffed his hands in his jeans pockets and tucked his arms against his sides. Closing himself off as if he was somehow the wronged party. "It's where I've always belonged."

Wes lost what little patience he had left. This wasn't the same person Wes had grown up with.

Not the brother he'd taught to fish or built tree forts with. Or the one he'd sung to sleep on storm-ravaged nights. So much animosity. So much anger. Where had it all gone wrong? And the sudden sadness. It encased Wes like a suffocating shadow.

Wes released Abby's hand and crossed his arms over his chest, unwilling to taint her. "So you sold the ranch to hit the open road?"

"I had to fund my travels somehow." Dylan's mouth pinched together even more, turning his words into sharp bites.

Wes ignored the stab of his brother's indifference. "That place was our home."

"It was my prison," Dylan spat.

Wes winced and rocked back. Beside him, Abby gasped. Wes had never known how his brother had felt. Wes had enlisted and found a place he'd belonged right after high school. He hadn't really looked back, or perhaps he simply hadn't wanted to.

Dylan had been a freshman and most likely believed Wes had abandoned him. There was so much Wes suddenly didn't know. He should've been there. Should've…

"That land you love so much killed Mom," Dylan charged on. "Even Dad didn't want anything to do with it. It was bad from the start."

Their dad hadn't wanted anything to do with

their family. It hadn't mattered whether they'd lived on the ranch or in the suburbs. Their father wasn't ever coming home. Wes had accepted that long ago. Now they also had no home to return to. A place to repair and rebuild their relationship. Just as Wes had feared, there was nothing left but a bond that had fractured long ago. Regret tugged at him. "Where's my share of the profits, Dylan?"

"Gone." That one word smacked between them like a gloat. A boast.

"You spent it all?" Wes widened his stance, steadying himself. There really was nothing left. The more Wes searched, the more he failed to find any trace of the brother he once knew. Not a sliver of the boy he'd grown up with and still wanted to hold onto. It was all gone.

"I've been racing." Defiance tipped Dylan's chin up. "Trying to win it back."

What had happened to them? There was right, and there was wrong. He refused to accept the blame for his brother's actions. "Were you ever going to tell me?"

"When I had something to tell." Dylan shrugged as if he hadn't planned anything. "I only needed a few more wins."

"Then what?" Wes dug his fingers into his skin. He wanted not to care. To be as remote and detached as his brother seemed. "You'd mail me a check and an apology?"

"I don't know. It doesn't matter much now, anyway." Dylan eyed him. A tic worked along his jaw. "Why did you keep searching for me?"

"I truly don't know. It doesn't matter much now, anyway." Wes launched his brother's bored words back at him. But his anger found its own voice. "That's not true. I wanted the money. And I wanted to understand what happened to us."

Dylan flinched, his eyebrows pulling together behind his tinted sunglasses.

Abby stiffened next to Wes. But Wes fully embraced the pain. The hurt. Better that than admitting he'd let down so many people.

"What now?" Dylan kicked at a pebble on the sidewalk.

"Seems your road is headed to Oklahoma and your overdue court appearance." Wes glanced toward the shadows and nodded to Gwen and her partner. "It seems racing isn't all you've been doing."

"Come on, Wes. I'm your brother." Dylan slapped his palm against his chest. A plea wove through his words. "Can't you tell your friends to look the other way while I disappear into the night?"

"No." Wes shook his head. He couldn't look

the other way anymore. Couldn't avoid his own truths. "I can't do that."

"You won't," Dylan charged. "You always were the saint in the family."

"Get in the car, and take some responsibility for your actions." Wes had to do the same. He stepped to the side, letting Gwen and her partner approach his brother. "A piece of advice, Dylan. When you're in front of the judge, try leading with an apology."

"Look, I'm sorry." There was more panic than regret in Dylan's words.

"It's a little late for that." It was too late for so much. "Good luck, Dylan."

Gwen and Thomas escorted Dylan to a black SUV. Gwen's partner climbed in the back seat with Dylan, while Gwen jumped into the driver's seat. The vehicle soon turned onto a side street, away from the town square and Wes. He watched until the taillights had disappeared.

"You can't leave it like that," Abby whispered beside him.

"He broke the law, Abby." Wes ran his hands through his hair, resisting the urge to take her into his arms. He didn't deserve her. "Dylan has to answer for that."

"He's also your family." Abby reached for him. Her palm landed on his chest. Just above what was left of his heart.

"There's no money." Wes leaned in to her touch. One breath. One last time and stepped back. "Nothing left to say."

"I don't believe you," she stated. Her hands flailed in front of her as if she wanted to catch those pieces of his heart. "It's been about more than the money. What about your mom?"

She made what he'd said sound colder. More ruthless. More heartless. As if only money drove him. If only it had. Maybe he wouldn't ache so much right now.

Wes lashed out against so many disappointments. "I was going to buy back my family's ranch in Colorado. Honor my mom. Don't tell me I never thought it wasn't about family."

Surprise stole across her face. He knew she'd thought he'd use the money to buy out Boone at the Owl. He'd never corrected her. Never set her straight about the rest of his intentions. Convinced himself it was in her best interest not to know. Perhaps it had just been in his.

There wasn't any money now. He couldn't keep Boone in his home. Or buy full ownership of the Owl. He had nothing. He'd failed his family. Boone. Had nothing left to give Abby. Nothing that was worthy of her.

"Don't you care what happens to your brother now?" Her voice softened. Her gaze searched his.

"Abby, you're reading too much into all of

this. I can't change anything." He rubbed his hand over his face.

"No. I don't think so." A different quiet framed her words. Dull and somber on the edges. But at its core, a resignation that tore through him. She saw his truths now.

He faced her. Arms at his sides, fully exposed.

She considered him. "I think I'm finally seeing things clearly for the first time."

She was finally seeing that he wasn't worth loving. That his love came with a cost. He'd let her down too, eventually. "What's that?"

She ignored his question and launched her own. "What now, Wes? You just walk away?"

He'd been running his whole life. Perhaps that was all he knew. All he was good at. "This place was always temporary."

"You didn't want to find your brother. Not really." She pushed into his space. Breached those boundaries until only a wish separated them.

A wish he was someone different. Someone she deserved. Someone whose heart was more than jagged pieces.

"You have to be relieved there isn't any money." Defiance and distress burst into her flushed cheeks and sparked into her gaze. "Now you don't have to worry about those pesky roots and putting them down anywhere."

She wanted roots. Family. She wanted to build something. With someone. It couldn't be him. Surely, she understood that. If not now, in the end she would. She'd walk away. And that he couldn't handle. Better she fly now.

"Well, the joke is on you." Abby pushed on his chest, then jerked herself away as if he wasn't worth the effort. "You've been putting down roots here in Three Springs this entire time. Are you honestly going to run from all that?"

He was letting her go. There was no running from the hole splintering inside his chest. He stepped inside it. Knew it was for the best. She couldn't want him. Not like he was. "What about you?"

She blinked and straightened. "What about me?"

"Since it seems like we're offering insights, as friends do…" There was a harshness to the word *friends*. He watched her recoil, the tiniest of cringes around her eyes and hardened himself against it. This was for her own good. She couldn't really want him. His own family hadn't wanted him. "I've got some of my own to share."

"Do your best." There was nothing yielding in her stance or her words.

"You've been so busy trying to be who you

think everyone else wants you to be, you can't see who you really are." But he saw. He'd always seen her. Been drawn to her from the first time he met her. Always would be drawn to her. Didn't make it right. She was made for a love story for the ages. Hearts like his weren't made for loving.

"And I suppose you know who I am?" Her words challenged him.

"Who you are is the woman leading a scavenger hunt, playing pin the tail on the bull and taking care of an entire town's well-being on her own." Who she was *was* amazing, inspiring and everything he would've wanted in a different lifetime. In a different time.

She inhaled. Never looked away from him.

He stepped forward. Close enough to know their breathing matched. Every inhale, every exhale in tune. In sync. As if they were made for each other. "Who you are is enough, Abby James."

She closed her eyes as if absorbing his words. Imprinting them inside her. Her gaze returned to his. "Except I'm not enough for you, am I?"

Wes swallowed his denial. Something inside her gaze deflated. Wes tumbled into that hole inside himself. The last of his heart crumbled.

She lifted her chin and turned her back on him. She never paused; she just walked away.

Her unrushed steps wrapped in so much pride and so much poise.

Wes let her go and watched until she melted into the crowd of dancers. Watched until his own gaze blurred and his own composure wavered. Then he headed toward the Owl.

It was complete. He'd finally lost everything.

CHAPTER TWENTY-THREE

IT WAS FRIDAY and the last day of Abby's first full week as Corine's assistant. Abby closed her laptop and stood up behind her handcrafted oak desk. Its brass pulls and deep walnut-stained wood matched the vintage vibe of her office inside the historic town-hall building.

Abby picked up her purse and phone, then glanced at the calendar she'd tacked on her bulletin board. Weekly movie nights in the square were booked for the next while. Along with a Halloween bash. Christmas decorations were being discussed for downtown, and a holiday festival was in the works.

She also had meetings scheduled every day right up until Labor Day weekend. Rebooting Three Springs Reunion Rodeo Days was going to be the best thing to ever happen to this town. She hoped.

That morning, Evan had even texted to inform her that he'd signed them up for September's trivia night, happening in two weeks. And she'd been tasked with providing a side dish for tomorrow's Roots and Shoots Garden Club meeting.

Her to-do list was lengthy. Her calendar full. She was satisfied. Perhaps not completely content, but that she would learn to live with. She'd already taken steps in that direction. She'd started making her own lemon and ginger tea and given up her decaf-coffee obsession. She couldn't avoid Wes forever, but she wanted to avoid him until she didn't ache quite so much. Until that pang inside her chest every time she thought of him wasn't quite so sharp.

Her cell phone buzzed. A hitch caught in her throat. The tiniest of catches. The smallest snag of hope. She swallowed around it. One day soon, she'd congratulate herself for not thinking it might be Wes every time her phone rang. Today was not that day. She cleared her throat, opened the text from Trey Ramsey, and scanned the pictures he'd sent.

A knock on her door startled her. She forced a smile for her cousin standing in the doorway and returned to her phone. "One sec. It's Trey. He's got several leads on cars for me. I'm thinking a small SUV or maybe something bigger like a full-size one. Something the baby and I can grow into."

Tess set a cardboard moving box on the side

of Abby's desk and hugged Abby. "I know what you're doing."

"It's not a secret." Abby had hung her to-do list on the refrigerator in the apartment. It was a reminder to keep herself focused and on task.

"But it's also not a five-alarm fire." Tess squeezed Abby's shoulder and focused on Abby's phone screen. "You don't have to rush into everything all at once."

"I'm not." Not exactly. But Abby had arrived in Three Springs determined to prove she could do things on her own. That's what she intended to do now. Now that she wasn't distracted. No longer sidetracked by a rambling cowboy and all the things she didn't need in her life. Like a relationship. Or love. "But we do need to hurry to meet Frieda's cousin at the house. Nora only has an hour for lunch and a firm one-o'clock appointment at the bank."

"The baby won't be here for months," Tess said, caution in her tone. "You don't need to find a place to live today."

"True, but I'd still like to get a quick look at the house." She had to have a home to raise her child and build memories together. It was part of proving she could do it all on her own. This was top of her to-do list. Maybe she was rushing. But was it ever too soon to prove herself? "Besides, Frieda said their great-aunt Esther has impeccable style and remodeled the interior. Aren't you a little curious to see it?"

"Fine. We'll have a quick look." Tess pointed at Abby. "Just remember you don't need to sign a lease today. It's not urgent you get out of my place."

It wasn't long before, charmed by the white bench-style swing and thick columns on the front porch, Abby followed Nora and Tess through the two-story craftsman. She peered into the furnished upstairs bedrooms and bathrooms. Each room charmed her more. She explored the downstairs office, then moved through the family room with the fireplace and built-in bookcases to the back of the house.

"The kitchen was our aunt's last big project several years ago." Nora led the way into the kitchen. "Before the dementia set in. She worked so hard on this as if she knew her time in this house was coming to a close."

Nora and Frieda's great-aunt had been moved to a full-time care facility, so the two cousins had banded together to look after their relation's property and finances. Abby ran her hand over the farmhouse sink and marveled at the round stained-glass window tucked in an alcove with a bench seat. Metal panels remained in the white kitchen cabinets as a nod to the past. "This room makes you want to cook and invite the neighborhood inside to eat."

"Aunt Esther was quite the chef and the entertainer. Her door was always open, any time." Nora opened and closed a drawer as if packing the memory away. "Let's see. What else do you need to know? You'll need to buy mattresses for the beds. We can remove any furniture you don't want. I'm sorry for the hodgepodge of antiques in here."

Abby wasn't. The two cousins had removed several heirloom pieces to put in their own homes, at their aunt's urging, then replaced those pieces. Abby adored the mismatched furniture and eclectic collection. Renting a furnished home also worked with her budget. "It's perfect."

"You can paint and certainly make it your own." Nora tapped her chin as if checking off her list of details to pass on to Abby.

"I'll take it," Abby blurted.

Tess frowned and shook her head at Abby.

"I thought it over. I really did." Abby lifted one shoulder. "And I want to live here."

Nora laughed. "You don't even know the rent."

"What is it?" Abby clasped her hands together, hoping she could afford the house. Now that she'd seen it and could see herself living here, she desperately wanted it.

Nora rattled off a number. Tess's mouth dropped open.

Abby blinked and gaped at the woman. Surely, Nora had missed a zero or two on that amount. "Are you sure that's correct?"

"Our family is happy knowing this house is in good hands. That it'll be treated well." Nora set her hand on the wall as if touching a friend. "It's a home that needs a family."

That was exactly what Abby was building. She touched her stomach. "When can I sign the lease?"

Nora and Abby arranged to meet on Monday at the bank where Nora worked. Abby would sign the rental agreement, put down her deposit and get the keys to her new home. She could begin moving in any time after that.

Tess and Abby grabbed pizza slices for lunch at the White Olive Pizza Shop. Tess headed for the general store, while Abby returned to her office.

Abby dropped into her chair, and the cardboard box caught her attention. She picked it up, noticed her name written in bold letters. The handwriting was vaguely familiar.

The box was taped and secure, unlike most of the ones in Tess's store. Abby sliced it open with a pair of scissors and gasped. A letter was taped to whatever was wrapped inside. And this time, she recognized the handwriting on the envelope. It was her Grandpa Harlan's, part cursive, part print. Her hands shook.

She unfolded the letter, rested it carefully on her desk. The date in the corner of the paper was the same month her grandparents had packed up the general store and moved north. Abby brushed at the tears leaking from her eyes.

Dear sweet Abigail,

Abby leaned back to keep the letter safe and dry. She couldn't contain all the tears for how much she still missed her grandparents. For the bittersweet surprise of this gift. Here was one more letter when she'd thought they had stopped forever.

Your grandmother and I wanted you to have the enclosed. We always believed we'd pass it along when the time was right. If you're reading this letter, then the time must be right.

Inside is an antique quill and ink set. I'd venture that many generations used it in the general store, but I can't count that far back. I never was good at math—that's one of your grandmother's many skills.

Find someone that complements you, Abigail. Someone who encourages your strengths, accepts your weaknesses and never tries to change you.

Back to the quill and ink set, suffice it to say your ancestors wrote their life stories with this set. Now, my dear, it's your turn. Be fearless. Be bold. And if the ink spills— and it will—never be too afraid to grab a new page and start again.

Lastly, if you've found yourself in Three Springs, and your grandmother and I sincerely hope you have, ask Boone Bradley and Sam Sloan about the McKenzie sisters and the Herring Gang. But keep in mind, the legend's not a treasure-hunt story so much as a love story, which reminds us that only with love are we truly rich. Don't believe me? Ask your grandma. Or your parents. Never be afraid to risk it all for true love. I promise you won't regret it.

Now, sweet Abigail, I must close this letter so you can write your own story. Make it a good one. Make yourself proud.

With love past the stars and back,
Grandpa Harlan

Abby reread the letter, cried for twice as long and then unwrapped the gift from her grandparents. There were two ink wells, a rocking blotter, a sanding jar and several dip-style pens with feathers or wooden handles that fit into a stand. Abby arranged everything on her desk and researched on the internet where to buy ink.

All the while, her grandfather's letter remained open on her desk. And all the while, his words stirred inside her. *Never be afraid to risk it all.*

Abby's ex hadn't fought for her. Hadn't really risked anything for their relationship. Abby stilled and turned one of the feather pens over in her hand. *Every coin has two sides, Abby. You have to have both to be complete. After all, there's no value in a one-sided coin.* But she hadn't risked either in her past relationships. She hadn't fought, but she had to fight this time. She had to risk it all like her grandfather advised. Because Wes was the one. Her true love. And she had a love story to live.

CHAPTER TWENTY-FOUR

WES JUMPED OUT of his truck and hurried toward Boone's house. Boone had called just after sunrise and told Wes that he had a bit of pain he wanted to talk to Wes about. In person. Then he'd hung up. Wes had yanked on his jeans, a wrinkled T-shirt and his boots before racing to his truck and making it to Boone's in less than five.

His truck still hot, Wes climbed the porch stairs and pulled up before he barreled into Boone. A fully dressed, hair-brushed and boots-polished Boone. Wes searched the old cowboy's face, taking in his good color and his straight posture. Wes's heart finally started to slow.

"Come on in." Boone opened the front door and motioned Wes inside. "Got your favorite biscuits, gravy and bacon ready and waitin'."

"If you're having pain, we should contact the doctor." Wes went inside and glanced over his shoulder at what appeared to be a healthy Boone. "We should head to the hospital."

"Don't need a hospital for this pain." Boone

set his hand on Wes's shoulder and guided him through the family room toward the kitchen.

Wes entered the kitchen and paused. Sam, Carter and Evan sat at the table. Each one dressed, hair brushed, and most likely teeth brushed too. Wes had omitted that part in his rush to get to Boone's place. He skipped his gaze around the table. "What's going on?"

"Now, listen up, son." Boone pulled out the chair at the end of the table and pointed to it. A silent command for Wes to sit down and pay attention. Boone continued. "You've been moping for a week. I'm tired of it. They're tired of it. You've got to be tired of it yourself."

"I haven't been moping." Moping implied he still cared. Still wanted Abby. Moping implied he'd been replaying their conversation. Rethinking every word he'd uttered. Moping implied he wasn't perfectly happy with the outcome.

Why couldn't he be satisfied? He'd gotten exactly what he'd wanted. Wes dropped into the chair and crossed his arms over his chest and the ache that wouldn't go away.

"Well, you've certainly been hiding." Boone walked to the stove, picked up a plate of homemade biscuits and scooped thick gravy over the top. The loaded plate he set in front of Wes. "Hiding in your office. In the barn. Can't deny that."

The others nodded. Wes concentrated on his favorite breakfast and stuffed a large bite into his mouth. The faster he ate, the sooner he could escape. Go back to hiding. The problem was there was nowhere to hide from himself. Or the pain.

"I've had heart surgery, and Wes looks more heartsick than me." Boone opened the refrigerator, took out a milk carton and filled a tall glass on the counter.

"Lovesick." Sam squinted at Wes. "The boy is lovesick."

Love. The bite of biscuit stuck to the top of Wes's mouth like sandpaper. The gravy clogged his throat. Wes wasn't lovesick. A person had to be in love to suffer like that. He set his fork on his plate and concentrated on swallowing and breathing.

"You love the woman, Wes." Boone set a glass of chocolate milk beside him, thumped him on the back and sat at the other end of the table. "No use denying what's more than plain to all of us."

Wes chugged the chocolate milk. Avoided looking at his friends. Tried to clear his throat. Nothing dislodged Boone's words.

"Love is what makes life worth living." Sam picked up a slice of bacon from the platter in the center of the table and pointed it at Evan, then Carter. "Would do you two some good to try it."

Carter grabbed a piece of bacon and held up his hands. "I'm here for Wes. This isn't about me."

"Me either." Evan grabbed his coffee mug and stood up to refill it from the pot on the stove.

The attention off him for a moment, Wes worked to remove the last of the biscuit from the top of his mouth. And return himself to rights. Except he hadn't felt right since Abby had walked out of his life. He hadn't realized his life hadn't been right until she'd barged into it on a backcountry road.

He concentrated on his plate of food. Life should be more like breakfast. Nothing complicated about biscuits and gravy. If the ingredients were kept fresh and simple, it turned out delicious every time. There was nothing simple about his feelings for Abby.

"Being left at the altar was a gift, Evan." Boone sipped his own coffee and considered the man. "You'll come to see that in time."

"That's right, it was." Sam smoothed his white beard into place. "Son, you can't give up on a chicken because of one bad egg. Same as you can't give up on love."

"Can we get back to Wes?" Evan sat and

poured enough sugar for ten cups into his coffee mug. "He's the lovesick one here."

"I'm good." His plate was half-finished. And he was almost feeling like himself again, that one part inside him that felt like a gaping hole aside. "Let's talk about Evan some more."

"You wouldn't know good if it stomped on you like a bull." Boone curved his hands around his mug. His thick eyebrows pulled together. "You were good with Abby. Now you're just…"

"Mopey." Carter bit into his bacon and chewed, then aimed an apologetic grin at Wes. "Sorry. It's true."

"Maybe I'm just tired." Wes aimed his fork at his own face. "This could just be my tired, overworked face."

Boone's burst of laughter was abrupt and brief. "Work energizes you. Always has. You're one of the most hardworking people I know. You ain't tired."

"It's his lovesick face." Sam's head shifted back and forth. Sympathy thick in his words as if he'd declared Wes's condition was never going away.

Not this again. Wes stabbed his fork into a fluffy biscuit. "What if I am lovesick? Whose business is it?"

"Ours." Boone spread his arm over the table and circled his hand in a sweeping motion to include everyone seated there. "This right here is family. When one of us is hurting, we all hurt."

Carter nodded. Evan too.

Family. Wes sat back and spun his fork in his hand. These were his friends. Mentors. Peers. They looked out for each other. Looked after each other. No questions asked. Something shifted and settled inside him. They were family. Wes's family. His appetite returned. He stuffed a piece of bacon into his mouth. "Whatever you want to call it, lovesick or tired, it'll pass. I'm handling it."

"Look, I let you handle that issue with your brother." Boone eyed Wes. His gaze wisdom-aged and assessing. "Don't think you're the only one who knows things around here."

Wes drank his chocolate milk, washed down the bacon and his surprise. "You never mentioned you knew about my brother."

"A man is entitled to his business." Boone brushed biscuit crumbs from the table onto his hand, then set them on a napkin. "I let you have yours."

Wes wiped a napkin across his mouth and crumpled it lightly in his fist. If that was true, they could move on from their conversation now. They could let Wes deal with his business of being lovesick on his own terms. "What about now?"

"That's simple." Boone leaned forward. Humor and affection crinkled the lines around his eyes. "I love you too much to mind my own business now."

There it was again. *Love.* Everything kept circling back to it. He supposed because love was the core. The foundation. And the truth that had been tracking him for the past week like a golden eagle locked on its prey. Wes loved everyone seated at the table. But the truth he finally stopped running from was something even deeper. Something precious. Something that he'd been missing. He was in love. In love with Abby.

"I said *love.* And nothing happened." Boone shifted his perceptive gaze from Wes to Evan to Carter. "Sam and I don't fear the word or the feeling."

Sam cradled one of his hands inside the other as if he recalled holding his wife's hand. His words wistful. "Not in the least."

He might've accepted the truth. Admitted he loved Abby. But he was still twitchy. Wes tossed the napkin on his empty plate. "It's not love I fear."

"What do you fear?" Carter's expression was somber. His tone serious. A marked contrast to his usual amused approach to life.

"Not being good enough for her." Wes tossed

his fear into the center of the table and clutched his empty milk glass.

"Is this about your lost inheritance?" Boone scratched his chin.

Wes flexed his fingers around the glass. He should've known Boone would have the details. He should've shared them with Boone. Trusted him. That's what families did.

The older man continued. "You do realize that money can't buy character. Honor. Respect. Values."

"You already possess all those things." Evan stacked his hands behind his head and leaned back in his chair. "Money or not."

Wes was letting go of his anger toward his brother. Knew it served no real purpose and changed nothing. Perhaps one day, he'd seek to understand the *why*s behind it all. But before then, apologies had to be given and accepted, including his own to his brother. That was for later. There was an important apology to give to Abby first. Yet more of those fears surfaced.

Wes studied the bottom of his glass. "What if I can't stick?" Same as his father couldn't stick. The same as his brother.

"Your father wasn't the man you are." A heat infused Boone's words. An intensity Wes hadn't heard before. Boone added, "Don't compare yourself to him. Ever."

"You already have stuck." Carter tapped his fist against Wes's shoulder. "Look around town to see all you've done."

"And if you need more proof, Abby put together a presentation for you." Evan hitched his thumb toward the counter and the folder resting there. "It's nauseatingly glowing and full of flattering things and all about you, my friend."

"Abby was in on this?" He shouldn't have been surprised. She was a fighter. He had to fight too.

"Family, Wes." Boone's voice was matter-of-fact. "We're all in on it."

"But you have to move. I have no land for the rescues." How could Wes make it all right? For his family. Boone had received word that the property was being sold to the land developers in a lucrative deal. He had thirty days to vacate.

"I have an idea about a sanctuary," Carter offered.

"It's a solid one." Sam tipped his coffee mug at Wes. "But you have to get the girl."

"I chased her away." Wes scrubbed his palms over his face. "Hurt her pretty bad."

"That you did." Boone chuckled at the frown Wes aimed at him but added, "I never said love was easy and pain-free."

"Now you have to make it right." Evan tapped his coffee mug against Wes's milk glass.

"How do I do that, exactly?" Wes heard the panic in his own voice. He was out of his league here.

"I was left at the altar, remember?" Evan held up his hands. "Don't look at me."

"Boone and I got our ladies to the altar." Sam slapped his palm on the table and laughed. Boone joined in.

Wes ignored the two chuckling older cowboys and looked at Carter.

Carter rubbed his hand through his hair, tousling the ends. "Can't say I've ever been in love like you. At least, I haven't wanted to win my exes back."

"This is not helping." Wes rose and picked up his plate. He was restless and uneasy. He'd lost Abby once. He couldn't lose her again completely. "What am I going to do?"

He rinsed off his plate and set it in the dishwasher. A simple apology wasn't going to cut it. *Sorry, Abby. I was stupid. Lost my common sense there for a minute. It's back now. Can you forgive me?*

"You have to do something big," Evan suggested. "Over-the-top romantic."

"Like an outdoor wedding. With an arch made of rare roses flown in from all around the country." Carter lifted his eyebrows at

Evan. "That was one romantic wedding you'd planned."

"And it failed." Evan's mouth thinned. "Let's keep that off the list."

"You have to show her you love her." Boone drummed his fingers against the table. "Give her more than words."

A wedding wasn't what Abby wanted now. Wes could see one. That was for later. Abby wanted roots more than anything. And Wes had to prove he had roots. That he wanted roots with her. He smiled. The real first smile in days. He dried his hands on the dish towel and glanced at Carter. "I've got an idea. But first, Carter, what's this about a sanctuary?"

"My grandmother gave my brothers and me forty acres across from the distillery," Carter explained. "It was passed down on her grandma's side, one daughter to another. But my grandma only had one son, then more grandsons."

"She loved her boys fiercely and fully." Sam touched his wife's wedding ring he'd worn on his pinky finger since her passing.

"We thought we could take thirty acres and turn that into a horse sanctuary." Carter leaned his elbows on the table and met Wes's gaze. "With you being our partner and managing the rescues."

Wes pressed his back against his chair and

exhaled. It was more than he'd expected. More than he'd hoped for. A permanent home for his rescues. "You're serious."

"My brother and I agreed. Grandpa too." Carter set his hand on top of Sam's arm. "We thought we could use your mom's first name and Grandma's. Call it the Martha Claire Horse Haven."

Words escaped him. Tears pooled in Sam's gaze. In Boone's and even Carter's. Wes blinked and failed to dry his own eyes. This was family. And how a family rallied.

"Are you in?" Carter stretched his arm over the table toward Wes. A scratch clear in his friend's low voice.

Wes set his hand in Carter's. "I'm in."

He was in. For the long haul. For the forever he'd never imagined he'd ever have. Now he just needed to show Abby he meant it.

CHAPTER TWENTY-FIVE

THE PIECES WERE falling into place. Wes stepped outside the bank and grinned. He'd spent his Sunday indoors looking over his finances, filling out paperwork for the new sanctuary and establishing those roots. He'd been at the bank before it opened. He'd greeted Nora Finch, the bank manager, with fresh coffee and Ilene's homemade blueberry scones to brighten her Monday morning. And secretly he'd wanted her to move quickly through the documents he'd submitted online for a loan last night. Nora hadn't disappointed and approved him within the hour.

Wes crossed the street and walked inside the Owl. The bar and grill was closed, but Nolan was in the kitchen, testing new recipes. Fresh coffee scented the air. Boone was seated at the bar, an empty plate and a half-finished soda in front of him.

Wes skirted the bar stools and set an envelope within reach of Boone. "This is for you."

Boone picked up the envelope and tapped

it against the bar top, his gaze fixed on Wes. "What's this?"

"Your retirement plan." And the start of Wes's future. He leaned an elbow on the bar top and nodded. "Open it."

Boone pulled the check from inside and studied it. Nothing passed across the old cowboy's weathered features. But a hint of approval tinged his words. "You buying me out, then?"

"Yes, sir." And he was investing in the town. In himself. In his family.

"Doesn't mean I'm going anywhere." Boone folded the check and tucked it into the front pocket of his plaid shirt.

"Never expected you would." Wes kept his smile restrained.

"Gonna offer my opinions too." Boone angled his soda glass at Wes and lifted one of his eyebrows. "Call you out when you're doing it wrong."

"I'm counting on it." That's what family did—counted on each other. Through the ups and the downs.

Boone eased off the stool and held out his hand to Wes. There was a mistiness in his pleased gaze. "Proud of you, son."

The two men grasped hands, then both stepped in to each other for a full hug. Wes held on for a long moment. "Thanks for not giving up on me, Boone."

"Never doubted you." Boone claimed his seat, then glanced at Wes. "We'll make it official later this week. Right now, I want to know if everything is a go for tonight's Operation Razzle-Dazzle?"

Boone and Sam had coined the silly phrase for Wes's plan to win back Abby during the lovesick intervention in the old cowboy's kitchen. Carter and Evan had enjoyed the nickname a little too much and started a group text chat under the same name. Wes had vowed that when his two friends found themselves on the lovesick train, he'd be there to revel in their trip. Carter told Wes not to worry, cows would fly before he erred and fell that hard for any woman. Boone and Sam had taken Carter's words as a challenge, to Evan and Wes's delight and Carter's dismay. "I'm meeting Tess in an hour for the rest of the deliveries."

"That's good. Real good." Boone stood and swallowed the last of his soda. "I'm off to see Delaney O'Neil."

Delaney was the town's best real estate agent and had built quite a photography business that she'd started as a hobby. Wes walked behind the bar. "Why are you meeting up with Delaney?"

"Got my eye on a nice little place in town."

Boone picked up his cowboy hat from the back of the stool and turned it around in his hands. "It's time to hang up the spurs and enjoy some front-porch sitting for a while."

"Don't hang up those spurs completely." Wes paused and studied Boone. The older cowboy hardly seemed upset or disappointed. He looked almost like he was up to something good. "I'll need you out at the sanctuary. I'm depending on your advice for the stable remodel and the shelters in the pastures."

"You can count on me giving it." Boone set his cowboy hat on his head.

"You know you can move into the apartment," Wes offered. Boone had to be out of the Dawson house before the end of the month. He had time yet to decide on where he wanted to live.

"I told you, I got my eye on a little place. Walking distance from downtown." Boone grinned and touched his shirt pocket. "And now the funds to make a purchase."

Wes hadn't given Boone the money so he could spend it the same day. "What else have you looked at? Maybe I should go with you."

"I already like the neighbor. I know that much. You keep on with Operation Razzle-Dazzle." Boone touched the brim of his hat. "Between my neighbor and this place, my plate is gonna be full. Just the way I prefer it. This retirement thing certainly isn't going to be boring."

Wes watched Boone amble outside. Swore he heard the old cowboy whistling. He would've followed, but his cell phone rang. Tess was back early and headed out to the old barn. Wes called goodbye to Nolan and headed to his truck. He had one afternoon to prepare the perfect evening. One chance to win back Abby and secure his future.

"YOU'RE SUPPOSED TO be helping me get Wes alone." Abby shut the passenger door of Evan's large truck and buckled her seat belt. "How is practicing trivia at Carter's house going to do that, exactly?"

"You could ask Wes out during trivia night." Evan steered the truck from the curb and headed away from downtown. "You could put your date request into one of the trivia topic squares on the screen."

"You want me to ask Wes out in front of the entire town? On trivia night? The busiest night of the month?" Abby set her purse near her feet and glared at Evan. She should've stayed home with Tess and Riley and played cards instead. How had she let Evan talk her into this? Trivia practice. She had to practice what she wanted to say to Wes.

"Sure, why not?" Evan tapped his fingers against the steering wheel and grinned at her. "It would be quite the declaration. Like asking someone to marry you during a pro basketball game on the jumbotron."

"And if Wes declines?" Abby ran her damp palms against her shorts. She wanted to fight for Wes. For them. But she didn't quite know where to begin. She'd thought the presentation in the folder would've earned some sort of response. She'd gotten only more silence. Now she had to make a second, bolder move, and she was terrified of making the wrong one. "It would be monumentally mortifying to be rejected in public."

"You don't want to date Wes, anyway," Evan said.

"Evan, you are so not helpful." Abby tilted her head back and stared at the ceiling. "You're like an aggravating little brother."

"I'll take that as a compliment." Evan laughed when Abby swatted his arm. "Okay. Seriously, here's the plan."

Abby shifted and faced him. She'd given up watching where they were going. All the country roads looked the same after sunset. They mostly looked the same in the daylight too, except Abby was getting better at finding her own landmarks from cactus to crooked mailboxes to cows in the pastures.

She'd even driven to Belleridge for her follow-up appointment with Dr. Carrillo and only made one wrong turn.

Evan spread his hand toward her like a game-show host with a prize. "The plan is a special breakfast at Boone's tomorrow morning. Only Boone won't be there. You will."

"Is that a big enough declaration?" Abby wrinkled her nose.

"The man likes breakfast." Evan scratched his forehead, moving his cowboy hat up and down. "Isn't the way to a man's heart through his stomach?"

"You tell me." Abby drummed her fingers on the console.

"Me?" Evan parked the truck, cut the headlights and the engine. "I prefer a grab-and-go kind of breakfast."

Abby groaned and reached for the door handle but paused and squinted out the windshield. "Evan. This can't be Carter's house. That's an old barn. How can you be lost? You've lived here your whole life."

"I'm not lost." Evan pointed out the window. "That's your destination."

"Half the roof is missing. No one is going

inside there. It's a hazard." Abby glanced from the old, dilapidated barn to Evan.

"Look closer." Evan tilted his head toward the old barn.

"Are there lights on inside there?" Abby squinted as if that would somehow improve her night vision. Something wavered in the shadows. "Wait. Someone is walking out."

"Abby." Evan's voice was soft.

Abby's gaze remained on the figure walking toward the truck. She knew that walk. That swagger. Those strong shoulders. That cowboy hat, exactly where it was faded and worn on the rim. Her heart raced. Her face flushed. Her entire body tingled.

"Abby," Evan repeated.

"What?" Abby snapped and tore her gaze away from the familiar figure.

"Get out," Evan urged. "Get out of my truck."

Abby focused again on the figure. On the man she'd know anywhere. On Wes. She reached for the handle and opened the door. Then looked back at Evan. "I don't think I'm going to need that breakfast, am I?"

"You won't know until you get out." Evan shoved her shoulder.

"I'm nervous," Abby admitted.

"And I'm late for poker night at Carter's,"

Evan drawled. "We all have our issues to deal with."

Abby's laughter overtook her. She squeezed Evan's arm, thanked him and stepped out. Stepped toward her future. To everything she ever wanted. Determined that this time she wasn't letting go.

Evan turned his truck around on the dirt road, honked twice and disappeared into the night.

Abby walked toward Wes. He never paused, just kept coming toward her. He didn't slow until he was close enough to wrap his arms around her and hold her against him. Where she wanted to be.

He kept his hands at his side. His stance relaxed, his words swift. "Abby, I'm sorry. It's not enough. I know it's not enough, but it has to be repeated. I'm so very sorry."

Abby absorbed his words. He was enough. She stepped up to him.

He held out his hand, stopping her before she could wrap her arms around him. "Can I show you something?"

"Sure." Abby slipped her hand inside his, and everything inside her finally settled. Her world finally felt right again. "Where are we?"

"The land belongs to Carter and his brothers." Wes tugged her closer into his side. "It's recently been converted into a sanctuary for horses."

Abby caught her breath, held it for a beat. But she had to know. "Whose horses will be here?"

"Mine. And the ones we rescue in the future." He held his other arm out. "Let me officially welcome you to the Martha Claire Horse Haven. Martha for my mother. Claire for Carter's grandmother."

"Wes, that's incredible." Abby scanned the horizon again.

"I'm still reeling." Wes squeezed her hand and guided her along a dirt path, weaving closer to the old barn. "The horses have a permanent home for generations to come."

Home. She wanted that too. With him. She chewed on her bottom lip, opened her mouth.

But the barn came into view and stole her breath. Hundreds of flowers in every kind and every color from roses to lilies to snapdragons and daisies filled the abandoned space, transforming it into a floral wonderland. Candles and tea lights along the rafters added the perfect glow. A bottle of apple cider sat on a small round table covered in a plaid tablecloth in the center. Abby pressed her hand against her chest and inhaled all the scents. "What is this?"

"I'm hoping it's the start of our future." Wes took both of her hands in his. "Dance with me?"

"Here?" Now. Always.

"Here." Wes went to a corner and started a record player. An old waltz played on a sole fiddle began, and he drew her into his embrace. "Just you and me. Under the stars."

Abby linked her hands behind his head. Grateful he held her. She felt her feet lifting off the ground. Felt those butterflies gathering to whisk her heart into the clouds. "Wes—"

"Let me say this first. You deserve to know all of it." He pulled her closer. "I realized this week that home isn't a place. It's a person. It's you, Abby James. You're my home."

Abby's heart took flight. Tears pooled in her eyes. Love washed away her voice. Those words. All she could do was hold onto Wes.

"Will you be my forever?" Wes set his forehead against hers. "Put down roots with me. Build a family, a future and our own legacy together."

"Yes. On a thousand shooting stars, yes." Abby pressed her lips against his.

"I love you." Wes pulled away and framed her face in his hands. "I loved you from the first moment I saw you. And I've been falling more in love every day since."

"I love you too, Wes Tanner." Abby gave her heart its voice. "You're my home. My safe place. My everything."

EPILOGUE

Early December

ABBY GLANCED IN her rearview mirror and watched the dust kick up behind the back wheels of her brand-new cherry-red truck on Old Copper Mill Road.

Boone sat beside her. His fingers tapped to the beat of the country song on the radio and the breeze from the open window made his gray hair sway. "Shouldn't be much farther."

Abby scanned the side of the road, looking for a familiar chestnut-and-white mare and a disgruntled cowboy.

"There." Abby pointed at the pair surrounded by cacti and tumbleweed. Her cowboy sat on a large rock, arms crossed over his chest. The Paint mare stood several feet away from him, her ears twitching. Abby put the truck in Park and leaned out the window. "Hey, cowboy, heard you needed some assistance."

"Wes needs more than that. He needs to update his horse training ways." Boone laughed. "Queen Vee got him good this time."

Her cowboy stood and brushed the dirt from his jeans, then walked over to the truck. "It was a rattlesnake that startled the horse. She bucked and I wasn't ready."

"And she threw you clear out of the saddle," Boone chuckled. "Wish I had been here for it. What was that? The third or fourth time Queen Vee has thrown ya off?"

"I haven't counted." Wes closed his eyes and inhaled.

"Well, I'm here now," Abby sing-songed and set her hand on Wes's arm. "Let's see if Queen Vee will let me close enough to grab her reins."

Wes opened the truck door and helped her out. "Every time I try to get near the mare, she backs away."

"At least she didn't run away." Abby grabbed a paper shopping bag from the back seat. She'd filled the bag at home and now set it near her feet. The ones inside her favorite pair of baby-blue-and-tan cowboy boots. "I brought carrots and apples. And her absolute favorite: sugar cubes."

"Wes, you should've put a jar of sugar cubes in your pocket before you left the rescue." Boone walked around the front of the truck and climbed into the driver's seat. "I'll take Abby's truck back to the house."

Boone had bought the house next door to Abby's in downtown Three Springs. Being neighbors, they enjoyed the occasional week-night dinner together and long conversations on the front porch on the weekends. Abby settled her cowboy hat on her head. "We'll be fine." Besides, she needed time alone with Wes. She always welcomed more of that.

Boone honked the horn, waved out the window and drove off.

Wes eyed her. "Are you sure you want to walk back?"

"It's not far." All in all it was less than two miles to the rescue. With Wes beside her, Abby knew she could handle anything. She linked her arms around his neck and stepped closer. "Besides, I'm off work. The bar is closed, and we have no where we need to be."

"The sun will be setting soon." His arms curved around her waist and he tugged her even closer.

"Can't think of a better view of the sunset than out here."

"Neither can I." He kissed her softly. Fully. Then brushed her hair off her cheek and smiled. "Thanks for coming to my rescue."

"Any time." Every time. Always.

"Ready to round up Queen Vee?"

Abby picked up the treat bag and took out an apple. She walked slowed toward the horse, praised the mare, commented on her calm manner and scolded the rattlesnake that had startled her afternoon exercise. When Abby was close enough, she stroked her between her ears and offered the mare an apple, then carrots. Abby kept up her whispered, one-sided conversation and reached for the reins.

Wes waited in the road, hands on his hips, his hat low on his forehead. "We're missing the sunset."

"Some things can't be rushed." Abby coaxed the horse out of the weeds and back onto the road. "But I think we're good now."

Wes came up to Abby and took her hand, linking their fingers together.

Abby slanted her gaze at Wes. "Did I wound your pride with how easy I made that look?"

"Not in the least." He grinned and squeezed her hand. "In fact, I couldn't be any prouder of you."

Abby smiled and a warmth filled her inside and out. Her heart sang. She had her cowboy and the beginnings of a new life. And it had all started on this very same back-country road. One wrong turn had become the best mistake she'd ever made.

Wes held out his phone. "Are you sure you don't want me to call for a trailer and a ride."

"I could use the walk." Behind her, Queen Vee trailed along, relaxed and docile as if she'd follow Abby anywhere. "I'm still full from Thanksgiving dinner." Their holiday feast had been four days ago. Abby was still laughing over the stories shared and the new memories made with friends and family—everyone she loved.

"We have to tell Tess to stop making her fudge and all those other candies." Wes put his phone in his pocket. Laughter lightened his tone. "Especially the homemade marshmallows. I can't stop eating those."

"I can't either." Still, Abby couldn't— wouldn't—tell her cousin to stop her candy-making ways.

Tess had unpacked her kitchen and was creating and baking for the first time in years. For the first time since her husband had passed. Tess was healing in her own way, in her own time. Abby wanted to support her cousin. If eating Tess's white chocolate raspberry fudge and red velvet truffles was the way to do it, Abby was all in. "Although, the baby's favorite seems to be the peanut butter drops."

Wes stopped and set his hand on Abby's stomach. "That's a good choice, little one."

Abby had made a really good choice too. She kissed Wes, then placed her palm against his cheek. "Ready to go home?"

"I can't think of anywhere else I'd rather be." He took her hand again, his grip steady and secure. The perfect fit.

Together, they walked the mare back to the rescue. Their pace slow. Unrushed. After all, there was no need to hurry. She was in love and planned to cherish every minute.

* * * * *

For more great romances from
Cari Lynn Webb and
Harlequin Heartwarming,
visit www.Harlequin.com today!

Get 4 FREE REWARDS!

We'll send you 2 FREE Books <u>plus</u> 2 FREE Mystery Gifts.

Love Inspired books feature uplifting stories where faith helps guide you through life's challenges and discover the promise of a new beginning.

FREE Value Over **$20**

YES! Please send me 2 FREE Love Inspired Romance novels and my 2 FREE mystery gifts (gifts are worth about $10 retail). After receiving them, if I don't wish to receive any more books, I can return the shipping statement marked "cancel." If I don't cancel, I will receive 6 brand-new novels every month and be billed just $5.24 each for the regular-print edition or $5.99 each for the larger-print edition in the U.S., or $5.74 each for the regular-print edition or $6.24 each for the larger-print edition in Canada. That's a savings of at least 13% off the cover price. It's quite a bargain! Shipping and handling is just 50¢ per book in the U.S. and $1.25 per book in Canada.* I understand that accepting the 2 free books and gifts places me under no obligation to buy anything. I can always return a shipment and cancel at any time. The free books and gifts are mine to keep no matter what I decide.

Choose one: ☐ **Love Inspired Romance**
    Regular-Print
    (105/305 IDN GNWC)

☐ **Love Inspired Romance**
    Larger-Print
    (122/322 IDN GNWC)

Name (please print)

Address   Apt. #

City   State/Province   Zip/Postal Code

Email: Please check this box ☐ if you would like to receive newsletters and promotional emails from Harlequin Enterprises ULC and its affiliates. You can unsubscribe anytime.

Mail to the **Harlequin Reader Service:**
IN U.S.A.: P.O. Box 1341, Buffalo, NY 14240-8531
IN CANADA: P.O. Box 603, Fort Erie, Ontario L2A 5X3

Want to try 2 free books from another series? Call 1-800-873-8635 or visit www.ReaderService.com.

*Terms and prices subject to change without notice. Prices do not include sales taxes, which will be charged (if applicable) based on your state or country of residence. Canadian residents will be charged applicable taxes. Offer not valid in Quebec. This offer is limited to one order per household. Books received may not be as shown. Not valid for current subscribers to Love Inspired Romance books. All orders subject to approval. Credit or debit balances in a customer's account(s) may be offset by any other outstanding balance owed by or to the customer. Please allow 4 to 6 weeks for delivery. Offer available while quantities last.

Your Privacy—Your information is being collected by Harlequin Enterprises ULC, operating as Harlequin Reader Service. For a complete summary of the information we collect, how we use this information and to whom it is disclosed, please visit our privacy notice located at corporate.harlequin.com/privacy-notice. From time to time we may also exchange your personal information with reputable third parties. If you wish to opt out of this sharing of your personal information, please visit readerservice.com/consumerschoice or call 1-800-873-8635. **Notice to California Residents**—Under California law, you have specific rights to control and access your data. For more information on these rights and how to exercise them, visit corporate.harlequin.com/california-privacy.

LIR21R2

Get 4 FREE REWARDS!

We'll send you 2 FREE Books <u>plus</u> 2 FREE Mystery Gifts.

Love Inspired Suspense books showcase how courage and optimism unite in stories of faith and love in the face of danger.

FREE Value Over $20

YES! Please send me 2 FREE Love Inspired Suspense novels and my 2 FREE mystery gifts (gifts are worth about $10 retail). After receiving them, if I don't wish to receive any more books, I can return the shipping statement marked "cancel." If I don't cancel, I will receive 6 brand-new novels every month and be billed just $5.24 each for the regular-print edition or $5.99 each for the larger-print edition in the U.S., or $5.74 each for the regular-print edition or $6.24 each for the larger-print edition in Canada. That's a savings of at least 13% off the cover price. It's quite a bargain! Shipping and handling is just 50¢ per book in the U.S. and $1.25 per book in Canada.* I understand that accepting the 2 free books and gifts places me under no obligation to buy anything. I can always return a shipment and cancel at any time. The free books and gifts are mine to keep no matter what I decide.

Choose one: ☐ **Love Inspired Suspense Regular-Print** (153/353 IDN GNWN)   ☐ **Love Inspired Suspense Larger-Print** (107/307 IDN GNWN)

Name (please print)

Address   Apt. #

City   State/Province   Zip/Postal Code

Email: Please check this box ☐ if you would like to receive newsletters and promotional emails from Harlequin Enterprises ULC and its affiliates. You can unsubscribe anytime.

Mail to the **Harlequin Reader Service:**
IN U.S.A.: P.O. Box 1341, Buffalo, NY 14240-8531
IN CANADA: P.O. Box 603, Fort Erie, Ontario L2A 5X3

Want to try 2 free books from another series? Call 1-800-873-8635 or visit www.ReaderService.com.

*Terms and prices subject to change without notice. Prices do not include sales taxes, which will be charged (if applicable) based on your state or country of residence. Canadian residents will be charged applicable taxes. Offer not valid in Quebec. This offer is limited to one order per household. Books received may not be as shown. Not valid for current subscribers to Love Inspired Suspense books. All orders subject to approval. Credit or debit balances in a customer's account(s) may be offset by any other outstanding balance owed by or to the customer. Please allow 4 to 6 weeks for delivery. Offer available while quantities last.

Your Privacy—Your information is being collected by Harlequin Enterprises ULC, operating as Harlequin Reader Service. For a complete summary of the information we collect, how we use this information and to whom it is disclosed, please visit our privacy notice located at corporate.harlequin.com/privacy-notice. From time to time we may also exchange your personal information with reputable third parties. If you wish to opt out of this sharing of your personal information, please visit readerservice.com/consumerchoice or call 1-800-873-8635. **Notice to California Residents**—Under California law, you have specific rights to control and access your data. For more information on these rights and how to exercise them, visit corporate.harlequin.com/california-privacy.

LIS21R2

HARLEQUIN SELECTS COLLECTION

19 FREE BOOKS IN ALL!

RaeAnne THAYNE
A COLD CREEK HOMECOMING

LINDA LAEL MILLER
SIERRA'S HOMECOMING

MOUNTAIN SHERIFF

From Robyn Carr to RaeAnne Thayne to Linda Lael Miller and Sherryl Woods we promise (actually, GUARANTEE!) each author in the Harlequin Selects collection has seen their name on the *New York Times* or *USA TODAY* bestseller lists!

YES! Please send me the **Harlequin Selects Collection**. This collection begins with 3 FREE books and 2 FREE gifts in the first shipment. Along with my 3 free books, I'll also get 4 more books from the Harlequin Selects Collection, which I may either return and owe nothing or keep for the low price of $24.14 U.S./$28.82 CAN. each plus $2.99 U.S./$7.49 CAN. for shipping and handling per shipment*.If I decide to continue, I will get 6 or 7 more books (about once a month for 7 months) but will only need to pay for 4. That means 2 or 3 books in every shipment will be FREE! If I decide to keep the entire collection, I'll have paid for only 32 books because 19 were FREE! I understand that accepting the 3 free books and gifts places me under no obligation to buy anything. I can always return a shipment and cancel at any time. My free books and gifts are mine to keep no matter what I decide.

☐ 262 HCN 5576   ☐ 462 HCN 5576

Name (please print)

Address   Apt. #

City   State/Province   Zip/Postal Code

Mail to the Harlequin Reader Service:
IN U.S.A.: P.O. Box 1341, Buffalo, NY 14240-8531
IN CANADA: P.O. Box 603, Fort Erie, Ontario L2A 5X3

*Terms and prices subject to change without notice. Prices do not include sales taxes, which will be charged (if applicable) based on your state or country of residence. Canadian residents will be charged applicable taxes. Offer not valid in Quebec. All orders subject to approval. Credit or debit balances in a customer's account(s) may be offset by any other outstanding balance owed by or to the customer. Please allow 3 to 4 weeks for delivery. Offer available while quantities last. © 2020 Harlequin Enterprises ULC. ® and ™ are trademarks owned by Harlequin Enterprises ULC.

Your Privacy—Your information is being collected by Harlequin Enterprises ULC, operating as Harlequin Reader Service. To see how we collect and use this information visit https://corporate.harlequin.com/privacy-notice. From time to time we may also exchange your personal information with reputable third parties. If you wish to opt out of this sharing of your personal information, please visit www.readerservice.com/consumerschoice or call 1-800-873-8635. Notice to California Residents—Under California law, you have specific rights to control and access your data. For more information visit https://corporate.harlequin.com/california-privacy.

50BOOKHS22R

Get 4 FREE REWARDS!

We'll send you 2 FREE Books plus 2 FREE Mystery Gifts.

BRENDA JACKSON
Follow Your Heart

ROBYN CARR
The Country Guesthouse

RICK MOFINA
SEARCH FOR HER

B.J. DANIELS
FROM the SHADOWS

FREE
Value Over
$20

Both the **Romance** and **Suspense** collections feature compelling novels
written by many of today's bestselling authors.

YES! Please send me 2 FREE novels from the Essential Romance or
Essential Suspense Collection and my 2 FREE gifts (gifts are worth about
$10 retail). After receiving them, if I don't wish to receive any more books,
I can return the shipping statement marked "cancel." If I don't cancel, I will
receive 4 brand-new novels every month and be billed just $7.24 each in the
U.S. or $7.49 each in Canada. That's a savings of up to 28% off the cover
price. It's quite a bargain! Shipping and handling is just 50¢ per book in the
U.S. and $1.25 per book in Canada.* I understand that accepting the 2 free
books and gifts places me under no obligation to buy anything. I can always
return a shipment and cancel at any time. The free books and gifts are mine
to keep no matter what I decide.

Choose one: ☐ **Essential Romance**   ☐ **Essential Suspense**
                  (194/394 MDN GQ6M)   (191/391 MDN GQ6M)

_____
Name (please print)

_____
Address   Apt. #

_____
City   State/Province   Zip/Postal Code

Email: Please check this box ☐ if you would like to receive newsletters and promotional emails from Harlequin Enterprises ULC and
its affiliates. You can unsubscribe anytime.

Mail to the **Harlequin Reader Service:**
IN U.S.A.: P.O. Box 1341, Buffalo, NY 14240-8531
IN CANADA: P.O. Box 603, Fort Erie, Ontario L2A 5X3

Want to try 2 free books from another series? Call 1-800-873-8635 or visit www.ReaderService.com.

*Terms and prices subject to change without notice. Prices do not include sales taxes, which will be charged (if applicable) based
on your state or country of residence. Canadian residents will be charged applicable taxes. Offer not valid in Quebec. This offer is
limited to one order per household. Books received may not be as shown. Not valid for current subscribers to the Essential Romance
or Essential Suspense Collection. All orders subject to approval. Credit or debit balances in a customer's account(s) may be offset by
any other outstanding balance owed by or to the customer. Please allow 4 to 6 weeks for delivery. Offer available while quantities last.

Your Privacy—Your information is being collected by Harlequin Enterprises ULC, operating as Harlequin Reader Service. For a
complete summary of the information we collect, how we use this information and to whom it is disclosed, please visit our privacy notice
located at corporate.harlequin.com/privacy-notice. From time to time we may also exchange your personal information with reputable
third parties. If you wish to opt out of this sharing of your personal information, please visit readerservice.com/consumerschoice or
call 1-800-873-8635. **Notice to California Residents**—Under California law, you have specific rights to control and access your data.
For more information on these rights and how to exercise them, visit corporate.harlequin.com/california-privacy.

STRS21R2

COMING NEXT MONTH FROM

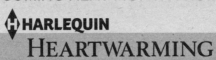

#391 A COWGIRL'S SECRET
The Mountain Monroes • by Melinda Curtis
Horse trainer Cassie Diaz is at a crossroads. Ranch life is her first love...until Bentley Monroe passes through her Idaho town and helps with the family business. Will this cowgirl turn in her boots for him?

#392 THE SINGLE DAD'S HOLIDAY MATCH
Smoky Mountain First Responders
by Tanya Agler
Can a widowed cop and single father find love again? When a case leads Jonathan Maxwell to single mom Brooke Novak, sparks fly. But with their focus on kids and work, romance isn't so easy...is it?

#393 A COWBOY'S HOPE
Eclipse Ridge Ranch • by Mary Anne Wilson
When lawyer Anna Watters agreed to help a local ranch, she wasn't supposed to fall for handsome Ben Arias! He's only in town temporarily—but soon she wants Ben and the peace she finds at his ranch permanently.

#394 I'LL BE HOME FOR CHRISTMAS
Return to Christmas Island • by Amie Denman
Rebecca Browne will do anything for her finance career. Even spend the summer on Christmas Island. But she didn't expect to have to keep secrets...especially from the local ferryboat captain she's starting to fall for.

YOU CAN FIND MORE INFORMATION ON UPCOMING HARLEQUIN TITLES, FREE EXCERPTS AND MORE AT HARLEQUIN.COM.

HWCNM0921

Visit ReaderService.com Today!

As a valued member of the Harlequin Reader Service, you'll find these benefits and more at ReaderService.com:

- Try 2 free books from any series
- Access risk-free special offers
- View your account history & manage payments
- Browse the latest Bonus Bucks catalog

Don't miss out!

If you want to stay up-to-date on the latest at the Harlequin Reader Service and enjoy more content, make sure you've signed up for our monthly News & Notes email newsletter. Sign up online at ReaderService.com or by calling Customer Service at 1-800-873-8635.

RS20